HAWKSWOOD describes herself as a 'wordsmith' who is
_really happy when writing. She read Modern History at
rd and first published a non-fiction book on the Royal
ines in the First World War before moving on to mediaeval
teries set in Worcestershire.

a&b

Ordeal by Fire

A Bradecote
and Catchpoll Mystery

SARAH HAWKSWOOD

Allison & Busby Limited
12 Fitzroy Mews
London W1T 6DW
allisonandbusby.com

First published in Great Britain by Allison & Busby in 2016.
This paperback edition published by Allison & Busby in 2017.

A CIP catalogue record for this book is available from
the British Library.

10 9 8 7 6 5 4 3 2 1

ISBN 978-0-7490-2097-2

Typeset in 11/16 pt Adobe Garamond Pro by
Allison & Busby Ltd.

The paper used for this Allison & Busby publication
has been produced from trees that have been legally sourced
from well-managed and credibly certified forests.

Printed and bound by
CPI Group (UK) Ltd, Croydon, CR0 4YY

Map of twelfth-century Worcester

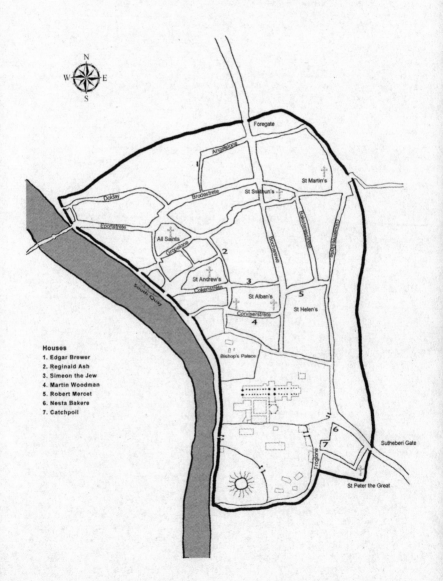

Foregate

Angelstrete

St Martin's

Dolday

Brodestrete

St Swithun's

Eportstrete

Baxterstrete

Newport strete

All Saints

Grapelone

2

Bocherewe

St Andrew's

Cokenstrete

3

St Alban's

5

Corviserstrete

4

St Helen's

South Quay

Bishop's Palace

Houses
1. Edgar Brewer
2. Reginald Ash
3. Simeon the Jew
4. Martin Woodman
5. Robert Mercet
6. Nesta Bakere
7. Catchpoil

6

Froglane

7

Sutheberi Gate

St Peter the Great

September 1143

Chapter One

'Fire!'

The cry spread almost as swiftly as the flames, from person to person as from straw to straw of the crackling thatch.

'Fire!'

Panic was mixed with action as anxious mothers dragged wide-eyed children from the spectacle. Neighbours, with as much an eye to preventing the blaze reaching their own property as to aiding the unfortunate silversmith whose workshop was alight, came running with buckets and pitchers to take water from the nearest well, and poles and hooks to pull down the burning thatch.

Serjeant Catchpoll was on his way back to the castle after visiting one of the burgesses. He had been sent by the sheriff to report the successful apprehension of the thief who had stolen the good man's three best pullets. It was a call of courtesy, and Catchpoll, who was not a naturally courteous man, was not best pleased, but William de Beauchamp, lord Sheriff of Worcestershire, was himself far too important to make such a visit. Instead, he had delegated his serjeant so that the next meeting of the burgesses would not lead to their whining petition for greater diligence in upholding the king's laws by the sheriff and his men.

The serjeant halted, making a swift assessment of the situation. Fire was the great fear of townsfolk, with their homes and businesses cheek by jowl, and nearly every one of them constructed of wood, and daub, and thatch. A fire that Catchpoll could remember from his youth, back in 1113, had cost dozens of lives, and livelihoods too. One of his own cousins had perished then, and there had been fire both accidental and intentional in the years since.

He considered running to the castle to bring the men-at-arms to assist, but it was clear that the alarm had been raised swiftly and it was a windless afternoon. Running was not something he did from choice at his age. The inhabitants of the street had pulled down the little thatched lean-to abutting the neighbouring premises, disregarding the pleas of the owner, and had created a small firebreak. Women were throwing water at the wall of this adjacent property, and already the smoke was more in evidence than the flames.

Catchpoll pulled a face. He could, as the sheriff's officer, make his presence known and take charge of the scene. On the other hand, the locals were doing pretty well on their own, and if the fire were not sufficiently damped down and erupted again later there could be no blame laid at his door. He held back and waited, inconspicuously; he was a man who could merge into the background when occasion arose. Eventually the number of people in the street began to thin, leaving only the tradesman and his immediate neighbours surveying the scene. Puddles of sooty water lay in every depression of the trampled earth of the narrow street, and the scattered thatch was strewn as if thrown randomly by a giant hand. Charred beams pointed accusing black fingers heavenward, and the frame of the lean-to stood precariously at a drunken angle. The owner of the structure was still complaining vociferously, but nobody was paying him any attention whatsoever.

Serjeant Catchpoll took a deep breath, and promptly coughed as the ghost of an acrid tendril of smoke caught in his throat. He had hoped to step forward looking official, but found himself being thumped on the back by an elderly and sparsely toothed woman, attracting the attention of the sorry-looking party while bent double and with streaming eyes.

The diversion caused the lean-to's owner to cease his complaint. After a minute, Catchpoll stood upright again. He hawked, paused, and spat into the soot-flecked dust.

'You know me. I am the lord sheriff's man, and he will want to know of this. How did the fire start?' he asked, still wheezing slightly.

'How do you think?' demanded the lean-to owner, grumpily. 'You'd think any man with a furnace in his premises would keep a better eye on it, not risk his neighbours through negligence.'

''Twas not negligence, as I and my journeyman could tell you if you would but listen.'

The silversmith, sitting on an upturned tun, wringing his

hands, roused himself from his gloom, and the journeyman, while having a burnt hand tended by a winsome maid who had eased his discomfort as much by her presence as her ministrations, looked round to confirm his master's words.

'True enough. The fire did not start by the furnace, and it was banked down low this afternoon. Master Reginald was selecting stones for setting in a chalice, and I was polishing. The fire was in the thatch at the rear of the shop when we first noticed it.'

Serjeant Catchpoll frowned. A fire was bad, but a deliberate fire was far worse.

'Don't you take what that longshanks says as truth,' piped up the old woman who had clapped Catchpoll on the back. 'He'd swear sunrise was sunset to keep in his master's favour. He'll not have the wherewithal to wed else, and he can't afford to wait long. She,' and the woman pointed a dirty-nailed finger at the journeyman's ministering angel, 'won't be able to hide the result of their sinning 'neath her gown much longer.'

The young woman reddened and threw her a fulminating glance, but the old woman merely laughed mirthlessly. Catchpoll's eyes, like everyone else's, dwelt upon the girl's figure, which was shapely in a voluptuous way. If she was carrying, well, perhaps another woman could tell, but the serjeant certainly could not, and the other men looked as surprised. Indeed, the owner of the lean-to stood agape, his jaw working silently for several seconds and his face assuming a purple hue, before he could find his words.

'You . . . You . . . lecherous, whoreson rogue! Ruin my daughter, would you! I'll have you whipped. Indeed, I'll do it

14

myself.' He lunged forward, and the girl placed herself smartly between father and lover, looking not chastened but belligerent.

'Out of my way, you ungrateful wench. What your poor mother would have—'

'My "poor" mother would have said I should have been wed long since, not kept to labour in her stead because you are too close-fisted to employ a woman to keep house for you. It's you who should be shamed, not I. Edwin has good prospects with Master Reginald, and is no mean match for the daughter of an idle, ale-swilling fletcher like you.' She turned to her lover. 'Will you take me dowerless, love?'

'You know that, Winflaed, but after this,' he waved his sound hand at the smouldering shop, 'I know not how we'll manage.'

Master Reginald, who had originally been contemplating the future in a very despondent fashion, seemed to have pulled himself together during the altercation over Winflaed, and now, though blackened of face and singed of brow, looked much more his normal, competent self.

'I'll swear not all is lost, Edwin. Whatever lies charred out the back, the flames have not done more than blacken the very front of the shop, so the ready pieces should be undamaged, and if it did not get too hot, the tools and gemstones will be there amongst the ash and soot. We can get the building repaired, even if I have to give bracelets and clasps in payment, but it'll mean a few weeks under an awning, and that's no place for a woman, especially if she is . . . Once there's proper chambers again you can bring your bride, and I'll make you my partner when your time is up next Lady Day. Let her stay with her father till all's ready.'

'As if I'd have her.' The fletcher curled his lip disdainfully. 'Giving herself like some cheap *forlegnis* in an alley, and behind my back too.'

Serjeant Catchpoll had been diverted by the unexpected turn of the conversation, but was keen to get back to the sheriff with a report, and now spoke up, his voice authoritative and calm.

'She'd scarce do so in front of you.' At his quip the old woman laughed, and choked as a consequence. 'You'll take her back, Master Fletcher, with a good grace, and make efforts to give her a dower if you value your own standing. And you,' he turned on the old woman, 'will keep your tongue between the remains of your teeth and not spread gossip. Many a child arrives a mite early, and nothing is said.' He dusted his hands together, dismissing the subject. 'Now, can we get back to the fire? If you and your journeyman are certain that the fire did not start in the workshop, could it have started accidentally to the rear, with a stewpot mayhap, Master . . . ?' He frowned, for Catchpoll liked to know the craftsmen of Worcester, and this one's name eluded him for the minute.

'Reginald Ash is the name.' The silversmith gave a bitter laugh. 'Fitting, today, eh? But the fire starting from a cook-fire? No, I'd swear not. A girl comes and sets a pot cooking slow for us during the afternoon, but she don't normally do that till the bell has struck for the afternoon service in the cathedral, and I did not hear her out back.'

'Nor I either,' agreed Edwin, 'and we weren't beating metal, nor any other noisy task.'

'Well, where would I find the girl to find out for sure?'

16

Catchpoll could foresee the sheriff wanting to be clear about this.

'Opposite, next to Adam Merlie, the coppersmith. She's Widow Wick's daughter, Agnes.'

'And would there be anyone you know of as would want you out of business, Master Ash?'

The silversmith shook his head. 'No, none. I keeps to myself, and have no bad blood betwixt me and any man that I knows of. My goods are well made and sold for a fair price, and there has never been any complaint otherwise. No, there is no reason anyone should want to burn me out.'

Serjeant Catchpoll rubbed his grizzled chin. 'Well, I will report all this to the lord sheriff, and let him decide whether it was malice or accident.'

He left the silversmith and his man, aided no doubt by the girl Winflaed, to begin the business of clearing and salvage, and went in search of Agnes Wick. She proved an unhelpful witness. The girl was slow-witted and vague, and her mother was much inclined to speak for her or suggest what she should say. She seemed unsure as to whether she had been to the smith's, but her mother, fearing blame might come their way, swore with more vehemence than veracity that the nasty business could have nought to do with her 'poor Agnes'.

Catchpoll was left with little that he could lay before the sheriff as good evidence for accident or crime. He returned to the castle unhappily aware that William de Beauchamp would most likely leave the decision whether to investigate further up to him, and knew the blame could be laid at his door if it proved he had made the wrong choice.

* * *

He was still pondering his unenviable position when he entered the castle bailey, and stopped short. He had left but an hour or so previously, and all had been quiet and everyday. Now the bailey was full of bustle, with horses, men-at-arms and a noticeable number of black-habited monks.

'What in the Lady's Name is going on?' the serjeant asked of the gate guard, who was taking considerable interest in a monk's spectacularly unsuccessful attempts to get an obstinate mule into the stables.

'Well, the Brother has been trying to . . .'

'No, cabbage-head, what is all this about?' Catchpoll waved an arm at the scene within the bailey.

'Ah well, the lord Bishop of Hereford has descended upon us all, in some state, because of some dispute. All above our level I expect, Serjeant.'

'Above yours, aye, but not necessarily mine.' He did not spare the guard another glance, but made his way through the throng to the kitchens. He knew the cook well, and also knew that the cookhouse was the hub of the wheel of knowledge within the castle. Drogo the Cook seemed to know what was going on before it even happened, and Catchpoll wanted to appear before the sheriff as fully informed as possible. Experience had taught him that being abreast of the news always gave the sheriff the idea that Serjeant Catchpoll was one step ahead, and Catchpoll enjoyed that.

Drogo was shouting orders at a scullion, while waving a ladle in the manner of a battling bishop with a mace. Catchpoll grinned.

'A few more for supper, then?' he quipped.

Drogo rolled his eyes. 'Ravenous wolves would be easier. Here's me, with Aelfred down with an ague, and two wenches sickening for heaven knows what, and the lord Bishop of Hereford arrives, without warning, with an army to protect him and half an abbey to pray with him. And then he sends down asking for herons! Not even just one! How much does this man eat? I thought men of God were meant to think of their souls, not their bellies! Where am I to get herons for tonight? Will they fall like manna from heaven or does the lord bishop think there is a fresh heron stall at the gate?'

Catchpoll sympathised, as one sufficiently up the scale of hierarchy to be called upon by name and given Herculean tasks to be performed instantly. His grin spread, ever more skull-like.

'Give 'em chicken and say they are stunted heron, friend.'

Drogo lobbed the ladle at him, but he ducked with surprising alacrity, and it caught the spit-boy on the back of the head instead. The lad yelped.

Catchpoll put up his hands placatingly. 'Fair enough, not a good suggestion. Just tell me in a few of your well-chosen words what is going on, and I'll leave you in peace.'

Drogo told him, succinctly, but with adjectives that made the girl shelling peas turn crimson. The bishop, travelling, so he said, with a large party for protection in such perilous times, had come to drag the sheriff off to the northern border of the county to sort out a land dispute where one of his holdings was involved. The sheriff would normally demur, but the thought of having the bishop and all his minions eating him out of house and home, and 'bleating' in his ear for days, swayed him.

'Well, I suppose I had best find out what the lord sheriff

wants me to do, pox on it. Hope he doesn't keep me kicking my heels for long. My wife has a nice fat partridge hanging ready to put in a pudding for tonight, and she makes a fine partridge pudding.' Catchpoll's mouth watered at the prospect.

'Puts plenty of gravy with it, I'll be bound, and not too much seasoning. Now I always say—'

'No time to listen to your sound cooking advice, Drogo. Must get to the lord sheriff and report.'

Before the cook could say another word, Catchpoll had gone.

William de Beauchamp, lord Sheriff of Worcestershire, was not a happy man. He found the society of clerics both boring and disquieting. He was a man who preferred action to pontification, and was distrustful of those who fought with clever words. He noted his serjeant's arrival in his hall with the relief of a man who sees reinforcements arriving to lift a siege, and drew him forth by an exchange of glances and a slight nod of the head. The bishop was in full flow, but the sheriff cut across him without compunction.

'You have seen Ranulf Fuller, Catchpoll? And he is content?'

'Aye, my lord. You'll have no moaning from him, leastways not more than usual, but as I returned there was a fire in the shop of Reginald Ash the silversmith.'

'Much damage?' The sheriff frowned.

'No, only to the silversmith's premises. The neighbours were quick about dealing with it, and prevented any real spread.'

The sheriff looked more cheerful. 'Good, then . . .'

'There was, my lord, some suggestion that the fire was not accidental.' Catchpoll kept his own face expressionless as the

20

frown reappeared between the sheriff's brows, and a grimace of annoyance twisted his mouth.

'You said "suggestion". Is it an idle claim to keep the man's neighbours from calling down curses on him, or are there grounds for thinking it was indeed a fire that was set?'

It was Catchpoll's turn to look unhappy. His grizzled, mobile face was screwed up into an expression of contemplation, and his head nodded from side to side as he weighed the matter. This was what he had feared might happen. The sheriff was going to leave the decision on action up to him. Catchpoll far preferred being given a task, a scent to follow, and then getting on with it without interference. Making the initial judgement was, in his view, much more difficult. If he said it warranted investigation and it turned out to have been a simple mischance, the sheriff would berate him for wasting his time. Yet if it was deliberate and he ignored it, well, the consequences could be too unpleasant to contemplate. He pulled at the lobe of his left ear, meditatively, and sucked his teeth.

'It's a tricky one, my lord, honest it is. The smith and his journeyman swear the fire started in the back of the premises, not in the workshop, and definitely not at the furnace, which they say was not in use today. I thought perhaps it could be a cooking fire. A girl comes to set a pot for them in the afternoon. Trouble is, the girl is about as bright as a plough ox, if that, and I would not like to say whether what she said was true, what she thought was true, or what she thought her mother and I wanted her to say. All I would vouch for is that if the fire was lit through malice, it was not the girl that did it.'

The sheriff was no fool. He knew that Catchpoll was now

trying to pass this potentially poisoned chalice back to him. His eyes narrowed for a moment, but then, to Catchpoll's surprise, he smiled; it was a small, grim smile. He was being called away by the Bishop of Hereford, and a suspicion alone was not sufficient to detain him. He cast a swift glance at the prelate, who still wore an affronted expression at having been abandoned in full flow so that the sheriff could discuss shrieval business with an underling. The smile twitched.

'Right, Serjeant. I am away north to assist the lord bishop here. In my absence you can keep your ears open in case of information that would prove this either way. I should not be gone for more than,' he paused, as the bishop made a sound between a cough and a growl, 'a week, or perhaps ten days. If there are further developments you can always send to my lord Bradecote and call him in. A little work would do my new undersheriff no harm. The harvest is in, and his brat should have been born by now. He would probably be glad to escape cooing women and a screaming infant in his hall.'

With that he nodded dismissal, and Catchpoll withdrew, muttering under his breath.

He had worked once with Hugh Bradecote, the new undersheriff, and had no real complaints about him, but he was still very green, and much inclined to get far too involved in what Catchpoll saw as his own remit. The old undersheriff, de Crespignac, had given the sheriff's serjeant pretty much a free hand, and Catchpoll preferred it that way. There had been no question about his methods as long as the result was satisfactory and de Crespignac could make it sound as though the inspiration were his own. The new man wanted to be far more involved; indeed he had taken the last case with little delegation at all. Serjeant Catchpoll heaved a heavy sigh, and ambled glumly back towards the kitchens, where he slipped into the dim brewhouse, and drew himself a pot of small beer under the indulgent gaze of the florid-faced, motherly woman who was busy filling pitchers for the sheriff's table. He gave her a slow, conspiratorial wink, with just enough of a leer to make her giggle and redden even further. She waddled out, still beaming, and Catchpoll, wiping the residue from his lips with the back of his hand, headed for hearth and home, and the consolation of partridge pudding.

Chapter Two

The sheriff's absence was not marked by any sudden increase in criminal activity within Worcester, and the first week of September passed without any incident worth calling upon the undersheriff. A successful hue and cry was raised over a cutpurse who attempted to empty the scrip of a wealthy townsman; a woman who claimed to have had her washing stolen from the drying grounds was found to have made up the tale to lay blame on a neighbour's servant, with whom she believed her husband to be having a liaison; and the thief who stole a leg of lamb from the butcher Cuthbert turned out to be a half-starved mongrel, whose owner had tried to use hunger to make it a more aggressive watchdog. Harsh words and the handing over of remuneration had ended the matter, though Catchpoll thought the dog would get a beating it did not deserve.

Serjeant Catchpoll was able to diffuse a boundary dispute

between two potters, former partners, by the simple expedient of taking Hammon, a man-at-arms of enormous proportions, with him on the visit, and suggesting, ever so reasonably, that if they did not come to an amicable agreement, Hammon would become very upset. When he was upset, explained Catchpoll conversationally, Hammon was inclined to throw his arms about in a very wild fashion. The potters looked at Hammon, who grinned innocently at them. He did not appear to be a man who would be easily upset. Catchpoll, on the other hand, looked just the sort of mean, malcontented bastard who would enjoy setting his tame giant to the wanton destruction of honest men's livelihoods. The potters, however little they liked each other, were not going to risk their goods, and, with fixed smiles and gritted teeth, shook hands and clapped each other on the back like brothers. Catchpoll's wolfish grin grew broader and the evil twinkle, detected by the disputants, became more pronounced.

He departed well pleased with the outcome, and convinced of the efficacy of his unorthodox methods. There were those who would have sought an end to the problem by negotiation and compromise, and oaths from all and sundry. The sheriff's serjeant regarded such disputes in the same way as he used to look upon squabbles between his children over a plaything. His method, which involved the removal, or destruction, of the article disputed unless both sides behaved, had been very successful, and had generally involved both parties uniting in their loathing of such a family despot. That numbers of the Worcester populace saw him in a similar light worried him not at all. In contented mood, he purchased a handful of plums from a market stall and deposited half of them in Hammon's huge paw of a hand.

'Just to keep you sweet, Hammon,' he laughed, biting into the soft flesh and spitting the stone at a mangy cur, scratching behind its ear. 'Don't want you upset, do we.'

The stalls were doing brisk trade, and Catchpoll threaded his way like an eel among the vendors and purchasers, soon outpacing the giant Hammon. Despite his swift progress, his sixth sense, the criminal-detecting one, worked as ever among crowds. Nevertheless, he was taken by surprise as a small boy, running at full pelt, cannoned into him from behind.

'Stop, thief!' The shrill cry of a woman, still hidden from Catchpoll's sight, made the serjeant grab the urchin almost instinctively, as he turned about. The child looked up, wary, fearful eyes staring from a grubby, undernourished face.

'Please, my lord. Let me go,' the boy whimpered, but Catchpoll's grip remained firm.

The owner of the shrill voice barged into view. She was a lanky, shrew-faced woman with glittering eyes and a skinny, heaving bosom, who ignored Catchpoll, and raised her hand to strike the boy.

'Steal my apples, would you, whelp? Well, I'll knock the teeth from your head so you'll bite into no more of 'em, and set you before the law. They hangs thieves like you.'

As her hand came down in the first blow, it was barred by the serjeant's arm. The woman started, suddenly aware of his presence, and sneered at him.

'Don't you protect vermin like him, or did you set him to steal?' She halted what would have been a tirade as she took stock of the man before her; grim face, hard, cold eyes and a thin-lipped mouth, which was set in an uncompromising line.

'What exactly did he steal?' The voice was slow, quiet and yet threatening, with lips barely parted.

The apple-seller looked less sure of herself. 'My apples.' She turned for support among the other vendors. 'How can an honest woman earn her bread if thieves, even small 'uns, go unchecked?'

There was a ripple of agreement, a vague murmur of general support.

Catchpoll looked down at the child. 'Show me.' It was a command, and the little boy, trembling, opened a dirty fist. Within lay a small, malformed, and bruised apple.

'It had fell off the basket, my lord, and rolled a bit. I thought nobody wanted it.' The piping voice was scarcely more than a whisper.

'It was still mine,' averred the apple woman, holding out her hand, with its thin, talon-like fingers, to take it back.

The urchin looked up at Catchpoll's harsh face. The man nodded, and with a sniff, the child handed back the purloined apple.

The woman smiled as if she had been given a silver penny. 'Now we take him for justice.'

Catchpoll's grip on the child tightened, and it cried out, but his eyes were on the woman.

'I am Justice.'

The woman's jaw dropped. The voice was so icy, the gaze so hard, Catchpoll could have claimed to be death itself and she would have believed him.

'You cry thief on a starved child for the sake of a wizened fruit most folk would feed to the swine, and take pride in it. Well, shame upon you, woman, and if the rest of your wares are as poor, I doubt you'll have many customers.'

The small crowd that had gathered to watch, took a step back from the woman, as if she carried contagion. She sensed the change, and bit her lip, but gave in with reluctance.

'Say whatever you will, I have the right . . . but no matter. In this case, since the fruit may have been damaged, I'll not take it further, but mind you give him a sound thrashing.' She turned on her heel and stalked away with as much dignity as she could muster, and little expectation of being heeded.

Within moments the attention of the crowd had dissipated, and Catchpoll, stepping back from the main thoroughfare, regarded his small captive. The child was confused, not knowing whether the man was his protector or the instrument of retribution. Catchpoll squatted down to be more of a height with the boy, and smiled, though the smile only made the scared eyes widen further.

'So, Master Criminal, what have you to say?'

'I thought it wasn't wanted, honest, my lord. I doesn't want to be hanged.'

'And why did you take it? What will your mother say, when I lead you home?'

The boy opened his mouth, but before he could answer another voice gave it for him.

'He did it because he'll starve else, and there's no home, nor mother neither, for you to take him to.'

Catchpoll turned. A girl, probably no more than twelve years

28

old, had come up behind him. She was ragged, and though her face was cleaner than the urchin's, it was as drawn and pale. Her voice was devoid of emotion, excepting perhaps the hint of a challenge, and her eyes ran him up and down, assessing him. Then they met his, and Catchpoll read in them all he needed to know. There was desperation, hopelessness and despair, as often amongst the destitute, but in addition there was a grim determination, and worst of all, a cynical condemnation. They were the eyes of a woman who knows how men can be at their worst, and counts all men as guilty, yet they were set in the body of a child.

'Leave go of him, my lord, and I am sure there's something better you could be doing than beating him.'

She smiled provocatively, while her eyes accused. The come-on was clumsy, and turned Catchpoll's stomach. He stood, slowly.

'I've a granddaughter your age, girl. What do you take me for?'

She shrugged. 'Same as the rest.'

'Well, I'm not, see. Now don't play off tawdry tricks on me and just answer honest. If you've no home, where do you rest?'

'Where we can. There's stores and outhouses enough if you're small, and careful, and I can make enough to keep us from eating the rats. There's not much, mind, so Huw scavenges what he can. But I've told him, and often, not to steal.'

'And how long has this been so?'

'Since second week before Easter, when our Mam died.'

'Your father?'

'Dead these three years, and we've no other kin. Mam was out of Wales. I promised her I'd look to Huw, and so I will, till he's old enough and big enough to take proper work.'

Catchpoll did not ask what the girl expected for herself. She clearly saw no future, and she was probably right. Disease or a violent man would see her end her days young.

It was not so rare a tale that the world-wise serjeant should have been shocked by it, yet he was, even as he chastised himself for being so soft. He dragged the remaining plums from his pocket and held them out to the boy, who snatched them lest the largesse be withdrawn.

'Do as your sister says, lad, and don't steal. I'd hate to have to take you up before the sheriff.' He returned his gaze to the girl. He could not tell her to mend her ways, as a priest might. The situation was as it was, and he could not show her a way out, but a thought did hit him.

'Since you range about the town, you might earn a little honest money from me. I am the lord sheriff's serjeant, and I likes to know what is toward. If you hear ought of thieves or killings, you let me know of it and if it is true there'll be coin for you. Serjeant Catchpoll, that's me, at the castle or the house next the cooper's in Frog Lane, just beyond the castle gate.'

The girl pursed her lips, and then nodded. Without a further word she took her brother's hand and slipped away amongst the crowd. Catchpoll shook his head.

'Never thought I'd grow that soft-hearted or soft-headed. Must really be getting old.'

He was still tut-tutting to himself when he reached the castle, where news cast all thoughts of the waifs from his mind. Just when he had expected the sheriff to return, a messenger arrived for the castellan with the tidings that the sheriff had broken his foot, slipping on a wet stair, and was holed up in the most northerly of his own manors, with the devil's own temper and a heavily bandaged foot. He could not be expected back in Worcester until the end of the month. Catchpoll prayed that all would stay quiet until the sheriff's return, but, despite his display of charity, his prayers were not answered.

It was a surprisingly warm night, lacking any sign of September chill, and with the merest sliver of a moon occasionally peering, furtively, from behind swathes of cloud, as if fearful of what it might witness. Few stars were visible amidst the velvety, blue-grey folds of the veiled night sky, and the narrow streets of Worcester were dark and oppressive. A dog was barking somewhere; its lone voice carried on the still air, but disguised its direction. From within some of the dwellings floated intimations of humanity from open upper shutters; a wailing infant being soothed by a crooning mother; a man and woman arguing; the giggling of a woman, and her lover's laugh; a snoring like the rumble of distant thunder. The sounds hung in the air for a moment before fading, ghostlike, ephemeral. Few souls were abroad. A pair of drunken men, arms linked in alcohol-induced amiability, wove a staggering course homeward, stopping briefly when one turned to vomit in a doorway. They almost collided with the dark-hooded figure who turned into Corviserstrete with steady, purposeful stride. They exclaimed as they reeled back, sending slurred expletives after him, but the figure ignored them as if they did not exist. One of the men crossed himself shakily, and muttered something about dark nights and hellfiends. His friend clapped him on the back and laughed, more from bravado than humour.

* * *

Catchpoll was woken from his bed in the early hours by an urgent hammering at his door. His wife groaned, and pulled the coverlet over her head, while he stumbled to cover his nakedness and, swearing as he stubbed his toe on a stool, went to open the door.

A breathless man-at-arms stood gasping for air on the doorstep. 'Fire, Serjeant! Fire in Corviserstrete! Come quick!'

Cursing, Serjeant Catchpoll finished dressing haphazardly in the darkness, and left his home at the run, the man-at-arms trailing behind. The fire was more terrifying by night than one in daylight. Several properties were well alight, and sparks showered down into the street. The faces and bodies of those attempting to douse the flames were illuminated by the red-orange glow like the damned from hell, and cast grotesque shadows on the walls opposite. There was a deal of shouting and some screaming, and it took the serjeant some moments to assess the situation. A tall, broad-shouldered man seemed to have taken charge of the firefighters, and it was he whom Catchpoll first approached.

'Anyone within?' he shouted, waving at the conflagration.

The man turned, his eyes streaming from the effect of the acrid smoke. Catchpoll recognised him as Corbin the Wheelwright.

'Can't say, and it'd be too late for any poor soul now. Wilfrid Glover got his family out in good time, but that was the last to catch.' He coughed, and shouted for more buckets. 'Ask Father Boniface, he was here early.'

Catchpoll could not tell priest from parishioner in the

weird firelight, but a small hand tugged at his sleeve, and he looked down to see Huw the beggar child, who pointed dumbly towards one of the men in the line passing pails.

'Father Boniface?'

A youngish priest, with a long, ascetic face rendered ghoulish by the shadow and light, turned at the sound of his name. His sleeves were rolled back and his gown kirtled to reveal white, scrawny knees, and hairy legs where no hose had chafed them smooth. Had the situation not been so serious, Catchpoll would have found him a cause for mirth.

'I am Father Boniface, yes.'

'Do you know if any were trapped within? The wheelwright says you were here quickly.'

'I raised the alarm, certainly. By then the first building was well alight, but it was the carpenter's wood store so I doubt there was anyone within. They would have been swift to cry "fire" if they had been there as it began. A woman and her children ran out of the dwelling when I shouted. I think her husband was not at home.' The priest was not watching Catchpoll now, but was once more engaged in the bucket chain. He wiped a grimy hand across his face as he handed on another slopping pail, wetting his sandals, his face now bearing sooty streaks. The sheriff's officer thanked him and set his mind on preventing the spread of the fire, and took charge of a dithering group of citizens armed with pitchforks and assorted implements.

It was only an hour before dawn when Catchpoll got back to his bed, shivering where he had sluiced himself down with a bucket of water. He still stank of woodsmoke, and was only glad that his wife was a sound sleeper. Had she woken and seen the state of him, he would have been turfed out of bed and into the floor rushes.

After an inadequate amount of rest, Catchpoll was about the sheriff's business once more, with a muzzy headache and a foul temper. He returned to Corviserstrete, where black puddles and charred wood marked the night's disturbance. The carpenter's wife and children had been taken in by a neighbour. Wilfrid Glover was standing before the ruins of his business, shaking his head, his family forming a sad group behind him. He did not take any notice of the serjeant's arrival.

'Have you been amongst the ashes to find anything worth salvaging?' Catchpoll hardly thought there could be anything left among the blackened and twisted remains.

The glover opened his right fist, in silence. Two or three palming needles and a small knife without its handle, black but recognisable, lay upon his palm. They both stared at the remnants of his craft.

'That's all I possess. I had a fair stock of fine soft leather ready for the autumn . . . when the chill creeps into the air, that's when I do my best business . . . but 'tis all gone, and the home with it. I'm sending my wife and the children to her brother, a tanner out on the northern road. There's those who'll help but it will be seasons before I can trade alone again, and I would not take a lease here.' The man heaved a great sigh, and Catchpoll left him with a consoling clap on the back. There were no words that could be of help.

In all, the glover's, the carpenter's wood store and workshop, his house and an almost forgotten, narrow dwelling between the carpenter's and a besom maker's, had been destroyed. A sudden horrible thought struck Catchpoll; nobody had thought about the little *cott*. It had been no wider than a doorway and a shuttered window, and only the door frame now marked where once it had stood.

'Who lived here?' The question was urgent enough to rouse the glover.

'Why, Old Edgyth, she's a widow and—' He stopped and blenched beneath the soot on his cheeks. 'Sweet Jesu, I never thought!'

'Has she been seen, today?' Catchpoll could feel grim foreboding rising like bile, and anticipated the shake of the glover's head.

Without a word, he took a half-burnt broom that the besom maker had leant against his shopfront, and trod gingerly over what had, only yesterday, been the widow's threshold. His eyes scanned the blackened debris, and he used the shaft of the broom to prod about, but it was his nose that warned him. The smell of charred wood was heavy and all-pervading, but in one corner there was another smell vying with it, faint but distinctive. Burnt flesh, once recognised, was an odour, slightly sweet and like roasting swine, never forgotten. Several large beams had fallen, one flat and the others interlocked above it. Catchpoll heaved at the nearest. The blackened, crumbling surface still retained warmth, but the core of the wood was sound, and it was very heavy. He called to the glover, who came, with every show of reluctance. The pair of them moved the timbers carefully, but the glover gasped as the last one came away, and dropped the end he carried with a crash and an exclamation of horror. He put a hand to his mouth and turned away retching. Catchpoll looked down upon the crushed, black and grotesque remains of what was still just about discernible as a human form, curled up with the fists before the face. Age and gender were indiscernible, but where once there had been lips a few gapped teeth showed. The serjeant shook his head. It could be the result of an accident. The old woman could have knocked over a rush light as she prepared for the night. But if it was not . . . The townsfolk would link this fire with the last, whether or not it was connected, and then with the death on top they would begin to panic, seeing fire-raisers at every turn. Much as he disliked it, he would have to call for the undersheriff after all.

Chapter Three

The rain fell softly, as if trying not to disturb the mourners, but it had continued long enough to penetrate the top layer of soil that lay ready to fill the grave, darkening it, clogging it, so that the first few loads slid from the wooden shovel and landed with a heavy, dull thud. Hugh Bradecote had stood immobile, staring down into the trench, an uncomprehending frown creasing his brow, and with the rain plastering his dark hair to his head, dripping in chill rivulets down the back of his neck and from the end of his long, finely chiselled nose, as the priest intoned the familiar Latin of the burial service. At its conclusion, the villagers and retainers slipped away almost silently, save for the sob-laden breathing of an older woman clutching a heavily swaddled baby to her spare bosom, and protecting the tiny face from the rain: Ela's baby; his baby; his son; his heir.

It required a superhuman effort for Hugh to leave the sexton and his lad to their task. Walking away was breaking the last tie, seeing the last red sliver of sun set on his unexciting but not unhappy marriage, and leaving him confused and blinking in the moonless night of guilty grief. Theirs had been a fairly standard marriage based upon family and land, beneficial to both sides, entered into with the barest knowledge of the other partner. He had seen a young woman who was quite pretty, and whose voice was soft. He had not loved Ela, but that only added to his guilt, because she had loved him so very obviously, for from the first she had hero-worshipped him. He had been fond of her, though more when parted, for she had irritated him to the point of madness with her mindless adoration. Whatever he said was right; whatever he thought a good idea must be implemented without regard to any obstacles, and at once. He had sometimes returned from duty with his overlord to find his household in uproar, and Ela fluttering like a netted bird, just because tasks she thought he wanted undertaken had been delayed. All she had ever sought, he knew, was his approbation and affection, and the more she had tried, the less she had achieved.

The pregnancy had calmed her a little, and given a serenity she had never previously possessed. She had been so proud of her increasing figure, proof at last of her success as a wife. Only at odd times had he found her fretful, and that was when she had feared the child might be a girl, even though he had kept on telling her he did not mind as long as she and the child were healthy. He had said it without great thought, merely as a soothing thing to a woman with child, never imagining what was to come.

He had been almost relieved to be called away for several weeks earlier in the summer, his service demanded by the sheriff to take part in an expedition to break up a gang of brigands on Bredon Hill. Then, purely by chance, he had become involved in the hunt for a murderer in Pershore Abbey. At the conclusion of the investigation the sheriff had set him in the place of his newly deceased undersheriff, and so, in the end, Hugh had only returned home for the last month before the baby was due. The time had sped by, with the harvest to be got in, and a myriad of manorial duties to catch up upon, and when the time of Ela's lying-in had come it was a complete surprise to him.

He had returned from a pleasantly tiring day with his steward, who was keen for both his approval of plans for a new barn, and to show him the success of the year in sheep and grain. He had been anticipating a quiet evening, with a good dinner and some wine to savour, but had arrived home to find his hall in a state of mayhem and, it seemed to him, full of women. They either ignored him, or cast him accusing looks as they busied themselves with linen and pitchers, and when, on finding the cause of the bustle, he had tried to see his wife, he had been unceremoniously bundled out of his own solar.

He had been stunned by this revolution in his household, and at the same time conscious of excitement and some trepidation. The sounds emanating from within were not pleasant, and could be heard through the solid oak of the door. Ela's time of travail was not easy. He left the hall, and wandered around the small, palisaded bailey like a lost soul. In the kitchen he found no sign of the dinner he had expected, and had to content himself with a fresh loaf, a wedge of cheese and a slice of some cake-like pudding with plums in it. He ate them, sat upon a bench in the golden sunlight of an August evening, and stayed thus, quiet and immobile, until the sun dipped and the evening chill crept in. He returned to the hall reluctantly, but in the expectation that events would be progressing and he would see his bed, even if not until the early hours.

In the end he slept, badly, in his chair upon the low dais, with his feet up on the trestled table and his cloak as a covering. When he had asked one of the serving women, early in the night, to bring him a blanket, she had berated him for his callous self-interest, and disappeared into the solar strident in her indignation at the selfishness of the male of the species. She had clearly imparted his crime to the other members of the sorority within, for he neither got his blanket nor peace. Whenever a woman emerged during the night, he was convinced they were especially noisy to keep him from sleep. He awoke a final time, with a crick in his neck and pins and needles in one arm, as dawn broke, a dawn that brought neither resolution nor rest. He had never imagined that childbirth took so long. In his masculine innocence and ignorance, he had assumed that it would take some hours as a battle took place over a number of hours. This was the battle that women fought, and at the end emerged exhausted but victorious. The small voice of reality inside his head that reminded him of the battles lost grew louder.

As the morning progressed, the atmosphere began to change. When he saw any of the women they were clearly tired, but there was a grimness to them that Hugh could not ignore. The groans and cries from the solar were weaker, though frequent, and it was just before noon that his ears detected a different cry, the surprised and indignant cry of the newborn cast from the warm security of the womb into the vastness of the world. He got up suddenly, and swayed, for he had been sitting a long time, and the blood rushed to his feet. He gripped the arms of his seat for support, excitement building. It would be a few minutes more, he told himself, for babes needed cleaning and swaddling. He thought perhaps his wife's tirewoman would bring the baby out to him if Ela was still being tended.

The door opened, and the youngest of the serving wenches hurried past, tight-lipped, without so much as a word or glance. A ball of fear began to knot itself in his stomach. He went to the door, left half open, and stood upon the threshold. Even a man could tell that the scene was not right. Ela lay back upon the bed, a small bundle tucked next to her head. Her tirewoman, who had been her own nurse, was stroking her brow and rocking gently to and fro, with tears coursing down her cheeks. The other women were silent. One was praying, her lips moving wordlessly, while another was bundling bloodied cloths out the way. There was an awful lot of blood; upon the linen, upon the midwife's arms, and upon the bed. The sheet was drawn up to Ela's chin, but a large and very wet, bright-red stain seemed to be spreading through it, like the petals of a scarlet flower.

Hugh said nothing. Words would not come, and he looked blankly at the women. The accusation was still there: you brought her to this; it is your blame. Now, though, there was also pity. A hand in the small of his back propelled him forward.

'She'll want to see you, my lord,' whispered the woman.

He drew close to the head of the bed. His wife's face was

unnaturally pale, and tinged blue around the lips. Her eyes struggled to focus upon him, and her voice, when it came, took all her strength yet emerged as a frail thread of sound. He had seen such faces before, but most had been men, or old. He had stood at his father's bedside, but that death had been a while coming, and was a relief in the end, and his mother, well, he had been away then, and another lord had informed him of his loss, and another lady had held him as he, at fourteen, wept in desolation. But this was his wife, this was Ela, who had not seen a score of summers, and had just given him a child. He had ridden out yesterday and she had even been laughing, happy, and now . . .

'See, my lord. I have given you a son. You are pleased?' Even now she sought confirmation of his approbation.

He reached out a trembling hand and touched her cheek, which was clammy cold.

'Of course I am pleased, sweet. Now you must rest and . . .' He halted, for the lies would not come. She was dying, and she knew it as well as he did.

Her hand crept with great effort to grip his own tightly, though he felt it as not more than a fragile clasp.

'You will see he is loved.' It was an affirmation not a plea. Ela Bradecote's voice was scarce more than a whisper, but level and calm. 'I would ask a favour, my lord.'

He made a strangled sound that she correctly interpreted as assent.

'Name him for my father. Gilbert Bradecote sounds well, I think.' She paused, and sighed. 'I am sorry, Hugh, but I have no strength left.' She closed her eyes. 'It is not so hard . . . dying . . . but I wish . . . our baby . . . so sorry, my lord. Hugh, I . . .' Whatever words were in her clouding thoughts, dimmed and disappeared. Her eyes closed, the lids drooping until shut.

Hugh felt a hand on his shoulder and jumped. It was the priest, Father Achard. The parish priest said nothing, but passed immediately round to the other side of the bed and knelt beside the dying woman. It must be like drowning, thought Hugh dimly; he was aware but unable to do anything, and all was taking place so very slowly. He watched, as the good Father gave the Last Rites; as the breathing grew more shallow; and ceased so softly that it was perhaps a full minute before he realised she was gone. It seemed so easy, as she had said, dying. There was no sound in the chamber for what seemed an age, and then the baby, still lying beside its dead mother, whimpered and broke the spell. The old nurse made to pick him up, but Hugh pushed her hand aside, quite fiercely, and lifted his son to look for a moment into the impossibly blue eyes within the tiny, puckering, red face. Then he held him close, the baby's cheek, soft as doeskin, against his own unshaven one, and shut his eyes as they filled with tears and a ball of angry misery filled his chest.

Eventually, the nurse took the infant, and Father Achard led Hugh Bradecote into the hall and sat him down. He leant forward, sagging.

'It is my fault,' whispered Hugh, looking down at his hands, which shook. He clasped them as if in prayer, but tightly so that the knuckles whitened, in an effort to still them. 'It is my fault.'

'No, my son.' Father Achard laid a hand on his arm. 'It

was God's will. Your lady wife was a good Christian soul, and departed shriven. God will look kindly upon her and show His grace upon those she leaves behind. I cannot tell you why she was taken now, for I have never truly understood how it can be best for a babe to arrive at the moment of its mother's departure, but I have been at many such bedsides. The boy will be a comfort to you; a gift from God and from her. Do not blame yourself. She would not want it, would she?'

'You do not understand, Father.' Hugh looked up, and there was horror in his wet eyes. 'It is because of my sin. That is why God has taken her from me, and from our son. *Mea culpa, mea culpa, mea maxima culpa.*'

The priest frowned. Grieving husbands were generally easy to comprehend, if not to solace.

'You take too much upon yourself. God would not take her life to punish you. I am—'

'Please, Father. Hear my confession; hear it now.'

So it was that Hugh Bradecote told the priest of his feelings, unexpected and intense, for a Benedictine Sister he had known, for a few days only, earlier in the summer, during the investigation of the murders at Pershore Abbey.

Father Achard listened patiently to the whole tale. In truth, he thought that Hugh Bradecote's sin was a minor misdemeanour in the catalogue of sins he had heard confessed in his time. The man had fallen slightly enamoured of a nun, rather for her spirit and her mind, he gathered, than carnal desires for her flesh, at a time when both were in a stressful situation, and the culmination of this four-day interlude had been a single kiss. Well, it was a sin, no doubt of it, but not one so dreadful that it would bring down damnation from On High. He supposed that, facing such a loss, Bradecote found it easier to have a reason than for it to be inexplicable. The priest gave him his penance, more to prove to the man that there was forgiveness than chasten him. It was evident that his conscience had already been far more rigorous than any priest.

After the funeral the lord of the manor withdrew into his hall, morose and monosyllabic. The baby gave the nurse distraction from her grief, and the wet nurse provided a focus for her complaints, but Hugh Bradecote felt superfluous in his own home. He looked at his son with a mixture of pride and incomprehension. He could detect no resemblance to either Ela or himself, whatever the nurse said, and sounds and movements that seemed to cause so much delight among the cooing women meant nothing to him. A newborn was not something, someone, to whom he as a man could relate. The pride that would normally suffice, the pride that said 'this is the living proof of my potency, the next of my line', was tempered by the knowledge that the simple and pleasurable act of giving his seed had cost Ela not just the months of sickness and carrying, but her very life. The women removed her garments, the clear signs of her presence, but he found little things, a comb, a half-stitched baby cap, things that chastised him for her absence. How often, he thought, bitterly, had he wished for peace from her fussing, and to be left alone. Well, now he was left alone.

His retainers tried to leave him alone, reading an unexpected depth of loss in his behaviour. Their very respectful withdrawal, and lowered voices in his presence, added to the atmosphere of gloom. Hugh himself did not miss his wife particularly; did not keep recalling things she had said or how she had looked, although sometimes, out of habit, he expected to turn and see her, anxiously adoring as ever. He was filled, however, with an enormous lethargy and inability to think, his brain clogged as though with the solid earth that covered her shrouded, coffined corpse. Whilst the priest had granted absolution, he still felt a weight of guilt, now because he had not loved Ela. That he had not been expected to love her was immaterial. If he had tried harder, could he have loved her? Had he expected too much of her? Should he have told her the soft, kind lie, as she departed life, that he did love her?

For the best part of three weeks Hugh Bradecote ceased to function properly. He ate sparely, slept badly, and began to look thin, hollow of cheek, sunken of eye, and unkempt. Then the message arrived from Worcester. Simon Furnaux, the castellan, was calling him in as undersheriff, to head the investigation into a series of suspicious fires in the absence of his superior.

Bradecote had to read the missive several times before he broke free of the fog within his mind. Then he roused himself, without enthusiasm but at least with a purpose. He shaved his rough-bearded chin, nicking the skin and swearing volubly as the blood dripped into the bowl of water. He had never been squeamish about the sight of blood, but the welling redness suddenly brought back the image of the bed, the bed from which he had sent all coverings, and the palliasse also, to be burnt, soaked as it was with blood, so much blood, her blood, and never a wound from which it could have come. He shook himself, thrusting the image into as far a recess of his brain as he could, dressed in fresh attire and called for his horse. He was actually on the point of departure when he remembered his son. He dismounted, and went back to the solar. The nursemaid was half asleep by the glowing brazier that warmed the room, for even the summer warmth did not pass through the thick stone walls. Gilbert Bradecote lay asleep in his cradle, one tiny fist, escaped from the swaddling, pressed against his cheek. Hugh bent and kissed his son very softly, offered up a prayer to God, and left without a backward glance.

Chapter Four

Serjeant Catchpoll was supervising the sharpening of blades on a whetstone in the bailey when Hugh Bradecote and the returning messenger trotted into the castle. Only when he drew close did the serjeant see the difference in the undersheriff, and his eyes narrowed. The man was sallow, and hollow of eye and cheek. He wondered at first if he had been ailing and had come from his sickbed. He nodded in acknowledgement of his superior.

'My lord.'

'Catchpoll.' There was no emotion in the voice, though it was strong enough.

'It's sorry I am to bring you in, my lord, but the lord sheriff is laid up on one of his manors, and the situation here needs delicate handling. If it is all mischance then the folk need someone in authority to convince them, and if it's malice . . . well, then we are in for a right time of it.'

'You can explain fully when I have seen the castellan and eaten.' Bradecote dismounted and gave his horse into the care of a waiting groom. His tone was matter-of-fact, even dismissive. Catchpoll ground his teeth.

The messenger was leading his own mount away, and saw Catchpoll's expression. 'S'pose you ought to make allowances for him being a cheerless bastard. He buried his lady a week or so back, and has a squalling babe in his hall. His people said he's barely slept since.'

Catchpoll merely grunted, not wishing to show any obvious interest in this information, but it made a difference.

The hall of the castle was not a place to share confidences, being both busy and noisy during meals. Catchpoll watched Bradecote, with the castellan spouting at length on his trials and tribulations, including the threat of an unsettled populace. When the meal was drawing to a close the serjeant took pity on the undersheriff and approached the dais. He requested Bradecote's attention with unusual politeness, though the castellan tried to wave him away. Bradecote was keen to make his escape, and would not delay the conference with the serjeant. He willingly assented to Catchpoll's idea that they should discuss matters in private, and left the hall with no small degree of relief.

'How does the sheriff put up with him? He'd drive a saint to murder.' There was weariness in his voice and he dragged his long fingers through his hair.

Catchpoll grinned. 'He does what he does best: he shouts loudly and listens not at all. It's not easy when the pair are in residence. The Earl Waleran made the lord sheriff his constable when they found themselves both supporting the Empress, and "suggested" the lord Furnaux as his deputy. It does not matter to Earl Waleran that the man is as much use as a shrivelled pizzle, since he is mostly concerned with his lands abroad these days. Of course, the lord Furnaux leaves off the "deputy". Would have mattered in the past, him being useless, but less so now. Earl Robert of Gloucester ain't likely to want to burn us out now that my lord sheriff is also for the Empress Maud.'

Bradecote smiled, though it was both brief and weak, and it did not touch the blue-grey eyes.

'Now you can tell me exactly why it is that you feel the need to call me in. I thought you preferred to hunt alone.'

'What "I wants" don't come into it on this occasion. There was a fire 'bout a week ago, in a silversmith's shop. Fires happen, and not as rarely as you'd think, but this one had a suspicion of being started with intention. It was only a suspicion, mind, and after some digging, it seemed not worth making too much of. Then, this night last, there was another fire, a bigger one this time, and with a death. It might be just mischance, them being so close together, but the townsmen are rattled. If there's another, heaven forbid, we'll have the burgesses in uproar and foolish women in every street crying out at the lighting of a lamp. So we needs to be seen to be doing something, and it will be up to you to placate 'em all if things get difficult.'

'Ah. So we don't know if there has been a crime at all?'

'No, my lord.'

'And even if one or both are the work of a fire-raiser, we don't know of any connection?'

'No, my lord.'

'I see. Well, I am not familiar with the town, so I am at a disadvantage to start with. I suggest that tomorrow morning you take me around and show me where the fires were, and we can speak to the people involved. Um . . . how exactly do you hunt down the culprit in a case like this?'

'Not sure yet, my lord. Never had to do it before. Catching them with a lighted torch would help, but otherwise . . .' He shook his head, grimacing, and Bradecote echoed the expression. 'Get yourself a good night's sleep then, my lord, and we'll get going tomorrow.'

No mention had been made of Bradecote's loss. Catchpoll turned away, and did not see the look on Bradecote's face alter. 'A good night's sleep' sounded like an impossible dream.

The morning brought a soft drizzle, and the sheriff's pair set out early. Catchpoll cast his superior a sidelong glance. His instruction of the evening before had clearly not been followed; the shadows under Hugh Bradecote's eyes were as deep as ever.

They headed first for the site of the silversmith's shop. Reginald Ash had wares laid out at the front of his premises and was actively seeking purchasers. He was by nature a craftsman who let his workmanship do the selling, and his efforts as a salesman would have been put to shame by any market stallholder. Nevertheless, when serjeant and undersheriff approached, he greeted them without a long face or complaining tone.

'I have been very fortunate, in the circumstances. I still have work to sell and have raised both money and bartered work for it. There's a man out the back sorting the thatch, and I gave the builder a cunningly wrought ring and a torque for his young wife. It's glad I am he is new wed and keen to please her. Members of the craft have been generous too, lending any spare tools to aid me. I reckon I will be back in business proper by Michaelmas.'

'I would like to show the lord undersheriff where the fire started, Master Ash. Is your journeyman at hand?'

'Aye, he's assisting the thatcher. It don't take two of us to sell, and I don't fancy working with the roof going back on above me. You take a look, my lord.' Master Ash made obeisance to Bradecote.

The silversmith waved them into the back of the premises, and turned his attention to a well-dressed young matron who was examining a cloak brooch.

Behind the shopfront the extent of the damage was visible both in the blackened beams and freshly whitened walls. The beams themselves had merely suffered exterior charring and were sound enough, although the inside of the premises would smell of charcoal, above that used by the smith, for months yet. The workshop area occupied the rear portion of the front chamber opening onto the street. It was here that the smith had his little furnace. To the rear was a door into the living chamber behind, with a ladder up to a small loft beneath the eaves, perhaps half the size of the area below. The hearth was near the division of the front and rear chambers, giving the maximum room between fire and thatch. There was a low back door, leading out to a midden and cramped yard. It was here that they found Edwin the journeyman handing up the straw to the thatcher. When he became aware of them he abandoned this task, and, rubbing the crick in his neck, asked how he could help.

There was not much to be gleaned that Catchpoll did not already know. Edwin pointed out where he had first seen the flames, which was some way from the hearth. If he was right, then it could not have started with an untended cook-pot. What Catchpoll had not seen on that first visit after the fire was the little wicket gate at the back of the yard. He and Bradecote exchanged glances, and Catchpoll went out to see where it led. Meanwhile, Bradecote bethought himself of the thatcher and called up to him. He himself had no knowledge of the material involved and how easily it caught light, or how swiftly a fire would take hold. After shouting up his questions, he was pleased that the thatcher came down his ladder and saved him Edwin's discomfort.

'When thatch catches, it burns fierce, my lord, but it isn't like tinder, not unless the weather's been unseasonably dry. This summer has given us enough rain to keep the outer layer damp half the time. A stray spark drifting up from a hearth wouldn't be likely to do harm, and besides, this roof burnt from this edge, and probably this corner, towards the front.'

Bradecote was stunned. He had not thought it would be possible to tell such a thing.

'But how can you know?'

The thatcher smiled; it was the smile of the expert faced with the ignorant public.

'Easy enough, my lord. When I first came to look at the job you could see the thatch pulled down from the front of

53

the place, which hadn't caught. The neighbours worked quickly, and dragged down more from the right side than the left. Much of that I could use again, and did so to give Master Ash a decent place from which to sell. The flames did not take, I should guess, to the front third, and, mark you, for this is important, there was less damage on the side where the hearth is set. If it had been a cooking fire, well then, the flames would have eaten away from the middle and the only salvaged thatch would be round the edge, like a priest's tonsure.'

He laughed at his mild wit, and Bradecote responded likewise, grateful for the information.

'If you had to start a fire in the thatch, how would you do it, Master Thatcher?'

The thatcher looked momentarily horrified, though Bradecote could not decide whether from fear of being suspected or revulsion that one of his trade could perform such an act of destruction. Then his features eased. 'I understand, my lord. Well, you couldn't just use tinder, a feather stick or such rammed in the thatch; it is too dense. No, I would light a fire beneath that would heat up the thatch to catching point and then . . . whoosh. It would give me time to escape as well.'

Bradecote nodded. What the thatcher said was very true. Assuming that the silversmith and his journeyman would be busy in the workshop, anyone entering the rear of the building could have climbed to the loft and set a fire going where the eaves met the boards. He thanked the thatcher for his assistance, and complimented him on his work. He then turned, in time to see Catchpoll come back through the wicket gate. The serjeant's expression was glum. Edwin cleared his throat, unsure as to whether he was still required or could go back to his task. Bradecote only had one question for him, and one that was simple to answer. With a small obeisance, the journeyman left the two sheriff's officers to discuss matters between themselves in low tones.

'The gate leads onto an alley, which runs behind all these plots right up towards St Andrew's, and with several side turnings onto the frontages. One comes out almost next door, right by where the lean-to was pulled down. Anyone could have used it unbeknownst.' Catchpoll pulled a face indicative of how fate had given them poor fare.

'But they would have to have knowledge of it. We can at least discount an outsider. Whoever set this fire knows Worcester.'

'That's good, then. And just how many hundreds does that narrow it down to, my lord?' Catchpoll sneered. He remembered just how irritating it was to have a 'superior' amateur teaching him his business.

Bradecote did not rise to the bait. His mind was trying to sort out all the information he had received into a semblance of order. When he spoke again, it was almost to himself.

'The journeyman slept in the loft space and had a palliasse there. Lighting that would be easy enough, and give time for the fire-setter to withdraw before the thatch reached the point of catching. It is possible that they simply took a good opportunity, but I would guess that they knew about the loft and sleeping arrangements. We should ask Master Ash who has been into his back chamber.'

Catchpoll gave his grudging agreement, but did not think much would be gained. He was right. Master Ash could name few who had entered the private part of the premises.

'There's the girl who cooks, of course, and I have had other smiths in of an evening, on Holy Days and such.' He grinned. 'And I dare swear that Edwin's wench, young Winflaed, has seen more of that loft than anyone else, aye, and been looking up at the thatch too.' He laughed, but then grew serious. 'I'd be hard-pushed to see any of them being involved in my fire.'

Bradecote noted the proprietorial term. Now the fire and its ravages had been overcome, and life looked set to recover, the master silversmith seemed to have relaxed, as if the fire were a contagion, that if survived, granted immunity thereafter.

There was no more to be gleaned from the silversmith's, and so serjeant and undersheriff made their way to the site of the second fire. Here the devastation was but a couple of days old, raw and rank; a wound upon the town. Those who passed by the blackened wreck of what had been the old widow's dwelling shook their heads and crossed themselves.

The glover was gone, but there were two labourers clearing the ground where his shop had stood, making ready for a new construction, and another on the site of the woodyard. A fourth man, who seemed less inclined to dirty his hands and more inclined to instruct, was in heated conversation with a harassed-looking woman with two small children clinging at her skirts.

'I know that face,' muttered Catchpoll to Bradecote, his lips barely moving. 'He's Turgis, a bully boy in the employ of Robert Mercet, who has a tidy holding in the town. Not a pleasant character.'

'Master or man?'

'Well, neither really. Come from the same strain of heartless, greedy bastards. It's just that Mercet's sires were more efficient.'

The woman was in tears now, wringing her hands. This did not have any effect on the man, except to make him smile in a particularly evil manner, and lean forward menacingly to whisper in her ear. The woman shrank back, her face flaming, and made to hit him. He was too fast, however, and caught the arm, laughing as she winced with the tight pressure.

Bradecote stepped forward smartly and laid his own hand, quite lightly, upon the man's shoulder.

'I do not think the lady likes your ways, friend. Best leave her alone, I think.'

The man, who was half a head shorter than Bradecote but of much heavier build, turned to see who had accosted him, and curled his lip derisively.

'And what do you have to do with it, my fine lord?'

'Quite a lot. He's the new lord Undersheriff of the Shire, and he's probably the only one who can stop me ramming your filthy teeth down your throat.' Catchpoll had picked up a rake that had been left against a charred cruck, and pressed the handle end into the man's neck. The eyes swivelled to Catchpoll, although the man remained very still. Serjeant Catchpoll was neither large nor heavily built, but conveyed an ability to inflict a remarkable amount of pain, very easily, and with no compunction about doing so.

'Ah, it's you, Serjeant.'

'Indeed, Turgis. So you'll be doing as the lord undersheriff says, and back off.'

Bradecote was appreciative of Catchpoll's introduction, but

did not wish to be left out of the encounter. He looked first to the woman, who seemed still fearful.

'Has this man threatened you, mistress?'

Her eyes widened, and she glanced first at the man, whose own eyes flashed warning.

'No, my lord. It was a misunderstanding.' Her voice was hesitant and the lie palpable.

'I see. And would it still be a misunderstanding if he was not stood here next to you?'

She coloured, but said nothing.

'Then you, Turgis, if I caught the name aright, had best be about your business elsewhere.'

The big man bridled. 'But I am here to oversee the clearing of the site, my lord.'

'Clearing it of wreckage or of people?' Catchpoll growled, and received a look of loathing in reply.

'It was not a suggestion, Turgis. It was an instruction.' Bradecote's tone was cold, and intentionally insulting. For a moment the man dithered, then he turned on his heel and swaggered off with as much bravado as he could muster.

One of the children began to cry, softly, unsettled by the angry adults he did not understand, and the woman bent to take him up in her arms.

'He will return, and then what am I to do?'

'If he does, we know where to find him, so I would not worry. Mistress Carpenter, is it?' Catchpoll's powers of deduction were reasonably acute.

'Godith Woodman, the carpenter's wife, yes.'

'And where is your husband, Mistress Woodman? Still not

returned?' Bradecote's voice was calming, even reassuring.

'No, my lord, but he was not expected back for a sennight. He has gone to his brother and then on towards Feckenham to choose timber for a commission from the cathedral. He was keen to select special timber.' Her voice cracked. 'And when he returns, it will be to this.'

'But you and the children have shelter, and food?'

She nodded. 'Our neighbours are good folk, but we cannot stay with them forever, and where is my Martin to work, and with his tools lost or ruined? And then Master Mercet's man comes and says he does not want us here. There are to be new premises here, not a woodyard. We have nowhere to go.' She was sobbing now. 'That man said,' she bit her lip, 'he might be able to persuade his master if I . . .' She shook her head and closed her eyes in anguish and shame.

'We understand. Can Mercet do that, Catchpoll? Build something else, I mean.'

'Not sure, my lord. Depends, I suppose, upon the tenancy. If the carpenter has a commission from the cathedral that is large enough for him to go that far for the wood, then they might have somewhere where he could work, or a vacant lease. The Church has a lot of property hereabouts.'

'Yes, that would be a good idea. Tell your husband that on his return, and if needs be, let me know at the castle and I will speak with Father Prior.'

Bradecote had no real idea if the solution was practicable, but was keen to give the carpenter's wife some hope while she was alone. He wanted her calm enough to give him fair answers, for a motive for the fire had occurred to him. A bench stood outside the besom maker's frontage, and he guided her to it and sat down beside her. Catchpoll caught his eye, and went to speak with the labourers, who had resumed their work now that the excitement was over.

'Has Mercet made any suggestion or threat to you about your tenancy before this?'

Bradecote was reluctant to use 'threat' but was not sure if anything less would gain a response. He was disappointed, however, because Mistress Woodman clearly knew nothing. All matters of business were conducted with her husband, she said, and she had never had speech with Master Mercet or any of his hirelings until today. She cast the undersheriff a nervous look, fearful of displeasing him, and trembled at the grim set of his mouth. It was not her answer that had made him so, but the manner, which had been so reminiscent of Ela that he almost caught his breath.

Despite the unsatisfactory response from the carpenter's wife, Bradecote was keen to investigate the possible involvement of the unseen but malevolent Mercet. He thanked the woman, reminded her to tell her spouse about the priory, and crossed to where Catchpoll was in apparently light-hearted conversation with the labourers.

Bradecote had seen Catchpoll at this ploy before, and knew how effective it could be in eliciting information. He was not surprised, therefore, to catch the meaningful twinkle in the serjeant's eye. Catchpoll disengaged himself gently from the conversation and left the men to their work.

'I take it you have ferreted out something interesting, Catchpoll.'

'Possibly, my lord. I say no more than that at present, but it may prove useful.'

'I, too, but I've no wish to discuss matters in the street. Should we return to the castle? I fear being trapped by the castellan.'

Catchpoll made a deprecating noise in his throat. 'You could come to my place, my lord. The wife will leave well alone and we can talk as long as we like.' He did not appear pleased at the thought, but had as little desire to be distracted by the lord Furnaux.

'Thank you, Catchpoll. That might be a very good idea.'

The pair walked in amicable silence through the streets of Worcester, parting like the current round rocks past the busy folk about their business in the town, caught up in their own cogitations and ignoring the bustle of the populace.

At last they sat at the bench table in Catchpoll's little *cott*. It was dark within, and motes of dust cavorted playfully in the shaft of sunlight that came through the open doorway. Mistress Catchpoll had been torn between anger at her husband bringing gentry to her hearth without warning, and delight at what she would be able to tell her cronies about her illustrious visitor. She kept out of the way, as Catchpoll had said, but only out of earshot, not view.

The two men settled themselves with a jug of ale and Bradecote set out his discoveries first. Catchpoll agreed that Mercet was worth watching and speaking to about the fire in Corviserstrete, but threw up the problem that the silversmith owned his own property.

'But did he perhaps buy the premises from Mercet and Mercet now regrets the sale or the price?'

Catchpoll scratched his grizzled cheek ruminatively. 'That might be so, but would be difficult to prove.'

'But if it had been his, then he, or more likely his man Turgis, would know the layout of the rear chamber well enough.' Bradecote was reluctant to let his theory drop.

'Fair enough, my lord. We should pay Master Mercet a visit, I'm thinking. Even if he wasn't involved in the fire, his activities since warrant our attention. It would be good to let him know that we know what he is about. But you are not the only one with a trail to follow.' Catchpoll halted, tantalisingly, but Bradecote only smiled drily, and forbore to look interested. Catchpoll shrugged and continued.

'The men clearing what had been the glover's shop told me about the old woman, the Widow Edgyth. It seems she had quite a reputation, not that I knew much of her. Some people were afraid of her, said she was a witch, but she certainly made balms and potions for the sick. What is even more interesting is that she was a woman visited by young women who found themselves with child and wished they were not. The men said it was common knowledge that she brewed draughts that would make a woman miscarry.'

Bradecote was frowning. 'So you think the object of the fire was to rid the world of Old Edgyth . . . a jealous leech or an angry man who wanted to be a father?'

'Unlikely to be the latter, my lord. Most men whose wenches seek to lose a babe are either married already or likely to be assaulted by the girl's kin for their lustfulness. No, what occurs to me is the connection between the two fires.' He saw Bradecote's perplexity and grinned; a death's head, mirthless grin. It was good to be ahead of his superior. This time the undersheriff did react.

'Come on, Serjeant. Don't play with me.'

'Well, my lord, when I was first at the silversmith's an old woman let loose the information that Edwin the journeyman's girl was with child. It wasn't something any man could tell, I assure you, and it caused quite a stir. I wonder if it was this Old Edgyth. When I saw the body, well, her kin would not have recognised the remains. The girl, Winflaed, might have thought to rid herself of the child and then changed her mind, or had Edwin change it for her.'

'What you are saying is that the motive would be that the girl or her lover wanted revenge upon the old woman for letting their secret into the open. It sounds rather thin, unless the girl has been cast out and Edwin punished.'

'That's not the case, though the girl's father was far from pleased.' There was a pause while Catchpoll sorted his thoughts. 'If the old woman had given the girl the opportunity to get rid of the child and Edwin had been firmly against it, he might well be angry with the person who had been willing to help.'

'But angry enough to set a fire? And what reason was there for the first fire if Edwin and Master Ash get on well?'

'There's the rub, I'll grant you, my lord, but perhaps there's undercurrents we don't yet know about. All I am saying is we have a connection, and that's more than we had an hour or so ago.'

Bradecote sighed and rubbed his chin thoughtfully.

'The body you found in the widow's dwelling was Old Edgyth? I mean, it might have been—'

Catchpoll raised a hand and interrupted. 'I'd swear it was so. The corpse was not recognisable except as human, but the size was right and the teeth showed clearly. Neither the widow nor the body had many teeth. The glover attested to that. The old crone I saw by the silversmith's also lacked teeth. If it was a different person it would have to be an extraordinary coincidence. And the woman has not been seen since.'

'Could the fire have been accidental?'

'Not if it started in the wood store, as Father Boniface said.'

'Who is Father Boniface?'

'The priest at St Andrew's. He said he raised the alarm, and that was because he saw the fire in the wood store.'

The younger man steepled his fingers together and stared at them for a minute or so. Catchpoll's wife set a fresh loaf, a heel of cheese and a platter of warm oatcakes before them and withdrew silently. The serjeant pushed them towards Bradecote, but the undersheriff was too lost in his thoughts to take notice. Catchpoll cut himself some cheese and a hunk of bread and began to eat, unhurriedly.

Eventually Bradecote roused himself and slapped his hands on the table.

'We have a lot to do, Catchpoll, though I do not know if it will advance our investigation. So much seems to be proving what did not happen and who did not do it. Have we much chance on this one, do you think?'

'Couldn't say, my lord. But the lord sheriff will be mightily aggrieved if he returns to find Worcester in uproar, and bits of it smouldering, so we had best hope we're lucky.'

Bradecote groaned, and Catchpoll grinned, proffering the food again. 'Eat up, my lord, and you'll work better on a full belly.'

Mistress Catchpoll was later able to tell her intimates that her noble visitor had complimented her on her baking, especially the oatcakes.

Chapter Five

After their repast, the sheriff's men split up; Catchpoll departed to find out what he could about Edwin and Winflaed, and Bradecote went to seek out the priest of St Andrew's. They agreed to meet again later, and pay a visit upon Robert Mercet.

Bradecote had little trouble in finding St Andrew's Church, but the incumbent was more difficult to track down. The church itself was cool and empty, and the advice of a woman passing by with a basket of washing, which was to knock at the door of the small adjacent dwelling, proved equally fruitless. The undersheriff had no wish to be idle, but he was also keen to have Catchpoll present when he spoke to Mercet. He sighed, and went back into the church. He was surprised to see a dark-habited figure trimming a candle.

'Father Boniface?' Bradecote's tone was uncertain.

The cleric turned. 'Yes.'

There was no welcome in the voice, nor softening of the austere features. Here, thought Bradecote, was a man who would not show much understanding of the errors of his flock. He was quite young, perhaps only in his late twenties, but the stern demeanour aged him. He was tall, almost gangly, and the robe hung from him as though his body were the clapper in a bell. The ring of hair about his tonsure was very dark, and showed a tendency to wave, but looked as though such frivolity was frequently chastised by water and comb. The dark brows beetled over a finely chiselled face with hard grey eyes. Bradecote felt that pleasure of any sort was anathema to the man.

'I am sorry, Father. I was here only a few minutes ago and could not find you. I tried your house also.' Bradecote wondered why he was apologising to the man.

'I came in through the sacristy door. How may I help you?'

'I am Hugh Bradecote, the undersheriff. I wish to speak to you about the fire in Corviserstrete the other night. You raised the alarm, it seems.'

The priest nodded.

'Yes. Heaven be praised that I was there! It is not the usual route I would have taken, but I had been considering a difficult problem, and, you know, I find walking is beneficial. My steps must have been guided.' He shook his head. 'I am glad that so many were spared, but, dear me, the old widow woman must have been hard of hearing or sound asleep, and in the bustle was forgotten. She died unshriven, and in the midst of her sin. It will go harshly against her.'

Bradecote was shocked by the stern edge to the priest's last words.

'Surely an old woman would have little left to confess?' He tried to sound cheering.

Father Boniface stared at him stonily. 'Assuming she had confessed all the earlier sins of her life, and not hidden them in her shame. The depths of iniquity suck many into it, and damnation is eternal.'

'Yes, well . . .' Bradecote had no desire to be given a lesson on the price of sin. He looked uncomfortable. A silence hung in the air until the priest broke it.

'What is it that you hoped to learn from me?' Father Boniface enquired.

Bradecote reassembled his thoughts. 'Only to find out where you saw the fire first of all, and whether you saw anybody else about beforehand.'

The priest clasped his fingers together, and thought for a moment.

'I certainly saw the fire in the wood store, and I think, yes, it may have already enveloped the dwelling next to it on the one side, but was only just spreading to the carpenter's house at that time. It must have begun in the yard on the furthest side from the house. Once the alarm was raised so much happened all at once. Alas, fire is a most crafty enemy that can move swiftly, and yet with furtiveness. It could have already been smouldering ready to take other lives even as I saw it. We were fortunate that no other souls were lost.'

'And did you see anyone else before you cried out?'

Father Boniface shook his head. 'I was not concentrating on

where I was walking, you must understand, so it is possible that someone could have stepped into the shadows and slipped past me, but I saw nobody.'

'I think you should be more wary if you walk in the dark, Father. Not all the citizens of Worcester are honest.'

Father Boniface gave a tight smile. 'Those that are less honest would also know that a priest would have nothing worth stealing.' He held open his arms. 'Would they steal habit and rope girdle?'

He had a point, acknowledged Bradecote. There seemed little more to be gained from the man, so Bradecote thanked him and withdrew.

Out in the open, he took a great gulp of air, though it was not as fresh as the country air he preferred. The cleric's manner had been oppressive to the spirit, like a heavy black rain cloud. Bradecote headed for his appointed rendezvous with Catchpoll, hoping the serjeant had spent a more profitable hour, but when he espied him there was nothing in his demeanour to suggest he was bursting with news.

Serjeant Catchpoll had made the same assessment as his superior, and was caught between a feeling of pleasure that the undersheriff had not made some astounding discovery alone, and the weary recognition that there was an awful lot more work to be done.

'So we can't return to the castle crowing of our success like midden cocks, my lord,' he concluded at the end of his report. He had tried the besom maker next to the Widow Edgyth's dwelling, but the man had been little use. He had seen a fair number of young women tap at the old woman's door, but then he had seen an equal number of men, young and old, and children too, with eggs or such to pay for the widow's remedies. Catchpoll had described Winflaed, but the man had shaken his head. Fair maids, dark maids, fallen maids or old maids, he had not the time nor indeed the inclination to gawp at his neighbour's visitors.

'And have you tried around the silversmith's?'

Catchpoll frowned. 'Of course, my lord. Do you take me for a bumblehead?' The question was clearly rhetorical. 'A woman who lives opposite the fletcher was happy enough to tell me about the arguments she's heard between Winflaed and her father, and says she thought the silversmith's journeyman was smitten with the girl, but nothing more. Master Ash and Edwin have nary a cross word, it seems, and master treats journeyman like a favoured son, so there is no sensible motive for Edwin to start a fire, or rather get Winflaed to do it for him since he was with Master Ash when the fire was noticed. I asked the woman if she knew the old widow, and if she had seen Winflaed or her swain seeking her balms, but that meant nothing to her, I swear.'

'And I have nothing wondrous to report from Father Boniface, other than I am heartily glad not to be one of his parishioners. They must pay heavy penance for their sins in that church, I tell you. But the priest could not say he saw anyone when the fire sprang up, nor if the wood store was actually the source of the fire.'

'Then I suggest we get on and cheer ourselves with a visit to Master Mercet, my lord.'

'Cheer ourselves?' Hugh Bradecote raised a mobile eyebrow.

'Indeed. He'll make you want to commit an act of violence upon him, on behalf of the good folk of Worcester, but we should be able to put paid to some of his plans, and that is almost as good.' Catchpoll's eyes glittered at the thought, and his death's head smile grew.

Mercet's house stood on a fine burgage plot amidst those of Worcester's wealthiest citizenry. The door was opened by a serving man whose demeanour was that of one keen to keep visitors out rather than usher them in. His gaze bypassed Bradecote entirely, as his eyes alighted on Catchpoll. They narrowed instantly, and he made to shut the door in their faces, but the serjeant stepped smartly forward, unceremoniously barging past his superior and keeping the door open by foot and hand. He smiled, which made the minion look even less comfortable.

'Good day to you, Serlo. We was wondering if we might be favoured with a few minutes of Master Mercet's so very valuable time.' The tone was soft, and had it not been for an undertone of pure menace, almost apologetic. Serlo, not bright enough to read the signs, grinned.

'My master is not seeing folk this afternoon. He is busy.'

'Ah yes. So many pies to stick his filthy fingers into; so many widows and orphans to cast into the streets, eh? Well,' Catchpoll paused and thrust his face forward into Serlo's, 'I think you did not understand. When I said "we wondered", I really meant "we will". Now run along like the faithful cur you are, and tell him the lord Undersheriff of Worcester and his old friend Serjeant Catchpoll are coming in for a little visit.'

Serlo rolled his eyes, caught between the knowledge that his master would be mightily displeased, and the growing fear that Catchpoll would do something unspecified but extremely painful. The latter prevailed. He bolted back down the gloomy passageway, and the sheriff's men followed, not waiting for a response.

'You have a way with words, Serjeant,' remarked Bradecote, with the ghost of a smile.

'Indeed, my lord, and it is closely linked to my ability to throttle the breath from vermin like Mercet and his underlings, given half the chance.' Catchpoll grinned, and was still grinning when they stood before Robert Mercet in his hall. He was a well-dressed, plump man, with noticeably pudgy hands, incongruously angel-fair wavy hair, and eyes that were both calculating and unusually pale blue. He was sat at a table with a harassed clerk, and they were clearly engaged upon accounts, because a chequered cloth piled with counters lay before them.

He looked at Catchpoll and Bradecote, annoyance vying with a desire to appear unconcerned at the intrusion.

'So you are the new undersheriff, my lord. Now what was it the last one died of, the flux or the pox?' The voice matched Catchpoll's for quiet menace, and the accompanying smile accentuated the insult.

Catchpoll said nothing, but Bradecote sensed him tensing. The undersheriff simply ignored the question.

'We are investigating the unfortunate fire in Corviserstrete, which involved a death. Since it appears that you own some of the damaged property, we thought we should speak to you, Master Mercet.'

'Quite so, my lord, quite so. A bad business.' Mercet shook his head and tutted.

'But not actually bad for your particular business, we find.' Bradecote's voice was very measured.

'My property was burnt to the ground. How can that be good for business?' The merchant tried to sound affronted, but it was not a good act.

Catchpoll gave a bark of mirthless laughter. 'Because you've got men clearing the carpenter's shop away to rebuild as a new lease, and undoubtedly at higher rent. No squabbling with Master Woodman about an increase, especially when he happens to be away on business and there's just his little mouse of a wife and the brats to deal with. What a good time to clear the ground.'

The aquamarine eyes flickered. 'Fair enough, there is an opportunity, a landholder's opportunity, and I am too good a man at making money to ignore it, but the idea that I would set a fire . . . Jesu, what if it had spread? I have several messuages in that street.' He paled at the thought.

Catchpoll was reluctant to leave the theory.

'You wouldn't have lit the torch yourself, but you employ enough gutter life who would do it without a thought if you willed it.'

Bradecote did not know Mercet, but did not think that the man was faking the edge of panic in his voice when he looked to his own person directly, and there was no trace of insolence or insult remaining.

'My lord, Serjeant Catchpoll would accuse me of any crime committed in Worcester, if he had the chance. I am not involved in this fire, I give you my oath. You must seek your fire-starter elsewhere, and I have a likely culprit.' He paused, aware that he had caught their attention.

'And that is?' Catchpoll did not disguise the wariness in his voice.

Bradecote tried to look only mildly interested.

'Simeon the Jew.'

Bradecote looked at Catchpoll and then back at Mercet.

'And he is likely to be guilty because . . . ?' The undersheriff could feel the disappointment rising inside him before a word was spoken.

'Because he is Simeon the Jew. They do not think like us, act like us. They do not care for the welfare of Christian souls.' Mercet was sounding almost philanthropic. 'They are guided by a desire for wealth, by whatever means. I have heard tales—'

'Yes, but tales are just that,' interrupted Bradecote. 'Why, exactly, should this man,' and he stressed 'man', 'have set the fire?'

'Why to discredit me, and to be able to buy up land at a good price, like a crow seeking carrion.'

Bradecote sighed. It sounded very unlikely to him, but he had never had any dealings with the Sons of Abraham, and knew he was no judge. Even if Mercet's belief was in part the desire to thrust blame upon an outsider and rival, there was no reason why the man should be excluded from their investigation. He glanced at Catchpoll, hoping to read scepticism on his mobile features, but there was a frown of thought. Catchpoll was not discounting the idea out of hand.

There was a brief silence, then Bradecote roused himself.

'Right. We will make enquiries, and I will see this Simeon. Thank you for your help, Master Mercet.' The irony of his tone was lost on Mercet, who smiled. It was a smile, thought Bradecote, of relief blended with pleasure.

Catchpoll growled something indeterminate, which Mercet might, if he were so inclined, interpret as thanks, but which could just as easily have been an expression of gruff disappointment. The pair left the merchant's house without another word, and only spoke when they had walked some way down the street.

'I take it that that was not as enjoyable as you hoped, Catchpoll.'

The serjeant grunted morosely.

'Was it because Mercet wriggled out from under your boot, or because you thought there was something in what he said?'

'I would doubt the sun sets in the west if that whoreson bastard told me that it did,' grumbled Catchpoll, 'but there might, and I say it very grudgingly, be something there for us, my lord. Most like he is just trying to get us away from his own shady dealings, whether or not they include lighting fires, but you never know.'

'I agree with your reading of his character, Catchpoll, but somehow I do not think this particular crime lies at his door. He was right that if the fire had spread further he would have lost other properties, and replacing several would be costly, even for him.'

'Perhaps he had his men set ready to prevent such a spread.'

The serjeant's tone lacked conviction. 'If it is not him it is surely a pity. He's one I'd love to see dancing at the end of a rope, though a strong rope it would have to be, with his weight.' Catchpoll sighed. 'One day I'll catch him.'

'But does he break the law?' queried Bradecote, and encountered a look of disbelief as answer. 'I make no claim for him being other than what you say, and morally corrupt, but he might manage that within the bounds of law.'

Catchpoll shook his head. 'He's clever enough to do trade that is legal, however unjust, but his love of making money, and at others' expense, of a surety leads him over the bounds. I know it, and he knows I know it. He would not be able to resist it. I will get him, my lord, if I bides my time.'

'And that brings us, in a way, to the trail he gave us. You did not jump down his throat at the suggestion that Simeon the Jew might be at the root of this, so what makes you consider it? What is this man like?'

'That's the thing, you see. I cannot tell you beyond where he lives and what he does for trade, and it is that that makes me wonder. I know something about most of the wealthier men in Worcester, and nigh on every shady character, which is sometimes one and the same but . . . but he is a mystery. He keeps himself quietly, not drawing attention to his dealings or person. That might be natural caution, but then again . . .' Catchpoll frowned.

'So you are simply saying you cannot vouch for him.'

The serjeant nodded. Then he halted, like a hound testing the air for a scent. For a moment Bradecote feared he might have caught a hint of another blaze, but the man was miles away in his own thoughts. After what seemed an age, he snapped his fingers and smiled at his superior.

'We're linking the wrong folk with these fires, my lord.'

Bradecote said nothing, and waited.

'We was looking at the link between Winflaed and Edgyth, but we should have been looking for a link between Reginald Ash and Martin Woodman. Just because the old crone died in the fire, it does not mean she was an intended victim. In fact, nobody remembered her at the time, so she was probably just an unlucky result of the fire.'

Bradecote frowned. 'But the only link we have is Mercet, and I thought we had just agreed that he looked less likely than you would have hoped. The carpenter and silversmith are in different crafts, in different streets, and not even of the same parish. Where do we start?'

He was floundering, and too worn to care that Catchpoll knew it. The serjeant smiled, but the smile was more conspiratorial than victorious.

'It might be best to leave the links between Masters Ash and Woodman to me, my lord, seeing as I know Worcester and, forgive me, you do not. Mind you, you're likely to get more from Simeon the Jew if you visit him on the morrow.' The smile grew to a grin. 'He'll appreciate being visited by nobility and your manners are much better than mine.'

Hugh Bradecote laughed, his weary pessimism suddenly dispelled, and did so without any feeling of guilt following it. Considering the fact later, he admitted to himself that throwing himself into an investigation was just the boost to the spirits that he needed.

Serjeant and undersheriff parted in the castle bailey. Bradecote wanted to sort his thoughts before having to sup with the castellan, and Catchpoll had to make sure that the men-at-arms on his watch-bill knew their duties for the next twenty-four hours. Before heading home, he slipped into the kitchen to share a jug of ale with Drogo, who was whiling away the lull between preparing the dishes for the castellan's supper, and the mad rush to serve them up still warm.

The kitchen was hot, with interesting smells of herbs and stewing meat vying for dominance. Drogo was not to be found within, but sat upon a stool outside the rear door, where the shadows cast cool fingers amidst the mellowing sunlight.

Catchpoll, having already provided himself with a beaker in anticipation, sat down on the threshold, groaning slightly as proof of his ageing bones. Without a word, Drogo pushed the ale jug towards him with a dusty foot, and for a few minutes the two men sat in companionable silence, drinking. Eventually, Drogo smacked his lips with relish, and wiped his hand across his mouth.

'Got your fire-raiser yet, then?' His tone was conversational rather than interested.

'Would it were that easy.' Catchpoll did not sound overconcerned. He scuffed his toe idly in the dirt. 'Investigatin' is a bit like your cookin'.' He raised his eyes to meet his friend's, who regarded him with good-humoured suspicion.

'Go on then, you old ferret. Tell me why that is?'

'Well, you see, the basic plan is simple enough, but every time the ingredients are just a mite different and you never know whether it will end in a triumph or something only fit to feed to the dogs.' Catchpoll's eyes screwed up in silent laughter.

Drogo feigned outrage, but his shoulders shook.

Catchpoll remained silent for a minute or so, and then came out with a question.

'Do you know Reginald Ash, the silversmith?'

Drogo squinted as he considered his answer. 'Not to speak to, as such. Heard of him, mind you, because his work is well regarded, and then my first wife was a silversmith's widow. That was a long, long time ago, God rest her. She knew the craft members, though of course Ash would have been only a journeyman then. Don't think she liked any of them, much. A good Christian woman she was, but you should have heard her on their lack of charity.' He shook his head. 'Poor Emma.'

'What about Martin Woodman, carpenter in Corviserstrete?'

'Now Martin Woodman, he built a good oak cupboard for my brother-in-law, and made a fine job of it. My sister wed a man of means, you know.'

'So you've often told me.' Catchpoll pulled a face, and turned the grimace into an exaggerated yawn.

'Alright, alright.' Drogo raised his hands.

'Don't suppose you've ever heard of a connection between them,' Catchpoll wondered, with studied nonchalance, 'and Robert Mercet?'

'Oh, so this isn't just a friendly chat. You are after something, fox-brain. And there was me thinking you just liked to sit in the shade and have a drink with a friend. Ha!' Drogo shook his head. 'I've nothing you'd like to hear, but if they choose to be involved with Mercet they had best have their wits sharp about them.'

Catchpoll drained his beaker and got to his feet. 'Oh well. I was only being hopeful. Best get home, and leave you to serve up something tasty for the lord castellan and my lord Bradecote.'

Chapter Six

Hugh Bradecote sat with his brain only half registering the castellan's monotone. The man clearly liked an audience, even a limited one. He droned on about a variety of subjects from the political turmoil between king and empress to the number of swans on the Severn. Much of it washed over the undersheriff, but he pricked up his ears when the subject of the fires arose. The castellan expounded a variety of theories, from a conspiracy to discredit him, to Welsh spies taking advantage of English internecine fighting, and even witchcraft. He complained about the lack of progress being made, waiving aside Bradecote's remonstration that he had arrived but twenty-four hours previously.

'Fulk de Crespignac would have had someone in the castle cells by now,' complained the castellan petulantly.

'Really, my lord. And would that have been the guilty

party or just someone who fitted his idea of a fire-setter?' Bradecote's tone was scathing. He had no wish to be compared to his dead predecessor, especially by one as ineffectual as the castellan.

The castellan choked over his goblet of wine, and began to bluster. Bradecote, who was weary of body as well as of spirit, made his apologies without any attempt at sincerity and withdrew upon the excuse that he had to plan his investigations for the morrow. In reality these consisted of making a mental note to ask Catchpoll for directions to Simeon the Jew's house and to draw a very rough map of Worcester within the walls, marking the streets that he knew and the location of the fires. It was not much, but it was all that he could think to do. Reviewing what he knew was but the act of a moment; the fire-setter knew their way through back alleys, so was local. He, or even she, had started one fire in the daytime and one at night. This cut down the likelihood of them being an apprentice or journeyman under a master's eye, unless set to the task by the master himself, and since they were able to walk out at night they were either wed to a heavy sleeper or slept alone. He could not even rule out that the fires were the random acts of a lunatic. On which unhelpful thought Bradecote blew out his light and lay upon his cot, expecting to lie awake until the small hours.

Surprisingly, he actually slept much better than Serjeant Catchpoll, who had worrying thoughts gnawing at his brain, and, try to dispel them as he might, they would not go away. He had returned home to find his wife grumbling over a broken ewer, and in less than welcoming mood. She rounded on him for the smell of ale on his breath, correctly assuming he had been drinking with his crony, the castle cook.

'I don't see why you should spend your time in idleness with that foul-mouthed sot,' she complained pettishly, going on to enumerate all the things she had heard to the detriment of his character.

Catchpoll grinned, which did not help matters.

'Oh yes, you can smile like a brainless fool, but if you had heard even the part of what I know, you'd not look so jolly. Why, only last week I went to her church with Agnes Whitwood, who used to work with her mother in the castle way back when she was scarce but a child. She told me Drogo the Cook had had three wives and was thought to have killed the first two. There, what do you say to that?'

'If every man who remarried was counted a murderer, there'd not be enough timber in the Malvern *weald* to make the gallows, woman. Idle gossip is what you've been listening to, and shame on you for it.'

She coloured, but held her ground. 'That's what the priest said, and sent me off with a penance, though not as heavy, I'll be bound, as the one he laid on Agnes. But idle this was not. She told me in church, when she went to say prayers and put in an offering for her poor mother's soul. She'd not talk "idle gossip" then.'

Catchpoll was not smiling any more. 'And why were you—' He stopped as his wife's face began to crumple. 'I'm sorry, sweet. I had forgot with all this business going on.' Belatedly, he remembered. September marked the anniversary of the death of their second son, who had died years ago as an infant. He had put the memory away and did not revisit it, but he knew that at this time every year his wife dragged the sorrow into the open, afraid to forget. He sat her down on a bench and then sat beside her, an arm round her shoulder.

'You tell me what she said, then.' He had no deep wish to hear, but it might distract her, and, for all that she had a sharp tongue on occasion, Catchpoll loved and valued his wife.

Mistress Catchpoll sniffed. 'She was talking about her mother, and the old days in the castle kitchens. I mentioned how you was friends with the cook, and she seemed quite shocked. She said that he had been married three times, and that at the time it was thought he had done away with them.

'The last wife died of a spotted fever and had been married a dozen years or more, but the first two lasted no more than a few months. The first was a widow herself, poor soul; left penniless and in debt when her husband drowned himself in the Severn. She sent her little son off, to relatives or the cloisters, I imagine, to avoid the shame and penury, but providing for him cost her dear. She took menial work in the castle and caught Drogo the undercook's eye, for she was a pretty woman. Rumour had it she caught the eye of others too, especially some lordling out of Shapwyck, but it was Drogo who married her, and she fell swiftly with child; perhaps too quickly. Not everyone thought the child his. While she was carrying she was more than usually sick, and he plied her with all sorts of pick-me-ups he made, and still she ailed. The healing woman tended her as well, and then she upped and died, and the unborn babe with her. If it was another man's, you know Drogo and his temper, he wouldn't

84

have taken it well. Jealous husbands make dangerous husbands. And then he married again, within months. The second wife was underground within the year, and not of any contagion or accident, either. Died much the same way, though she was not carrying. It is hardly surprising that tongues wagged. He did not wed again for several years afterwards. Now tell me that is not suspicious.'

Catchpoll said nothing, although a tight frown knitted his brow, and his wife continued.

'Agnes said there was more, but the priest interrupted us. Most aggrieved he was, so he must have heard quite a bit. He ranted at us, quoting scripture over and over, and then almost threw me out, having set penance. I dare not think what penance he must have set poor Agnes for I have been so occupied I have not spoken to her since.' Mistress Catchpoll looked sideways at her husband, her head on one side. 'Don't tell me that there's really something to the tale after all.'

Catchpoll was silent but shook his head absently. Strands of thought were weaving through his brain, making and breaking contact. He suddenly had too much information, and gut instinct told him that there was something on which he should fasten; but a dull disquiet, one that forced him to admit that Drogo had entered the web of suspicion, was fogging his judgement. He could think of no possible reason for his friend to be the starter of fires, nor was he a man Catchpoll would put down as one who would kill, or try to kill, in cold blood. Drogo had a temper, for sure, and Catchpoll could see that if goaded too far he might be a man to strike out in anger, but no more. Yet he formed a possible link between the incidents he was investigating.

His wife, misreading his silence for old memories, patted his hand and rose with a sniff to ladle out his dinner with her former anger forgotten.

Bradecote lay upon his bed with his mind busy, but free from the grey and formless misery that had beset him. The seemingly insoluble mystery of the case gave his brain something new upon which to focus, and in doing so gave him ease. He slept, and if it was a little late then at least the slumber was not haunted. When he awoke to the new day he was aware that the lassitude that had enfolded him had been cast aside. He might still bear dark rings around the eyes but his brain was working at normal speed, unfettered at last. It was therefore an undersheriff in positive mood who greeted Catchpoll after a brief breaking of fast.

The serjeant was, in contrast, more than usually morose, and acknowledged his superior with the briefest of nods and a grunt, which Bradecote might, if he had the inclination, interpret as greeting. Bradecote thought him preoccupied, and attributed it to his plan for the morning's investigation, so made no comment. After a brief exchange, the pair split up; Bradecote to Simeon the Jew and Catchpoll to undisclosed addresses within the town.

Simeon's house was a good-sized property at the end of Cokenstrete away from the Severn. It was clearly kept in good order but there was nothing to show that the occupant was wealthier than any other in the street, nor different in any way. Only when Bradecote stood at the doorway did he notice the small gouged hollow in one of the thick upright beams, with a thin roll of vellum nestling within it. He frowned, wondering what it might be, and the look of perplexity was still present when a serving man opened the door to him. The man was polite but wary, casting glances both up and down the street before asking the visitor's business. He bid Bradecote enter, and another surprise awaited the undersheriff. There was a heavy carved screen across much of the room, thereby creating a small area at the front of the hall where clients might wait until Simeon chose to receive them. Bradecote appreciated the ploy. It put clients at a disadvantage if Simeon so wished. On this occasion the servant led Bradecote straight round and into the main part of the hall, which was lit by the pale light from the upper windows at the front of the hall, above the height of the screen, and by several large candles on tall stands. The sheriff's officer was conscious that the house smelt different to any he had been inside: sweeter, but not like honey; rich and slightly exotic. Well, the man was a merchant with goods coming from distant lands, so perhaps he kept some of the most valuable in his home.

The master of the house was seated at a table towards the back of the hall, with a small boy upon his lap reciting in a language that Bradecote did not know. The child's face was pinched with concentration, and he did not register the arrival of the stranger. The servant did not announce Bradecote, but stood still and waited. The child rushed the last phrases of whatever he had committed to memory and then looked up to his father's face seeking approbation, only relaxing and grinning back when his father smiled and nodded at him. The movement broke the spell, and the servant announced the undersheriff.

The father looked up, paternal pleasure replaced by wariness. He patted the little boy's cheek and dismissed him with some comment that set the child laughing as he was put down and half skipped to a chamber at the rear of the hall, where a woman's voice could be heard from beyond the partially closed door.

Simeon rose unhurriedly, and greeted Bradecote with formal courtesy. The undersheriff felt guiltily surprised, for the man spoke with only the suggestion of an accent. Without reason, Bradecote had expected someone distinctly foreign. In appearance, Simeon would certainly stand out among the citizenry, having a warm tone to his skin that Worcestershire natives might only get after a summer of labour in the fields, but without the weathering. More striking still was the blackness of his hair and the full, well-kept, glossy beard, unlike the thin, jaw-edging variety that was worn by most men who chose not to be clean-shaven. He had deep bay-brown eyes; eyes that assessed the undersheriff swiftly and accurately. Simeon depended upon his judgement of his fellow man, both in his trading and for his own security. He sensed Bradecote's uncertainty but could see that it did not spring from diffidence. The tall, dark man before him exuded competence and probity; a man whose word could be trusted. Such decisions on character came easily to the merchant. He smiled a little more broadly, although the eyes remained watchful, and invited Bradecote to be seated with a broad sweep of his hand.

'Forgive me, my lord. I try to make a few minutes each day to hear my son's learning, and if the hour is late he makes mistakes and is frustrated. He is a good boy and tries hard. You have sons?' It was a conscious manoeuvre to link himself with his visitor.

Bradecote caught his breath as he was about to answer in the negative, and coloured.

'Yes. I am now the father of a son, but he is no more than a swaddled babe.' There was a suggestion of pride in his voice, but Simeon had caught the grey shadow that had passed across his face and made a wise guess.

'A son is a man's comfort. May he grow strong and be always a credit to you.' He spoke as if it were a formal benediction, and looked Bradecote straight in the eye. The moment was all that was needed to convey understanding and sympathy, and then it passed and Simeon assumed a more formal tone. 'And how may I be of service to you, my lord Undersheriff? It is official business, I take it.' The use of the title and Bradecote's demeanour had immediately dispelled any idea that this was a man seeking the services of a usurer.

Bradecote cleared his throat. 'Indeed it is, Master Simeon. There have been several fires in the town in recent weeks, probably not mischance. I am seeking to find out if this is so, and who it is who puts the town at risk. I am asking questions among the merchants and those linked to the locations of the fires.' He spoke carefully and without emphasis.

'I see.' Simeon's full lips pursed. 'The fires, as I have heard, were at the premises of Master Ash the silversmith and in Corviserstrete. I have made purchases for my wife at the silversmith, but I have no connection with Corviserstrete. I trade, my lord, but I own no property beyond my own house and wharfage. I assume, therefore, that I have been pointed out to you merely because I am "Simeon the Jew". It is always so much easier to blame the outsider.' There was a weary understanding in his voice.

'That is true, but I do not seek someone to blame, only the truth, and I would be neglecting my duty if I did not speak to all those who were brought to my attention,' Bradecote paused for an instant, 'even if I questioned the motives of the informant.'

The two men said nothing, each gauging the other. Then Simeon nodded. 'That is fair, my lord. I will give you any answers that I can, but I cannot see that it will aid you, for I fear I have nothing pertinent to say.'

'Then I will start with the obvious. Have you ever been in dispute with Reginald Ash, over his work, or had financial dealings with him?'

'No, my lord. He is accounted a prudent and honest member of his craft, I know.' He smiled ruefully. 'It is in my best interests to know about the other tradesmen in Worcester, so that I can judge whether they would be good "clients" if ever they did come to borrow money. But in truth, much of my livelihood still comes from "honest trade", however difficult it is for us in these times. I have goods come up the Severn from Bristow, where I come from, or rather, where I was born; spices from the Mediterranean; citrus fruits and other rare commodities that other merchants do not often carry. My grandsire came to England from Portugal, and I have good family ties there. The family works together. So far none has tried to prevent us continuing in this trade and of course we "enjoy" royal protection, as long as we pay our taxes for the privilege and accede to requests for royal loans. I sometimes wonder how this strife would be paid for without us to pay the soldiery.'

He could see that he held Bradecote's interest. The information might have nothing to do with fire-setting, but it was useful background if the undersheriff was to work in the town in future.

'We have a false reputation, we Jews. Because our faith, though far older than yours, is alien to you, because our language is foreign and because we do things in a different way, we are regarded as untrustworthy, even dangerous. I have seen mothers shield their children as I passed as if I carried foul plague, as if I were some fierce monster.' He opened his arms and shrugged. 'Yet I am merely a man. We lend money because in many places that is all that is left for us to do. One day perhaps, I will have to exist upon it if my trading is forbidden, and I will make the best deal that I can, for the sake of my business and my family. It does not make me greedy.

'I have even loaned money, once, at no interest at all, but I would be obliged if you did not make that common knowledge.' Simeon's eyes twinkled. 'There was a good woman, many years ago now, only a few years after I came here, whose husband died in debt. He was persuaded into an enterprise by others who made sure that any risk lay with him.' Simeon shook his head at the man's foolishness. 'The widow was pious and honest, and once did my Rebekah, my first wife, a kindness. She knew who Rebekah was, but did not hold back from helping her. When the husband died she lost everything to the creditors and was reduced to taking menial work to survive. She wanted to spare her son the poverty and the shame and sought to put him into the cloister, but she did not even have the money to provide the "gift" that would accompany his application. I provided the money . . .' He laughed without mirth. 'A Son of Abraham funding a Benedictine. How strange is that? But that woman paid back every silver penny within a year, though I am sure she often went hungry. She married again after that, but I do not know what became of her thereafter. She deserved better fortune.' He was half talking to himself by now, but roused himself to gaze at Bradecote. 'Perhaps it was a godly deed, perhaps mere soft-heartedness. I do not care to judge, but can you imagine a "Christian" man like Robert Mercet, doing the same?'

Bradecote was actually relieved to hear the merchant's name. It brought the conversation back to the current problem without him having to labour the point.

'No, having met the man I would not say that was even possible. I take it that you and he do not engage in pleasantries.'

Simeon gave a crack of genuine laughter. '"Engage in pleasantries", no indeed. He would slit my throat as soon as look at me, and I . . . well let us say uncharitable thoughts have been known to pass through my head. It was he who brought my name to your attention, wasn't it.' It was a statement not a question. 'No need to answer. He would love to see my downfall, and pick the rich scraps from my business.'

'And is the feeling mutual?' The question was almost casually put, but Simeon was nobody's fool.

'Would I ruin him? Of course, my lord, of course, but only

by good business means. You are going to say he has holdings where the fires occurred? Well, my lord, I would see him sink in debt as deep as the Severn and laugh, but I would not risk honest business or innocent lives. You must look elsewhere for your fire-raiser.'

'Can you think of anyone else with feelings like yours, but less compunction?'

'I would be surprised if there were more than a handful of townsfolk, outside those who work for him, and perhaps not even them, who would not call a holiday at his fall, but I could not point a finger at anyone prepared to do violence, except upon his person directly, that is.' Simeon had relaxed. Bradecote's questions had not been those of a man keen to find a scapegoat. He was, as he had claimed, merely a seeker of truth.

The sound of a baby's insistent cry came from the rear chamber, followed by a woman's crooning. Bradecote winced and Simeon, conscious of not having offered hospitality, knew that the undersheriff would not choose to linger. He rose.

'If there are no more questions, my lord, then I would be about my business. I have a boat due in this morning. I apologise for not having offered you refreshment.' He bowed.

'It is no matter, Master Simeon. May I walk with you to the riverside?'

'Shrieval approval, my lord?'

'Let us just say that I would not want others to be incited to take the law into their own hands.'

'Then I thank you. Your company would be an honour.' He bowed again, and called for his cloak.

The two of them made their way unhurriedly to the riverside

wharves, the tall undersheriff and the Jewish merchant, and Bradecote knew that eyes followed them and made note. It was a good thing. He could not see Simeon as a fire-raiser, though facts might yet emerge to the contrary, but he did not want Mercet to be able to achieve his ends by rousing the townsfolk against Simeon simply because he made an easy target. The warehouse was busy, and assailed the nose with a myriad of exotic smells. On the riverside the doors were open, and men were unloading sacks and bundles from a sailing vessel. Simeon stopped a man with a small box on his shoulder and opened the lid. Inside, nestled in straw, was a handful of bright-yellow fruit. He took one, squeezing it gently and then holding it to his nose. He inhaled and smiled.

'I did not offer you refreshment in my home, for which lack of hospitality I ask forgiveness, but perhaps I may atone for it here. It would not be corruption of the sheriff's office if I were to offer you this?'

Bradecote smiled. 'No, I think not. But,' he looked at the strange thing, 'what is it?'

'A fruit. A laymun. It grows on trees in Spain and Portugal, but long before that in Lebanon and in groves even about Jerusalem. You will not have seen one.'

Bradecote shook his head.

'This laymun, it is very sharp to the taste but good in cooking. I will please my wife very much by presenting her with one as a gift.' He proffered it to Bradecote, who rubbed the skin gently and smelt it. 'The flesh inside is sharp, as I said, and the "*pépins*",' he used the French word, 'which are pale, are towards the centre. You could not plant the seeds to make it grow

94

here, though. England is too cold a country. Sometimes in the winters, I agree with the laymun.' He smiled. 'Take it back with you to your manor and have the cook take off the thin outer skin and put it in butter to flavour it, and the juice mix with honey to sweeten it, and warmed English wine. I would say you will be one of the only men in the shire to have come across it, though those who have been to the Levant will know of them. I have purchased a small box. They will fetch an extremely high price with the lord Bishop of Worcester, and the lord sheriff perhaps, higher than nearly all of my spices.' Simeon smiled in anticipation.

Bradecote thanked the merchant and left him to his business. The interview had been interesting, but he could not see that it had advanced his hunt for the fire-setter. He wondered if Catchpoll had gone back to see Reginald Ash, since Martin Woodman the carpenter would not yet be returned, and so made his way to the silversmith's. The craftsman was at work, but had not seen Serjeant Catchpoll that morning. Bradecote decided to ask the relevant questions himself, but they availed him little. Ash had only met the carpenter on a few occasions, the last being some six months previously, when Woodman had been making a casket in which a fine goblet was to lie before being presented to a visiting prelate. In addition, the premises were the property of Master Ash himself, who had inherited them from the master silversmith whose apprentice and journeyman he had been.

''Tis one of the reasons I am content to make Edwin my partner. In the fullness of time, and may that be a long time, mark you, he will take the business as I did before him. It seems very fitting to me, my lord. Sort of natural. He's a good fellow is Edwin. I could not have had a son I would be more proud of, all in all. It wasn't that way with my master; not close we weren't, but Master Long recognised a good craftsman.' Ash shook his head at his memories. 'Gave me a few rare beatings in my youth for my errors he did, and he was a warm one at business, but he left me a fine inheritance here. So may God have mercy upon his soul, I say.'

Chapter Seven

The sun was now high and the shadows short. It had been a most frustrating forenoon, and Bradecote hoped that Catchpoll had had more success, even if it meant the serjeant gloating upon it. When he came up with him before the castle gate, however, there was no look of triumph on Catchpoll's weathered face. If anything, he looked even more glum than earlier.

'I had thought to find you with Reginald Ash, Catchpoll. Did some more likely quarry draw your attention?'

'Not quarry, merely checking details.'

'Thorough checking it must have been then, if you did not get as far as Master Ash.' There was an edge to his tone.

Bradecote's eyes narrowed a fraction, for he thought that Catchpoll looked uncomfortable, and he had not seen that before in his dealings with him. It occurred to the undersheriff that an investigation outside of the usual criminal suspects might involve ferreting closer to home than was the norm, and perhaps even such an old hand as Catchpoll might dislike it. Part of him would have liked to put Catchpoll on the spot, but at heart he knew it would be unfair. If anything relevant turned up, he trusted Serjeant Catchpoll to bring it to his attention at once. If he could not trust him to do that, then their working relationship would be worthless. The serjeant said nothing, so he continued.

'Well then, I have to say that other than having been making the very interesting acquaintance of Simeon the Jew, and been given this,' he held up the fruit, 'which is, it seems, called a laymun, I do not think I have made any advance. I went to Reginald Ash, who apparently took over the business from his old master, a craftsman called Long. There seemed nothing that would help us. Any luck your side?' The question was casually put, but carefully so.

Catchpoll spoke half to himself. 'Not that you could call definite advances, just possibilities. Trouble is, the more you scrabble around in this case the more suspects you can find. Let's face it, my lord, half of Worcester needs proof of innocence, and cannot provide one neither. I get the feeling I'll be suspecting myself next, and I know it wasn't me.'

Bradecote pulled a wry smile. 'That's a relief, at least.' His tone was light, hoping to rouse Catchpoll from his dismal mood, but he was concerned. He needed Catchpoll's mind as clear and dispassionate as he had been on their first case in Pershore. The undersheriff felt he was warming to the role of law officer, but recognised his own inexperience.

The older man did not acknowledge the mild jest, and merely

grunted. In truth, he was not sure how much of his morning's questioning had proved useful and how much muddied the waters. After a troubled night's rest, he had gone in hunt of Agnes Whitwood. He had been reluctant to approach her, for she was a loose-tongued woman whom he did not really like, and he had no desire to have it passed around Worcester that the castle cook was under investigation. He compromised by eliciting information by stealth, ostensibly berating her for having brought down her priest's anger upon his wife when she was beset by her old loss. As he had hoped, Mistress Whitwood had bridled and excused herself, commencing with 'But I was only telling her . . .' and thence recounting the tale afresh. From there it was easy enough to delve deeper by the simple expedient of saying that such tales were ridiculous. This, Catchpoll decided, both brought out any corroborative details Agnes Whitwood possessed, and made it clear that Drogo was definitely not under suspicion by the law.

The story recounted to him was, shorn of the repeated avowals of not being one to spread untruths, and pleas to the Almighty to strike her tongue from her head if a word was malicious, the same as his wife had given him the previous evening.

'But you were only a slip of a girl back then. You might have not heard aright.' He actually thought she must have been nigh on twenty, but he knew she had wed late, not being a well-favoured woman and of shrewish temperament, and reckoned she would prefer not to be reminded of the fact. He almost smiled when she simpered, though it was not a pretty sight.

'Why, Serjeant Catchpoll, how right you are . . . about my age, I mean. However, the story was oft repeated, and my dear mother always gave it credence. She knew the first wife quite well, and never understood how such a godly, respectable woman could have married one as intemperate as Drogo. Prone to throwing things about the kitchen, he was, when his rages took him, and that was often enough, because everything had to be just so with him. You'd think cooking was an art.' She snorted her dismissal of the idea.

'She was a widow, wasn't she? One whose husband took his own life?'

Mistress Whitwood nodded. 'I don't recall the scandal, but I know there was one.' Her voice held regret that such information had escaped her.

'Do you recall her name? Or his?'

'Her name was Emma, but I could not say her husband's. She was simply "Emma" in the kitchen, her position being just that of an underling, and she never spoke of him – not in my hearing, at the least. Must have gone hard with her, having been a craftsman's wife and used to directing her own home.'

Catchpoll filed the information. Drogo had mentioned his 'poor Emma' when talking of the local silversmiths, but if it were that long ago, Reginald Ash would have been merely learning the trade.

'And as for the second wife,' continued Agnes, 'well, she did not come from within the castle and we never really saw her or anything, so I never knew who she was other than she was a redhead with freckles, which would, of course, account for Drogo getting rid of her.' She presented this final scrap of knowledge as if it were a vital fact.

Catchpoll's eyes boggled. It was rare for anything to surprise him but this threw him completely.

Agnes Whitwood smiled at her superior understanding, and explained as if to a dim child. 'Redheads. You know, Serjeant. Redheads have tempers on them. Why, if I had a penny for every time that Amice Pottes, that flame-haired shrew across the way . . . But, Drogo, he must have found all the arguments too much to handle, him being tempersome also, and done away with her.'

Catchpoll relaxed, and smiled his death's head smile. No, he had not failed to pick up on something important. Mistress Whitwood took it to be appreciation of her sagacity, and coloured.

'So tell me, why did he get rid of the godly Emma, then?' he asked.

'It must have been because the child she carried was not his.'

'But if she was a respectable woman . . .'

'Even respectable women are not strong enough if a man is set upon having them, poor souls.' She tried to look affronted by the insult to her sex. 'By all accounts, one of the lord of Shapwyck's sons was mightily taken with her and loitered under the feet of the kitchen staff till the cook, not Drogo, who was just the undercook, had words with the steward. After that he was more circumspect, but if his ardour got the better of him one evening . . . Nobody would give credit to the word of a kitchen maid against one such as him.' She shrugged. 'It would be a sound reason for her accepting Drogo.'

Catchpoll's smile had become fixed into a rictus. This did have a sense to it. He did not like it, not one tiny bit, but it had a certain logic. And yet his friendship with Drogo, which went back well over a decade, did not give him the impression of a man who would slowly poison a woman. If he had hit her with a skillet, or the poker from the fire, while in a drink-fuelled rage, well that he could have understood, but not slow poisoning. This fitted, and at the same time was all wrong.

'The deaths were not investigated. I was new to it all back then; just a man-at-arms the serjeant thought more useful than some. I had barely begun to learn, but I would have remembered queries about two deaths involving a man from within the castle.'

Agnes Whitwood sniffed. 'Drogo's a good cook, they say. Mayhap the castellan and the lord sheriff were too taken by his cooking of venison and goose to want to stir up a pot of trouble.' She laughed at her own witticism, but then shrugged as Catchpoll made no sign of appreciating the jest. He left her with thanks that were polite but not effusive, and a recommendation not to let her tongue earn her greater penance. She sniffed.

From Mistress Whitwood, Catchpoll had headed for Corviserstrete, where he asked directions for the dispossessed glover. Mistress Woodman clearly knew nothing, but it was possible that the glover had greater knowledge of how affairs stood in his own street. Hunting him down led Catchpoll first out of the Foregate to the north of the town on the Wich road, where he hoped to find him with his brother-in-law, the tanner. Unfortunately, it turned out that the industrious glover was calling in favours from other members of his craft, and

Catchpoll spent the best part of two hours scouring the town before he caught up with him.

In need of slaking his own thirst, Catchpoll suggested an adjournment to a neighbouring alehouse. Wilfrid the Glover needed no great persuading, for his own morning had produced a disappointing degree of success. Over a beaker of ale he was only too happy to call down curses on the head of whoever had set the fire, and on Robert Mercet for taking every advantage from his misfortune. Catchpoll understood his ill feeling, and concurred with his reading of Mercet's character, but he was interested in other information. It had occurred to Catchpoll that the glover, rather than Woodman or the old woman, might have been the target of the fire-setter, and he was keen to discover anyone with a grudge against the man. Wilfrid considered the matter with furrowed brow.

'None as I'd reckon have taken against me enough to set a fire. I'll admit there are a couple of fellows who have swung a fist at me when both of us were the worse for ale, but such disputes disappear with the sore head next day. There's never been anything of a feud or a grudge against me.'

Catchpoll eyed the glover sceptically. The response had come with a fraction of hesitation and a deepening of colour. Wilfrid Glover was a bad liar. He made a calculated guess.

'You are a good husband?'

'I've got four children.' The tone was mildly affronted.

Catchpoll raised his eyebrows. 'I didn't ask if your loins were fruitful. Being a good husband and siring four brats do not have to go together. Many a father fathers elsewhere. So you haven't let your eyes, or more importantly, any other part of your body, stray?'

'No.' There was an unspoken 'but' left hanging in the air, so Catchpoll voiced it.

'But . . . ? Never once?'

'Well, perhaps once. But that was some years back, and her husband never knew. Besides, the woman is dead these two months, God have mercy on her.'

Catchpoll raised his eyes heavenwards at the stupidity of his fellow man. 'And just supposing he knows now. A deathbed confession, or a "friend" who didn't want to cause trouble when she was alive but can't bear the widower going on about how wonderful his wife was?'

Wilfrid looked suddenly uncomfortable.

'Name the lady, then.' Catchpoll sighed. 'I'm not a priest interested in men's souls, just a man whose job is to keep folk from murdering each other, stealing, oh, and setting Worcester aflame.'

'Maud, the wife of Edgar Brewer,' mumbled Wilfrid.

Catchpoll ran the name through the filing system of his memory.

'Sultry looking piece, all raven locks and drooping lashes. If her husband is after every man who got the come-on from her, I'd best have a man-at-arms with a pail of water set at every corner in the town.' Catchpoll sniffed discontentedly, but then broke into a smile at the glover's shocked expression.

'Thought it was just you, eh? There now. There's no fool like a man who thinks another man's wife who strays, strays only for him. Well, I hopes you've learnt your lesson and look to your own bed in future.'

He stood up to leave, but then bethought himself of another question.

'Old Edgyth,' the serjeant began, and the glover crossed himself and shuddered at the memory of the charred corpse, 'was a healing woman, and one who was popular with young women who found themselves in tricky situations, by all accounts. Did you see anyone looking . . . well, suspicious, visiting her in the last few weeks?'

'No. Just the usual folk as visited . . . except of course . . . there now, I had almost forgotten him, and me and the wife had a fine old time wondering what he was about and who he was at the time.'

Catchpoll could not quite keep the eagerness from his voice. 'Yes?'

'Mmm. Most of those who sought Old Edgyth were townsfolk, just the ordinary sort. Your rich men and lordly sort go to Roger the Healer and his sort, and pay more for worse advice, if you ask me.' Wilfrid paused, half expecting Catchpoll to do just that. Getting no response, he continued. 'This man was different. He wore a cloak, with the hood up too, though it was a fair day. It was an ordinary man's cloak, nothing fine, but his shoes were good-quality leather and he wore gauntlets, heaven knows why. They cost him a pretty penny, though they weren't my work. He was just, well, all wrong; a man trying hard not to draw attention to himself. So of course, he did.'

'Were there raised voices when he went inside?' Catchpoll asked.

'Oh no, nothing like that. It was who he was, not what he did that drew our attention. I thought it might be a man with an ailment best kept private, keeping himself disguised. My wife thought he might be a spy come to the old widow for poisons, but she's a fanciful sort and disliked the old crone. Whoever he was, he came twice, and not thereafter.'

Catchpoll's interest was caught. 'Describe him to me.'

'I can't. As I said, he wore a cloak with a hood.'

'So tell me the colour of the cloak; how tall he was; how he walked.'

'Your sort of height, and he walked upright enough and without a limp. Cloak was just sack brown, but the gloves were a good chestnut with a fine finish. If they came from Worcester, then I'd guess the leather came from Gilbert, the tanner out on the Sutheberi road, not my brother-in-law, who makes mostly leather for saddlery.'

Catchpoll thanked the glover, and left him hunched over his ale pot, wondering about both Edgar Brewer and the fine leather gauntlets.

It was the information from the glover that Catchpoll divulged first as he and Bradecote sat in the chamber allotted to the undersheriff. Bradecote listened attentively, but agreed that the information provided more threads than leads.

'We can speak to Edgar Brewer, but even if he were guilty he has but to deny it and we are stuck. There is no evidence.' Bradecote sighed.

'Might be best to get back to the silversmith first, my lord. If Ash, or more likely young Edwin, had dealings with Maud Brewer, it would be a mightily good motive, and a widower would have no problem being out late at night.'

'And if that is the case, do we have to be swift? From what you say, there could be plenty of other victims in waiting.'

Catchpoll groaned. 'If he denies it, we had best set a watch on him, at least until we have a stronger suspect.'

'That leads us to the disguised man with the fine gauntlets. Is that a fair lead?'

'To what? I have no doubt the glover spoke true, but if the man was seeking some potion he would have no cause to burn the woman, and we have to find a connection with Reginald Ash. What's more, it would have to be a connection with a reason to set fire to the silversmith's.'

Bradecote's expression was now nearly as morose as that of Serjeant Catchpoll. 'We are running in small circles. I just cannot see how we are to find the answer to this one, Catchpoll. I am afraid you have to be unhinged of mind to want to set fire to things, and if that is so there need be no sense to any of it. Our fire-raiser could be working on a whim. How can we catch a man whose acts are random?'

'By luck, if that be so. But even things that look random may not be, my lord. I mean, however unconnected they look to us, the fire-setter will have his reasons, be they nary so weird.'

Bradecote smiled wearily. 'So we think like madmen. Thank you, Catchpoll. With the suspects, or non-suspects, we have, that will be easier than I would have thought a few days ago.'

Catchpoll regarded his superior steadily. 'There's another "non-suspect" as you call them, to add to the list. Drogo the Cook, as runs the castle kitchens. There are connections with the healing woman and the silversmiths, however much I dislike it.'

He set out the information from Mistress Whitwood plainly, though Bradecote could see how uncomfortable he was about it. At the conclusion they sat in silence for a few minutes, each ruminating upon possibilities. Catchpoll's expression had never been more lugubrious, but Bradecote frowned as he tried to unravel the problem. At last he brightened.

'Serjeant Catchpoll. All this about the castle cook may be true for all we know, but we could never prove it. Only God can bring him to account if he did kill his wives. But even though there is a loose connection with the two fires, there is no motive for any attacks, and even if you could concoct one, it existed some twenty years ago, man. Why, in Jesu's name, would anyone wait that long for revenge or whatever other motive it was? It makes no sense, and even more so if Drogo is the hot-headed sort.'

Catchpoll felt a wave of relief wash over him, but it left him feeling no happier.

'Aye, my lord. You have the right of it, and yet . . . I believe Drogo is no fire-raiser, nor murderer either, but there is something there. It's like in the gloaming, when you see something out the corner of your eye. If you look straight at it, there's nothing there. If you looks at this there is no sense to it, but at the edge of my mind I know I should see something, and it grates with me that I can't say what.'

Bradecote half understood, but could provide no answer. Instead he opted for banishing Catchpoll's unease with more tangible threads to follow.

'We can't hunt the invisible, so we had best be about the mundane and obvious. As you said, we have a link between Brewer and Wilfrid Glover, if he was the target of the second fire. So we establish if there was a link between Brewer and Ash or his journeyman. We then find out if there is a link between our gauntleted man and the silversmith, though it seems grasping at a straw. If there is anything at all, then we have to find out who he is. That will mean speaking to the tanner and then whoever the tanner sold the leather to, if that is possible. And then . . .'

'What, my lord?'

The undersheriff smiled grimly. 'We pray that it rains in Worcester . . . rains heavily.'

Chapter Eight

Reginald Ash was a little surprised, and also irritated, at the reappearance of the undersheriff, and now accompanied by the sheriff's serjeant. He wanted to put the upheaval of the fire behind him, and to re-establish himself as 'Reginald Ash, the fine silversmith' rather than 'Reginald Ash, the man whose business nearly burnt down'. He was a fair way to achieving that aim, but having the officers of the law hanging around like crows round an ailing sheep set him back. The smile with which he greeted the pair was brief and clearly forced, and he returned his attention to his client, an ostentatiously dressed man who was discussing the design of a large cloak clasp. Bradecote's lips twitched, for Master Ash was struggling to prevent the man ordering something of such size, complexity and weight as to tear any cloth to which it was attached. He could detect the conflict between the businessman's desire to supply an expensive item, and his craftsman's soul writhing at the prospect of being associated with a ghastly and tasteless piece of work, which would have the purchaser returning to complain that it damaged his clothes. By the time he had concluded the deal for the clasp he was clearly agitated. He wiped a faintly charcoal-smudged cloth over his face, thereby leaving dark shadows that altered the planes of his face. He gazed dolefully at Bradecote.

'Wasn't one visit enough for the day, my lord? I take it you aren't here to purchase. Unless your wife . . .' He halted at the look that appeared upon the undersheriff's visage.

Bradecote sensed rather than heard the beginning of the low growl in Catchpoll's throat. However much Catchpoll disliked having to work with an active superior, he was jealous of the office of sheriff's man, and took most unkindly to anyone treating it with disrespect. The undersheriff did not know whether Catchpoll knew of his bereavement, but assumed that by now he did. It was not something he was going to share with the silversmith. He understood the silversmith's lack of enthusiasm, and silenced Catchpoll with a small movement of his hand.

'My apologies to you, Master Ash. It is not our intention to keep you from your work, nor,' and he pulled a wry face, 'work from you. Even so, we have to make sure that Worcester does not burn down, so whether it pleases you or not, we are back with more questions.'

Reginald Ash's cheeks assumed an even redder hue, and he mumbled an apology, which Bradecote also waved away.

'What we need to know now, Master Ash, is whether you, or your journeyman, have had dealings with a woman called Maud Brewer.'

The silversmith raised his eyebrows and looked enquiringly.

'That depends on what you mean by "dealings", my lord. And if you're thinking what I suspect you are, the answer is no, never. In terms of honest trade though, yes I have, when her husband has been by, mind. Always happy to purchase little pieces to keep her sweet he was.'

'Keep her in his bed, you mean.' Edwin the journeyman had come from the rear chamber as his master spoke. He stood with his thumbs tucked into his belt, and a grin on his face.

'And I thought you a betrothed man,' Catchpoll murmured, with an even more lecherous leer.

'I am that, and faithful to my Winflaed too, but it don't mean I don't see what's put before the end of my nose. Some women can't help themselves; making eyes at every man they come across. She was one such. Brewer never saw, or pretended he didn't. Instead he prided himself on her looks, and thought how many were jealous of his position.' Edwin winked. 'Never seemed to strike him that her favours might be widely spread, like her . . . and he a cuckold.' Edwin shook his head. 'Poor fool. Maud Brewer was a woman well "known" in Worcester.'

'She died some months back. Have you seen Edgar Brewer since?' Bradecote wanted to know if Edgar Brewer was still under this delusion of his wife's fidelity.

'No. What use should he have now of my work?' Reginald Ash frowned.

'I only wondered if he seemed the same . . . believing in her being a good wife.'

'Couldn't say,' replied Edwin. 'You'd think he'd have to be deaf, aye and blind also, not to know her reputation, but some folk choose to be deaf and blind, if you see what I mean.'

Catchpoll nodded. Such denial of reality was common enough. It did not help the discovery of culprits.

Bradecote hid his disappointment, though in honesty his expectations had not been high.

'We are also interested in a man, probably wealthy, perhaps some local lord, who wears gauntlets.' Catchpoll was already working on the next trail of evidence.

The silversmith looked puzzled.

'Not uncommon, that. Why should I note one man more than another?'

'We think this one has been wearing them even in fine weather, when others would not . . . fine leather gauntlets perhaps, and chestnut in colour.' Bradecote was working on the assumption that the man did not possess too many pairs of such an expensive item.

The look of perplexity remained on the silversmith's face, and was echoed by that of Edwin. They shook their heads, and Bradecote turned to Catchpoll, whose face contorted into a fleeting grimace of resigned disappointment. The sheriff's men left the silversmith's and set off at a relaxed pace for the Sutheberi road below the castle and cathedral. Bradecote was suddenly aware of the isolation of their work. The everyday life of Worcester was continuing just as normal all around them, and they were largely ignored, although he noticed a couple of surly fellows who stepped back into the shadows or turned away when Catchpoll approached. They existed in a different world of threat, deception and death that was ignored by the world at large, and complained of when it intruded into normal daily existence. Catchpoll had inhabited this other world for many years and seemed unconcerned, but Bradecote was conscious of having been part of the unaware majority until only a few short months ago. He gave thanks that at least he was not investigating in his own manors, and could keep home and this duty apart. Home . . . there was a moment of realisation that 'home' was no longer the same, but the image of the bloodless pallor of Ela's dead face was swiftly supplanted by the fresh pink of his son's. He must adjust, he told himself, just adjust and move on.

It was not long before they reached the Sutheberi gate, with the hospital of Bishop Wulfstan's founding just outside. The roads divided, and they set out up the hill. The houses soon petered out and, beyond a small enclosure, Gilbert the Tanner had his business. It was a foul-smelling trade that put filthy water into whichever watercourse it used. There were small tanneries on the riverbank at the northern edge of the town, but Gilbert had a large business and steady clientele, which led to his presence beyond the town boundaries and by a stream that entered the river a mile or so below Worcester. The combination of putrefying flesh, ammonia and animal excrement produced an eye-watering stench. It pervaded even the front building where the finished leather was kept for the artisans to select as suited their trade. Bradecote had of course purchased from saddlers, cobblers and glovers, whose premises smelt sweetly of worked and waxed leather, but he wondered how anyone could work in a place such as this, as the foul air assailed his nostrils and brought tears to his eyes. His gorge threatened to rise. Catchpoll smiled as the undersheriff coughed. A tannery was not the sort of place that the upper classes visited. Mind you, it was not one he would choose to come to either unless duty so demanded.

A lad who was carrying a stiff and malodorous hide, stared at them as he passed, and Catchpoll asked after the master. The youth, who was heavily set and remarkably bovine in appearance, tossed his head in the direction of the rear door of the chamber. Bradecote groaned inwardly. He had no wish to advance further into this miasma, but had no alternative without losing face. Gritting his teeth, and taking as shallow breaths as possible, he led the way into the rear yard. The scene was one of industry, and to his amazement there was even a man whistling. The undersheriff studiously avoided looking closely at the large pits, wherein lay the soaking hides, and which were dotted about the yard as if the products of corrosion by the liquid contents. In one corner men were actually treading up and down in a shallow pit, rather as he had seen done in a fuller's vat. Elsewhere men were scraping the hair from sodden hide, or stretching it to cure. A man, better dressed than the labour force and clearly in charge, was handling a hide that had just been taken down from a frame. He looked up as his attention was drawn to the visitors by one of his workers.

He registered the two men, the one tall and of lordly bearing and apparel, the other shorter, with grizzled hair and dour expression. He recognised that face as belonging to the sheriff's serjeant.

'Good day, Serjeant Catchpoll.' He looked to Bradecote and made a correct assumption. 'My lord? I take it that you are my lord de Crespignac's replacement.' He shook his head. 'A great pity his loss was, to be sure.'

Bradecote contrasted his words with those of Master Mercet.

'Yes. Well, that's as it is.' Catchpoll did not actually want to linger any more than necessary, and de Crespignac's replacement needed no eulogies about him. 'We were hoping you could give us some information about some leather that has been made into gauntlets, good quality and chestnut in colour. Wilfrid Glover said they were not of his making, but that the leather was so good he thought it must be yours, if local.'

'If Wilfrid Glover speaks so well of my workmanship then I am mightily pleased, but such leather is not uncommon. I have sold much of it over the years.'

'The glover thought it new,' interposed Bradecote, keen to put himself into the conversation.

'Well, I sold some very good chestnut hide at the end of Whitsuntide, but that was for boots, I know. The only chestnut leather sold to a glover was fine kid, such as a lady would wear, not for a man's gauntlets. They want something tougher for regular riding and hunting. The kid would be soft, fit for a lady's soft and delicate skin. It would be a strange fellow who wanted gauntlets out of it.'

'Who was the purchaser, Master Tanner?' However unlikely, it was the only lead to the disguised man the law officers possessed, and Bradecote, whose eyes were now watering, was very keen to end the interview.

'I sold it to Walter Typcote. Ask him by all means what he made with it.'

The undersheriff thanked Gilbert Tanner and hastened to withdraw. Once outside and far enough down the hill not to be seen from the tannery, he stopped and took great draughts of air. Catchpoll, who was more discretely breathing through his mouth, laughed and choked. After a few health-giving gulps, Bradecote turned to him.

'Jesu, Catchpoll, how do they work there?'

'They gets used to it, as I suppose. Mind, they are probably sick when they start.' Catchpoll was observing his superior's greenish tinge, and the next minute Bradecote turned aside quickly and could be heard retching in the narrow alley between two dwellings. Catchpoll grinned, but schooled his expression into one of concern by the time Bradecote rejoined him.

'Feeling better now, my lord?'

Bradecote nodded, ignoring the hint of tremor in Catchpoll's voice. 'If ever, and I mean ever, there is a death in a tannery, by accident or design, then you can investigate alone, Catchpoll, if it costs me my position.' He swallowed hard. 'Is that understood?'

'Indeed, my lord. I will make a mental note of it.'

'I know bathing is not healthy, but that stink gets right into you. I will be calling for hot water and herbs when we get to the castle. Could there be a more lingering and revolting smell?' Bradecote's question was rhetorical, but Catchpoll's expression hardened.

'Aye, and that's the smell of burnt flesh. Once in the nose it is remembered forever.' He shook his head, all joviality banished. It was a suddenly sombre pair who came back into Worcester, and headed not for the castle, and water, but to Walter Typcote the glover.

Their visit did not give them the name of their mystery man, but considerably heightened their interest. He had come, said the glover, been measured and selected the leather, and returned some days later to collect them. His clothes and manner proclaimed the lord and there was no reason to ask his name, especially in the circumstances.

Undersheriff and serjeant raised eyebrows in unison, and the glover smiled but also shook his head.

'Poor man, I was glad to do what I could for him, truth to tell. He looked well enough at distance, if a little drawn, but when he revealed his poor hands . . .' Typcote crossed himself, and shook his head. 'If ever such a thing befell me, I'd starve.' There was a short silence, that even Catchpoll felt loth to break, and then the craftsman continued. 'Normal gloves were impossible and I had to pick the very softest leather, of course. It took some time to design the best fit, not being able to draw round the hand in the normal way.'

'Why?' Bradecote was unable to conceal his interest.

'Because his hands were all gnarled and contracted, and the skin red and angry, burnt as they were. I suppose you would have to say he was fortunate to survive such injury, but seeing his constant discomfort, I am not totally convinced. They would be useless if he were a craftsman, and I doubt even he can hold his horse's reins proper now. His face bore burn marks as well, though not as bad, about the chin. Must be an awful thing for any man to bear.'

'Do you suppose the injuries were recent?' Catchpoll tried to sound as if the answer would not be important.

'I'm not one as has seen much of burns. It's mostly cuts and slips with awl and needle in this trade. Can't have been too recent or the scars would not have drawn, but the skin looked raw new so perhaps a few months or so, no more. It's a complete guess, mind.'

Bradecote thanked the glover for his help, and he and Catchpoll headed slowly back towards the castle. Neither spoke for some minutes, assessing and working upon the new information. The undersheriff spoke first, musing almost to himself.

'It seems too odd a chance that we are dealing with a burnt man. Perhaps it was the result of an attempt gone wrong, or an ill deed that made him want a similar fate for others.'

Catchpoll stared at his superior in patent disbelief.

'You're not saying this man is our fire-raiser, surely? No, my lord, the tannery fumes have addled your wits in that case. We agreed the fire-raiser knew Worcester, but this man is from out of town, and a lord too. In addition, he has no connection with the silversmith, and if he did it would seem unlikely that it provided a reason to set a fire. All we have is the connection with Old Edgyth, and we can explain that. If his hands were as bad as Typcote says, then no wonder he sought the old woman's salves to ease his pain. Even if they did not work as well as he hoped, he would have no cause to burn her out. A man who had suffered from flame like that would be more like to cringe at the sparking of a log in his hearth than want to set fires. No, my lord, this is one of those peculiar coincidences that just happen. There is no connection between this burnt man and our fires. We dismiss him here and now and hunt elsewhere. I'll go to Edgar Brewer tonight, if you think it best, and see what he really knew of his wife. You go and wash away these flights of fancy with hot water and sweet plants.' His tone was firm and almost paternal.

Bradecote disliked being told that his ideas were madness, but Serjeant Catchpoll made sense. Perhaps the stench had indeed muddled his brain. The thought of hot water, infused with any strong-smelling herb that the kitchen had to hand to drive away the clinging foulness, was very tempting, and he assented to the idea without demur. Their two paths diverged, with Catchpoll heading back into the narrow streets to find the cuckolded widower, as Bradecote returned to the castle. He hoped to go straight to his chamber, but was waylaid by the castellan in the outer bailey. Bradecote heaved a heavy sigh at his approach.

'I am not at all happy about this.' The castellan's voice was raised peevishly, and he pursed his thin lips, making his small mouth look like a scrip drawn tight. His arms waved in a vaguely encompassing gesture. 'I have had the burgesses knocking at my door, and blaming me for letting them be burnt to a cinder in their beds. If you hadn't made such a fuss about the fires the townsfolk would be none the wiser even yet. The weather has been hot and fair, so they could have been mere accidents.'

Bradecote gazed at Simon Furnaux in amazement, succeeded by rising anger. Here was the man who had proposed improbable and even impossible theories, and pestered for greater action, now complaining about action being taken. He stepped close, intentionally, glad to contaminate the man's nose with the stench he had been forced to bear.

'So you now think it would be best if we sat quiet and waited for more charred corpses to pile up?' Bradecote's tone was scathing, and deliberately insulting. He had spent an unpleasant and seemingly useless afternoon, and was in no mood to be civil, whether the castellan outranked him or not.

The castellan's face grew purple. 'I will not take such words from you, a mere . . .' His sentence petered out as he could not find a term that fitted his opinion, and even more from the choking cough that rose as the odour from Bradecote's person reached his senses.

Bradecote smiled, although the smile was largely a sneer. 'Mere undersheriff will do, my lord Castellan.' His voice was quiet, unlike the castellan's bluster, and very deliberate. 'But it is no matter. I take my orders from the sheriff of this shire, from whom I also hold land, not from you. For your information, there is no doubt in my mind, nor in that of Serjeant Catchpoll, whose experience is beyond doubt, that there is a fire-raiser at large in Worcester. Pretending there is nothing amiss will not work. Until we catch this man, and it is most probably a man, the risk to lives and livelihoods remains.' His voice dropped. 'And we will do whatever is necessary to catch him, whether it sets the burgesses, or you, aflutter or not.'

He stepped even closer to the castellan, intimidatingly. Simon Furnaux's nose wrinkled in distaste as the all-pervading smell now overwhelmed him. He took an involuntary step backwards. Without waiting for the castellan to comment upon the odour or formulate a response, Bradecote turned smartly to his left, into the kitchens where he could order washing water and a large bowl.

If he felt afterwards that he smelt of the evening meal, which was pork heavily laced with sage and wild garlic, it was an improvement. It had taken quite a lot of rubbing of his skin to believe the smell of the tannery had left him, and its ghost haunted his nostrils. He took a fresh undershirt and his spare tunic from his blanket roll, yelled for a servant, and then cast out their predecessors to be washed. The serving wench who came running and caught him before the chamber door was closed, stifled a giggle at seeing him with the undershirt half over his head and clinging to his damp torso, and then gasped when she picked up the soiled garments. The undersheriff said nothing, being just glad to be free of the tannery. It was then he remembered the scented fruit he had been given by Simeon the Jew. It lay in his scrip still, and the merchant clearly considered it of great worth. He took it from the bag, smelt the skin, and then wrapped it in his spare linen undershirt in his roll of belongings. He could just imagine some castle maid coming across it if left on display, and casting it out as some dangerous devilment. He smiled, briefly, then sighed. Today he had learnt nothing of real use to his investigation and only that tanneries were to be avoided at all cost, and that there was a strange yellow fruit that grew upon trees in hot climes.

Chapter Nine

Serjeant Catchpoll was regretting his offer to see Edgar Brewer, for it meant trailing to the northern edge of town, just to the west of the Foregate, and the air held the sultry foreboding of a storm coming. Perhaps the undersheriff's prayers had been heard, but the serjeant had no desire to be out in the consequences of that success.

Brewer was a tall but stoop-shouldered individual whom Catchpoll assessed to be rather younger than he looked. The serjeant had decided it would be best not to ask the man outright if he knew his wife had possessed the morals of a whore, and so began his conversation with questions about a totally fictitious theft of a barrel from elsewhere in the town. Having opened the interview, he was invited into the brewer's house. As he did so the brewer drew back slightly and pulled a face. The vestiges of tannery still clung to Catchpoll's person.

The serjeant murmured an apology and made a quip about the less than joyous reception he would be likely to receive at home from his wife, which turned out to be prophetically true. From this it was simple enough to steer the brewer into talking about his late spouse.

'You must miss her,' he commented, noticing the unnatural tidiness of the chamber, for the home of a widower of recent date. It bore all the signs of habitation by a house-proud woman, excepting a dirty knife that lay beside a cheese with an irregular chunk cut from it, and a broom rested at a drunken angle beside a heap of dust and old rushes that had got no nearer being swept out than being gathered in one place, as though the sweeper had left in a hurry, with the work half done. Edgar Brewer shook his head, and Catchpoll was caught wondering if he was refuting the idea or was being doleful.

'My poor Maud. Such a beauty she was, and with a laugh like little tinkling bells. The place is not the same without her.' He sighed, rather dramatically in Catchpoll's opinion.

'A very well-favoured woman as I recall, and very popular.' Catchpoll did not say with whom, and watched the brewer closely. For an instant he thought he saw a flicker of displeasure cross the man's face. He risked delving deeper. 'Very lucky to have such a woman as a faithful helpmeet.' There was just the slightest stress on 'faithful'.

This time the change of expression was more definite.

'Did you know her, yourself, Serjeant?'

Catchpoll caught the inflexion. Brewer had at least had suspicions of his wife, then, if no more. Their eyes met.

'Not better than being able to say "good morrow" in

124

the street, Master Brewer, but I am not blind.' Read into that what you will, thought Catchpoll. His attention was suddenly drawn to a basket of washing on a stool by the rear door. Here were further signs of domesticity; everything was neatly folded, and with a repair clearly newly and tidily darned. It might be that Brewer was simply paying a woman to do his washing, though few would then do repairs, or clean house so well. The central hearth was swept and with a fire laid ready to light, but with no sign of cooking. By this hour there should be pottage bubbling away, even if it had been made and set to boil by a wench from elsewhere, as at the silversmith's. The brewer clearly got his sustenance, if nothing else, by another hearth. So there was a replacement for Maud Brewer in the offing, was there? He returned his gaze to Edgar Brewer.

'I don't think I can be of any more help to you, Serjeant, when it comes to missing barrels,' said the man slowly, keeping eye contact. 'Good luck with hunting your thief, and if I lose any of mine I will, of course, be sure to tell you straight away.' He made to show Catchpoll to the door, and the serjeant did not demur. On leaving, he decided that Maud Brewer's demise, which had occurred when he and the sheriff had been absent, warranted further investigation, whether or not her husband was currently about with flint and steel. Just because they were hunting down one criminal did not prevent him taking interest in other crimes, and murder was murder.

He did not report to Hugh Bradecote, leaving him to his ablutions, and so headed straight for his own cooking-pot and hearth, but just before entering his home he halted and knocked instead next door, at the cooper's. The man's youngest son opened the door, and smiled up at him, recognising the neighbour. Catchpoll, seeing that the meal would shortly be served, made his apologies to the mistress of the house with much more sincerity than most got from him, and requested a few words with her husband. She indicated his presence out in the yard that separated work from dwelling, and Catchpoll found him with a pail of water washing his muscled forearms and sweat-stained face.

'Evenin', Will. Hot work today.'

William the Cooper blew the water from his top lip and nodded, sending droplets of water from the wet hair hanging over his forehead.

'Come on a friendly visit, eh? Either your good wife has cast you out and you need a meal, or you are after information.'

'It's a cynical man you are, Will,' grinned Catchpoll, 'and it's the information. You have plenty of contact with the brewers, so I was wondering if there was any gossip about the death of Maud Brewer.'

'Plenty of gossip while she was alive, surely,' answered Will, with a wicked smile. 'I could keep you here all evening with tales of what she got up to, and with whom.' He sniffed. 'Edgar Brewer is an odd sort of man. Very quiet for one of his trade. His wife died in a fall, as I heard. No interest to you there, though he's not the broken-hearted widower you might imagine. Of course, how he remained ignorant of his wife's reputation, or lack of it, remains a mystery, but despite outward shows of grief he seems very settled, and has his feet under the table of Widow Fowler. Not a woman you'd pick for her looks, but maybe he

wouldn't want that second time around.' Will cast an anxious eye indoors, where his wife was gesticulating.

Catchpoll saw the look on the cooper's face, and clapped him on the back. 'My thanks, friend. I'll not keep you from table, not when your wife will tell mine and I'll be on bread and dripping for delaying you.' He smiled, nodded amiably at the harassed housewife as he came back through the house, and saw her wrinkle her nose and frown a little as he passed her close. He went home to his own repast, hoping that the inviting smell that greeted him would mask any lingering foul odour. It did not, though if scathing words alone could cleanse him, he would have been more fragrant very swiftly.

The storm was taking its time brewing. A waning moon peeped cautiously and sporadically from behind scudding clouds, bathing Worcester with deep dark and ghostly silver by turn, though in the narrow street the light scarcely reached. There came rumbles of distant thunder, giving warning of the approaching army of raindrops, but then they ceased. A dog was howling, but it would have been difficult to pin down where. The sound of footsteps, firm and purposeful, reverberated from the walls of the buildings to either side of the narrow thoroughfare, and a dark figure headed eastward along Cokenstrete. The wind whipped the black cloak around the muttering form, which half stumbled and slackened its pace. Pale hands drew the hood more securely over the head and then held the cloak from flapping. In the all-enveloping blackness the dwellings looked much alike and the search for one particular house was unexpectedly difficult. A man

127

emerged from a narrow alley, head down and fumbling with his clothing. He almost collided with the person in the cloak. The pair performed an odd sequence of sidesteps like a bizarre dance as they tried to avoid each other, and the fumbling man passed by with a mumbled apology.

The cloaked figure made its way slowly along the street, peering at the buildings on one side only, and came to a halt. The moon was now totally obscured and the figure became almost invisible. There was a sudden flash as a fork of lightning zigzagged to earth somewhere beyond the far bank of the river. Taken by surprise, the lone mutterer looked up and, for a fraction of a moment, the face was illumined, ghoulishly pale in the white light. It was followed in a moment by a sharp crack of thunder like an enormous whiplash of sound, and proved that the storm had crept up on the town and was already almost overhead. The figure made the sign of the cross, as if to deflect the wrath from the heavens, and stood, clearly uncertain, looking up and down the street. Then the rain began; slowly at first, with great drops pitting the trodden earth and scattering like the shards of broken glass. The house seeker gazed heavenwards, and then clearly thought better of the nocturnal visit, turning back the way they had come with long strides, stopping for a moment to peer into the darkness of the alley whence the man had emerged.

In the alley shadows, the girl covered her ears and trembled at the sound of the thunder. She too then crossed herself as if the noise were the wrath of God, and directed against her. She did not like plying her trade in the dark, for if the risk of public discovery was less, the risk to her life was greater, and

Huw hated being left alone in whatever bolt-hole she had found them. For all that, the men who were busy making money by day had time to spend it in the hours of darkness, and so here she was. She had seen the strange, sinister figure, whose ghostly face had been unknown to her, 'dance' with her most recent client and had shrunk back into the shadows, fearful. Now the storm sent her scuttling to the dry security of the stable loft where she had left her brother nestled in sweet hay, and where, curled beside him, she could banish the harsh realities of what she had to do.

Serjeant Catchpoll had not taken much notice of the weather, warm and dry as he was in his own home, and with a good meal inside him. His slumbers had only briefly been interrupted when his wife had woken with a start at the first clap of thunder, and thereafter hidden her head beneath the blanket. He arose, therefore, as refreshed as the dawning day itself, and was about his business in good humour. As he approached the castle gate he saw Drogo the Cook letting himself out of a house further up the street, and sniffed and pursed his thin lips. That was something he had heard no whisperings about. He increased his pace to come up beside his friend.

'You old dog, Drogo. How long have you kept that little secret?'

Drogo did not look well pleased. 'Long enough, and I'd be grateful if you'd let it stay a secret. She's a good woman, Widow Bakere, and don't deserve her name being dragged into gossip. Aye, and she's a fine baker too.'

'So you were just helping her get her buns to rise, eh?'

Catchpoll could not resist the lewd jest. 'There's scope for a fine riddle there, you know.'

'And if you concoct one it will be your teeth, not a loaf, that's rammed down your throat.' Drogo was clearly put out, and Catchpoll clapped him on the back reassuringly.

'No fear, Drogo. It's none of my concern. Keep your warm Welsh widow and good luck to you.'

They parted in the bailey; Drogo headed to the kitchens and Catchpoll to the guardroom, and sometime thereafter to wait upon the undersheriff. He found him sweeter smelling than the previous evening, but hardly well rested.

'Good morning, my lord,' opened Catchpoll, cheerily, noting the heavy eyes and deep shadows around them. 'Dipping deep with the castellan were we?' He had good reason to know this was not the case, but kept the foreknowledge to himself.

'No, Serjeant, "we" were not. In the course of the night there was another fire.' Bradecote paused, as Catchpoll's face registered unfeigned horror.

'But nobody called me,' the serjeant bemoaned, shaking his head.

'Correct. That is because they called me instead. The good news, Catchpoll, is that this particular fire-raiser was a bolt from the heavens. The bad news is that one of the watch – and I am glad to see you have been sending out patrols through the night – thought any fire worthy of rousing me from my bed, and in truth, being a potential danger as great as one set by man, I suppose it was not a bad thought. The long and the short of it is that Worcester boasts less of one alehouse, and I have a head that feels as though there's a cleaver stuck in it.'

'Which alehouse?' Catchpoll homed in on the most important information, and exhibited no sympathy for his superior's state of ill health.

'The one with the sign of The Goose by the town wall. Nobody was killed, though there was considerable damage and many barrels lost, mostly to the fire. I could not vouch for a few not being rolled away having been "rescued". It took some time to put out, despite the rain. The roof was good and wet and is sound apart from the hole where the lightning struck, but it destroyed much of the taproom. It will not serve the thirsty within for some time.'

'More's the pity, then, for he sold good ale and kept out of our way . . . few fights or such.' Catchpoll was silent for a minute, and then continued. 'Talking of ale, I went and saw Edgar Brewer last evening, before it rained. We should have been told of that death, the wife's that is, but with the sheriff and my lot up beyond Bredon, and nobody raising a cry because it had the appearance of accident, well, it slipped through the net.'

Bradecote frowned, wishing his head were clearer. 'You mean, it was not an accidental death at all?'

'Oh, the husband, he killed her. I would lay you odds on that. Whether we find out how and whether we can prove it is another thing, being this late after the event, but I could feel it.'

Bradecote raised his eyes heavenward. 'Holy Virgin preserve us, you are going to give me the "mystic serjeant" act now, I presume. All intuitive powers and subtlety. You'll want incense burners and chanting priests next.' He was not in a good mood.

Catchpoll prickled at the sarcasm. 'No, my lord, there's

nothing mystic about it, just the better part of twenty years' experience as sheriff's serjeant and the fact that more killings are domestic than anything else. All I claim is years of doing the job, and doing it thorough. Maybe you'll have it one day.' The barb in the comment was obvious enough. The amity that had woven between them was still fragile enough to be torn by the pressures of the case.

'Does it mean that he rises as a suspect for our fires?' The undersheriff had too great a headache to rise to the insult, but kept his response clipped.

'That is not certain, my lord. They could as easily be two different things entirely. Mind you, if we keep a watch on Master Brewer, we will either be able to catch him in the act or discount him; and I will do some investigating as to what really happened back in June.'

Bradecote shook his head, partly in refusal and partly to try and clear it of the muzziness. 'No, I cannot spare you from the fire-setting case. That must take priority over a two-month-old murder that nobody reported as murder anyway.'

'It's not taking me from the case if they are linked.'

'And it is if they are not, Serjeant. We are going to have enough trouble sorting this out before the sheriff returns, and I don't want to have to tell him that Worcester is in ashes but you have solved a domestic murder.'

Catchpoll bit a lip, meditatively. 'That's fair enough, my lord, but what if I select a likely lad from among the men-at-arms to keep a watch on Brewer and do a little probing? He'd be less obvious than me, even if less wily. It gives us the chance to nab Brewer if he sets out with fire in mind without keeping us from other trails. It's how I started in this line, and I do have a candidate in mind. As for the murder alone, well, if you give me the odd hour over the next few days so I can speak to the neighbours and the local priest, then I think we will soon know if my hunch is right.'

'Why the priest?'

'Because when someone dies he is the first person called by the family. They see a lot of bodies in their vocation, and notice things without knowing. Yes, if you want to know about a corpse, ask their priest.'

Catchpoll's chosen man was one Walkelin, a well-set young man in his early twenties with a shock of ginger hair, a slightly turned-up nose and an open, innocent expression. Bradecote was at first surprised by the choice; the man-at-arms did not look particularly promising, but when he was briefed on his task his questions showed that appearances were very deceptive.

'Don't you worry, my lord. Young Walkelin will do well enough, and better than many. He's a bright lad, and I've noticed he has a good eye for detail and a good memory. He will make mistakes here and there, but he won't make the same one twice. It's a pity about the hair, of course, but you can't have everything . . . the colour doesn't really make for blending in and being forgettable.' Catchpoll shook his head at the errant hair. 'I have been thinking for some time he would be worth training up for when I've no longer a care to go chasing round the shire.'

'Intimations of mortality, Catchpoll?'

The serjeant gave a puzzled look, and Bradecote explained.

'You have an idea that you won't live forever.'

'None of us does that. We all reach the end at some point.

But you won't go before your time comes,' Catchpoll replied with perfect seriousness.

'And murder victims?'

'Ah.' Catchpoll paused. 'Their time came earlier than expected.'

Walkelin was sent to his duties fired with enthusiasm and dreams of glory, and undersheriff and serjeant spent the rest of the forenoon in unprofitable attempts to make any advance in the hunt for the fire-setter.

'It's no use,' sighed Bradecote, rubbing his hand to and fro across his jaw ruminatively, 'I still say we're just doing a May dance. Every suspect we raise we then immediately discount, and no linking motive appears either. Why anyone should set fire to Master Ash's workshop eludes us completely. Nobody seems to dislike him. You'd as well say the fire-raiser didn't like the shape of the building. When we get to the Corviserstrete fire we cannot tell whether the intended victim was the glover, the old woman, the carpenter or the plot on which the buildings stood, and our suspects have been Mercet, because you dislike him—'

'And he is an evil guilty bastard, my lord. Be fair.'

'And he is, as you say, an evil and probably guilty bastard, Simeon the Jew because he is an unknown quantity, and Edgar Brewer because his wife was a whore and you have decided that he killed her, despite any proof. Then there is the unknown lordly man with soft-leather gauntlets and badly burnt hands who visited the old healing woman.' He ticked them off on his long fingers. 'And your friend Drogo, who is innocent because you say so.' Bradecote shook his head, miserably. 'You know, I hate to say this, Catchpoll, but I have an awful feeling that what we need to get further is another fire.'

Catchpoll groaned.

Chapter Ten

Catchpoll would at least have been cheered by the actions of his protégé, who threw himself into his exciting undercover work with a passion. Apparently as aware as his mentor of his memorable hair, he thoughtfully took with him both a woollen cap and a floppy-brimmed hat, and purchased a supply of Widow Bakere's best oatcakes. Thus prepared, with a short plank of wood, and a small sack slung over his shoulder, he set off towards Edgar Brewer's.

He found himself a likely spot with a good view of the front of the property and was fortunate in that the street opened out into an area that could, at a pinch, be termed a square, at the point where the brewer's premises stood. It was therefore possible for him to observe the comings and goings without being in the way of passers-by. He then took the short plank of wood, cut two notches at either end with his very serviceable knife, and looped some twine around it to make a tray that he could hang around his neck. From the small sack he withdrew several little wooden animals, stylised rather than purely representational, but just the size for a child's hand to grasp. Walkelin was a whittler, and the results of his labours were certainly good enough to present for sale. During the morning he plied his trade, selling three or four small horses and a couple of ducks. Around noon, a couple of lads emerged from the brewer's premises and sat against the south-facing wall to bask in the sun and partake of bread and cheese. They acknowledged Walkelin's presence, and after a while ambled over to see what he was selling. It was easy enough for the enterprising Walkelin to then join them in their respite, sharing his oatcakes in exchange for swigs of beer, and enjoying a companionable chat until the sound of a raised voice within drew the brewer's labourers indoors. Walkelin grinned. It had been a profitable morning's work, and not just from the silver fourthings in his scrip; he felt confident enough to delve further. Serjeant Catchpoll would, he felt sure, applaud his initiative.

The morning in the castle having availed them of nothing, undersheriff and serjeant took to the streets of Worcester in the afternoon, and found themselves, like birds of ill omen, eyeing potential targets for anyone who wished to set the town ablaze. Bradecote was not a town-dweller, and was conscious of a desire to get away from the bustle and stale air. He found himself thinking of being back at Bradecote, listening to the skylarks in the open skies, and then felt guilty both for dead wife, and worse, living son, whom he had shut out from his thoughts so much in the last few days. He had seen the summons to Worcester as freedom, but suddenly, today, felt it as imprisonment. Until the fire-setter was caught he would not be able to see his son, and a wave of sudden and unexpected paternal yearning washed over him. He sighed.

Catchpoll misread the reason behind it. 'We'll get there somehow or other, my lord, even though our path looks dark as the pit of hell just at present. It's the "why" that has me muddled. If we had a motive we would have "who" fast enough, but the deeper you delve into it, the more it must be the random workings of a madman.'

Bradecote stopped, and frowned.

'But as you said, just because the fire-raiser is mad doesn't mean that his actions are random though, Catchpoll. To him they make perfect sense, but we do not see the connection because we, as far as I can tell, are not mad.'

'So we really do have to think like lunatics?' Catchpoll gave his most death's head grin and rolled his eyes. A passing woman quickened her step and muttered under her breath.

'Think, perhaps, but not try and look like them, Serjeant. It gives the law a bad name.' Bradecote smiled wryly. He felt suddenly light-headed. The seriousness of the whole thing could only be dealt with by jest.

They had reached the gate that gave onto the bridge across the river, and turned to return by way of the quays and wharves. Here there were not just more people, but they were also engaged in labour, not merely going 'about their business'. Men were lifting, shouldering sacks, guiding ropes and shouting instructions. The blood of commerce flowed along the artery of the Severn, and kept Worcester vital and vibrant.

The sheriff's men were forced to weave their way in single file in places, and it was some minutes before they could converse.

'Plenty to burn down here,' noted Catchpoll conversationally, 'and easy to melt into the throng, but difficult to get a fire going and not be noticed.'

Bradecote nodded. 'I'd like a couple of men-at-arms to do a special turn up and down here at night, mind. Get the castle watch on to it. It would be easy to set a fire going in the dark, and as you say . . . plenty to burn here; wood, wool, all sorts. It would have the burgesses in far more of a flap than the death of an aged widow if they thought their trade at risk.'

They turned up towards St Andrew's church, getting into step once more. At the priest's house Bradecote turned and grimaced.

'You didn't have the pleasure of meeting the priest of St Andrew's.'

'No, though I exchanged a couple of words with him at the Corviserstrete fire. He's only come within the year, and not my parish, thanks be. The old priest, Father Ambrose, I came across occasionally, and he was firm but understanding, if you get my meaning.'

'I wouldn't think understanding is high on Father Boniface's list of attributes.'

At that moment the door of the house opened, and the subject of their comments emerged. Father Boniface's eyebrows rose in mild surprise.

'How strange. It is providential that you should be here, my lord Undersheriff. It has shown me the path that I must take, and I suffered from indecision.'

Bradecote exchanged a swift glance with Catchpoll.

'You see,' continued the priest, 'I did not know whether to report the loss . . . the theft . . . to you or not. Of course, judgement will be delivered by the Almighty for such a sin, but your presence has shown to me that the secular authority should know of it.'

'Father, you have us in the dark. What exactly have you decided to tell us?' Catchpoll tried not to grumble. He preferred simple speech to 'holying' about things as some priests were wont to do.

'Why, the theft of a bottle of holy oil from the sacristy. I only received a new bottle last week, in anticipation of my current bottle running out. It is most worrying, because I use it for important sacraments. I cannot think why anyone should wish to steal it; it is both priceless and without price. It is for God's work, and anything less is sacrilege.' The priest frowned, and Bradecote felt that the furrows were habitual. Joy did not seem to feature in Father Boniface's life.

'Thank you, Father. When did the bottle disappear?'

'A couple of days ago. I have put in a request for a replacement, of course. I know it cannot be a priority for you, my lord, and I was in two minds about coming to you, but there, you have appeared before me, so I have told you.'

The priest nodded, and without waiting for any response, turned down the street and stalked away.

'Happy soul, ain't he,' Catchpoll murmured.

'Told you.' Bradecote grinned, but then grew serious. 'Mind you, he gives us worrying information.'

'He does indeed. Holy oil soaked into a rag would help any fire and be easy to carry about without drawing all eyes.' Catchpoll shook his head despondently. 'Setting fire to property is not as easy as you'd think, from the outside. Inside is a different matter, of course, or with a supply of wood like the carpenter's wood store, but if the fire-raiser wants to set a place aflame from without, well, I had been hoping that would be too time-consuming and chancy.'

'He would still need more than just an oil-drenched cloth though, Catchpoll, to get most things ablaze, unless they were cloth. Solid oak would perhaps char a little on the surface but . . .'

'I have been thinking about that, my lord. They had it easy the first two times, what with getting into the back of the silversmith's and with the wood store, and at night, but with more men-at-arms out in the town, and the difficulty of lighting fire when not inside or hidden, I am thinking if there are any more fires, they will be like your lightning, striking at night.'

The pair headed on a meandering but purposeful course back towards the castle, each gloomily conscious that they were still reacting to events rather than taking positive action. As they drew close they were aware of raised shrill voices. An altercation was taking place before Catchpoll's front door, and they hastened their steps to see what was toward.

Mistress Catchpoll, very red-faced and with a besom in hand, was berating a small figure trying to defend itself against word and broom. It was little Huw's sister, and Catchpoll swiftly intervened.

'Lay off, woman, for heaven's sake. What are you about?'

Mistress Catchpoll rounded on her spouse. 'How dare you, husband, have whores come to my door. For shame to drag my good name into gossip.' She raised the broom to him, but he grabbed it firmly.

'Quiet now. Let's see to this seemly, and inside.'

'Her? In my house? Never!' Mistress Catchpoll was outraged.

Catchpoll ignored her, and bundled her back into the house. He then turned to Bradecote and the girl. 'Come you both in,' he commanded, for command it was.

The girl hesitated, and turned as if to run, but Bradecote blocked her path. He looked at her without any trace of emotion on his face, which she found peculiarly comforting. With reluctance, the girl edged into the cottage as if into the den of a wild beast.

Mistress Catchpoll, trembling with anger, stood intimidatingly with folded arms, but at the rear of the chamber. Catchpoll sat at the two stout planks that formed a trestle table and invited the girl to sit down, but she shook her head.

'You have something to tell me?'

She nodded, and wetted dry lips, suddenly shy. Catchpoll wondered if it was his wife's judgemental presence.

'I've not been inside a house, a proper house, all summer,' whispered the girl, and her eyes were moist.

So that was it. This brought back the old life, the ordinary, everyday life of childhood that had been snatched from her. Small wonder it affected her, but best not to let her dwell on it.

'Well now. What is it that you have seen?'

'Last night, just when the storm began, I saw a man and . . .' She paused and bit her lip.

'And?'

'He scared me.' Her eyes dilated at the memory, and Bradecote frowned.

Catchpoll was focusing on the details. 'In what way? By what he did?'

'No, I mean not exactly. What he did was odd, but it was the look on his face . . . horrible it was.'

Mistress Catchpoll's face was a blend of disgust and fascination, but her husband kept his gaze holding that of the girl, and his comprehension was quicker.

'This was not a man you were with, was it.' There was no question in the statement.

'Oh no, no. I just saw him.'

'Then tell us where you were and exactly what happened.' Catchpoll's tone was a surprise to Bradecote, for it was unexpectedly sympathetic, without any trace of a command. The undersheriff was impressed. Whether Catchpoll felt any sympathy or not, and he suspected not, he was able to portray it convincingly. The girl relaxed, and ceased twisting the loose threads of the frayed cuff of her grubby gown.

'I was in a little alley off Cokenstrete, up toward the Bocherewe. The man I . . . I was doing business with, well, he was leaving. As he did, he and another man nearly bumped into each other. It was quite funny, really. Both stepped one way and then the other to pass each other, so it looked like dancing.' A fleeting smile, an innocent, childlike smile, flitted across the careworn face. 'Then the other man came on along the street, peering at the houses on the north side as though he was looking for a particular one. He stopped a bit beyond me and faced a house. He stood there for a while, wondering whether to knock, I suppose, for it was rather late to visit, and then the lightning struck and the dark was bright light for a moment. It made me jump, and him too, I think. He looked up suddenly, and that was when I was frightened. The look on his face was,' she paused and frowned, trying to find the right words, 'like a man who is wild drunk; dangerous and unthinking. Sort of mad. But this man was for certain not drunk, because he walked straight and with purpose, not weaving or wobbling. And his face was like Death, all white in the light, and with mad eyes.' She shuddered at the memory. 'As he came back along the street he looked down the alley, but I do not think he saw me, for he carried on.'

'Had you ever seen him before?' Bradecote could not resist the question, though his interruption drew a warning scowl from Catchpoll. The girl looked at Bradecote as though she had forgotten his presence.

'No, my lord, never to my knowledge.'

'Then just describe him to us.' Catchpoll wanted her attention fixed and not wandering.

'I can't. It was dark and I only saw his face in that flash. He was all dark too.'

'Of what height? What did he wear that was dark? A cloak? A hat?'

'He was tall, yes. Taller than you,' she averred, staring at Catchpoll. 'Much more like him,' she pointed at the undersheriff, 'but perhaps not quite so tall. He had a dark cloak with the hood drawn up over his head so I didn't see much of him. He walked well, confident I'd say, not creeping around. He had no beard and I could see his eyebrows in the light so they were not the pale sort. Does that help, my lords?' She included Bradecote in her question, astutely thinking more largesse might be forthcoming from a man clearly of lordly status.

The sheriff's men exchanged glances. It did not give them an awful lot of detail about the suspicious figure, but it did give a probable target.

'You did right to come to me, girl. It might be nothing, but it might as easily be important. Now if you see him again, anywhere, keep out of his sight and come to us. This is the undersheriff, my lord Bradecote. Either of us will do, but make sure you come quick, yes?' Catchpoll proffered a ha'penny, which the girl accepted with a serious expression. She then turned her eyes to Bradecote in dumb request. It was, he decided, a clever piece of blackmail. Since Catchpoll had given a ha'penny, anything less would look mean-spirited. He ruefully handed over a silver penny. She bobbed a small curtsey, but her eyes signalled that she believed herself to have made a good deal.

'You get back to your little brother, straight away now. And you really shouldn't leave him alone at night. I take it you have him somewhere safe?' Catchpoll was in fatherly mode.

'Safe, yes, and warm too. In a stable down by the quay, where the carts and horses of one of the wealthy traders are kept. It's the best place I've found yet. There's good hay to sleep on in the hayloft.'

145

'You take care. If it's where I am thinking, it belongs to Mercet, who is not a generous man, nor his men neither.'

Her face clouded suddenly, and the pinched look returned. 'I knows that already, but we are safe enough as long as the rent is paid, see.'

Bradecote opened his mouth to speak, and then shut it tight. The girl was not talking of a money transaction. He remembered the fair, fat features of Robert Mercet, and revulsion rose in him.

Catchpoll did not so much as blink. 'And who "collects" the rent, child?'

'Master Turgis, he calls himself,' her lip curled in disdain, 'but he's no better than a hog.' She stared at the two men, accusing them as men in general, and then glanced at Mistress Catchpoll, whose mouth was set in an uncompromising line. Unsure whether this was indicative of anger towards herself or against the male sex, the girl made to leave.

'Wait.' Bradecote's voice halted her, although he was looking directly at Catchpoll. 'I will go to Cokenstrete and leave warning there. I will see you back at the castle after supper, and Walkelin too, if he is back in.' He turned then to the girl. 'You'll accept the protection of the undersheriff as far as Cokenstrete? You can point out the right house to me.'

For the briefest of moments he sensed her questioning his motives, and then she nodded. The unlikely pairing departed, leaving Mistress Catchpoll to combine a diatribe on the wickedness of men against poor girls, and her annoyance at having a whore in her chamber.

The girl did not speak a word as they made their way through the streets of Worcester. With unexpected consideration, she did not walk beside the undersheriff, but followed a few steps to the rear. She thought it respectful and also fair. In Cokenstrete she pointed out the alleyway and then the house before which the frightening stranger had stopped. As Bradecote had expected, it was the house of Simeon the Jew. The girl declined the offer of escort all the way to the stable, announcing that she would buy supper on the way. Bradecote warned her, smiling, to avoid cutpurses, and saw her slip away down a side street. That penny ha'penny would feed them for a day or so on more than just bread.

Returning to the matter in hand, he knocked heavily upon the door of Master Simeon's house. The same servant as before opened the door a fraction, but threw it wide with a courteous bow when he saw who it was. Bradecote asked to see the master immediately upon an important matter, and the servant led him straight into the main part of the hall and then halted, uncertain whether the situation warranted intrusion or not.

At the end of the hall the family were about to eat. Simeon was clearly intoning prayers, and frowned as he looked up to see his visitor.

Uncomfortably aware of the invasion of something with both a family and religious significance, Bradecote approached with apologies but firm in his determination to speak without delay. Simeon excused himself from his table and came forward to meet his unexpected and unwanted guest, his face mirroring Bradecote's grimness.

'I am sorry to disturb you, Master Simeon, but the matter cannot wait.'

Simeon bowed his acceptance. 'What is it that you require of me, my lord?'

'Nothing but your vigilance. Information has come to light that leads me to believe that your property, and thus your family, stand in immediate danger. An unknown man was seen hunting for your house last night, as the storm broke. He stopped outside, but the violence of the weather sent him off. I assume you do not encourage trading visits after dark, and it therefore seems likely that the visitor meant no good. If it turns out to be our fire-raiser, well, it is best that you have a close watch kept to the front and to any rear access.'

Simeon nodded, his dark brows knit. He cast a swift glance back towards the family at his table. 'Should I send my family from here until the matter is resolved, my lord?'

'I cannot truly judge. Perhaps, but then where would you send them?'

'Down the river to Bristow and my brother if I must, though there is discord enough down there.'

'It must be your decision, but for tonight simply keep a careful watch.'

'That I will, my lord. And thank you for coming in person. I fear we will not enjoy a peaceful Sabbath.'

Bradecote looked puzzled. 'But . . .'

Simeon gave a tight smile. 'Ah, of course I mean our Sabbath. You Gentiles have the wrong day, you know.' He judged the undersheriff would not take umbrage, and was correct in his assumption. Bradecote was more astounded to hear that another faith observed a sabbath.

'Oh.' Bradecote was at a loss how to respond, and took

refuge in repeating both his apology and warning. Master Simeon showed him to the front door in person, and bowed him out respectfully and with genuine thanks. The merchant's face, when he returned to his table, was clouded and serious.

Chapter Eleven

In sober mood, Bradecote returned to the castle and headed for his supper, though with a curtailed appetite. He was relieved to find the castellan absent, nursing an aching tooth in his chamber, and when Catchpoll entered, with Walkelin in tow like an eager hound, he pushed his trencher aside and rose to meet them.

They adjourned to the privacy of the guardroom, and round a small glowing brazier that kept out the evening chill, the recent developments came under review. Bradecote sat upon a narrow bench, and invited Catchpoll to do likewise. As befitted his lowly rank, Walkelin remained standing and kept his own counsel as his superiors discussed the information about the stranger in Cokenstrete. They agreed that the Jew's house was a clear target, and Catchpoll remarked that he had instructed the watch that was going to do the rounds of the quay area at some point during the night to take in Cokenstrete on its patrol. They then wondered about how much further they had got in identifying their potential fire-setter. Assuming the girl had seen him, and not just some debtor with a grudge, then the culprit was now confirmed as male, of tall stature and not blonde-haired. At this point Walkelin could not resist commenting that Edgar Brewer was not fair-haired, but though tall, walked with a stoop.

'Would that be visible if he wore a flowing cloak, do you think, my lord?'

Catchpoll's train of thought had been disturbed, and he rounded on the man-at-arms. 'You just wait till we're ready for you, young Walkelin, or else I'll send you to stand out in the bailey yard and your keenness can cool off out there. You've fair thrown my thinking, so you have. Keep your mouth shut and learn. Where were we, my lord?' He turned back to Hugh Bradecote.

'Accepting that whoever it is, it is not Mercet's tame bully, Turgis. He's probably not tall enough, but more importantly the girl would have recognised him at once.'

'Mercet has other men to do his dirty work though, so it does not necessarily rule out the master even if it does rule out the man.'

'True enough. And Walkelin does not rule out Brewer, even though he casts doubts.' Bradecote rubbed his chin, thoughtfully.

'Not doubts, my lord, just questions. Besides, as I have it, if the fire-raiser is Brewer, then his motive is against those he thinks usurped his bed. Are you seriously suggesting Maud Brewer sold her body to a Jewish merchant?'

'If he had plenty of money I don't suppose it would have stopped her. Why should it? If adultery meant nothing to her it would be unlikely that a man's religion would get in the way. More to the point is that I do not see Master Simeon, respectable husband and clearly doting father, falling in sin with a brewer's wife, especially of her reputation. I'd swear an oath he has eyes only for his wife, and his profitable business.' Bradecote shook his head. 'No, that doesn't work.'

Catchpoll was thinking, his face contorting as it always did. Walkelin watched the spectacle with slackened jaw and wide-open eyes. Bradecote fought the sudden urge to laugh.

Catchpoll's face ceased its movements. 'Of course, there's always the possibility that any action planned against the Jew is just using the fire-raiser as a cover for another motive entirely.'

Bradecote rolled his eyes and groaned. 'Don't, Serjeant.'

'So Brewer can be followed up further?' Walkelin was keen to keep his first target in view.

Catchpoll looked to Bradecote, who shrugged.

'Can I tell you what I discovered today then, my lord?' The puppy-like eagerness of the man-at-arms was difficult to suppress.

'Go on, then.' Catchpoll kept his features very straight, although a muscle in his cheek quivered.

Walkelin stood as straight as possible, cleared his throat and addressed a point some inches above Bradecote's head.

'As ordered by Serjeant Catchpoll, at the beginning of my watch I set out for—' he began in a colourless monotone.

'Halt. Stop.' Catchpoll shook his head. 'You've been talking to Gyrth, haven't you, lad?'

Walkelin coloured and nodded. Catchpoll sighed.

'Gyrth is a sound man-at-arms. He's a good man in a fair fight and,' Catchpoll admitted grudgingly, 'an even better one in an unfair fight, but he is not, and never will be, the man to make a report. Tell us what you know in your usual voice, and stop talking to the wall. Now, get on with it.'

'Sorry, Serjeant,' mumbled Walkelin, his reddened face clashing with the flame colour of his hair. He began again, describing, with a tinge of pride, how he had disguised himself in front of the brewer's, and even drawing a small wooden horse from his scrip. 'I make them when there's not much going on . . . and all sorts, not just horses. There's ducks and pigs and . . .' His voice petered out under Catchpoll's withering stare.

'At what point is your report going to tell us something about the brewer as opposed to you, Walkelin?'

'Ah, right. Sorry, Sergeant. Yes. Well, I watched the house all morning and a woman entered and remained there for several hours. She was not particularly young, or indeed comely, as I see it, too broad in the hip for—' Catchpoll's expression brought him back to the point. 'I later found this was the Widow Fowler, when I changed my disguise in the afternoon. Her cottage lies on the lane behind the brewer's. It seems she is none too popular with her neighbours. They were all keen to point her out as one that had found herself a cosy billet, so to speak, as soon as Maud Brewer was cold, and several remarked that she and Edgar Brewer had been on "comfortable" terms for some time prior to that. Oh, but before that, I sat and chatted with the brewer's workers at their noontide break. There was two of them came out, and they said that the widow and Edgar Brewer get on very well, and she has been "looking after" him since his wife died. There was some bawdy comment made at this point, my lord, but that might just be the usual sort of jest men make on the subject, and could not be taken as fact. I further discovered that it was the Widow Fowler who found the body of Mistress Brewer on the day of her death. They, the workers that is, said they heard humming from the upper chamber of the house that morning, and then a thump, but that Master Brewer, who was with them in the brewhouse out back, laughed it off as his wife dropping the old palliasse, the one that was going to be replaced, down the stair. Some short while after, there came the scream when Widow Fowler, coming to ask for a pat of butter, found the corpse at the bottom of the ladder stair. Then the priest was called, of course, because she was clearly dead.' He paused, and frowned. 'Mistress Brewer, that is, not Widow Fowler.'

Serjeant Catchpoll was listening attentively, but wisely ignored Walkelin's muddled conclusion to the report. 'That would be Father Anselm of All Saints. Brewer was in the brewhouse when the thump was heard, you say.' He pulled a peculiar face and rubbed the back of his neck, meditatively. 'And how, I wonder, was she found?'

'By the widow, Serjeant.'

'No, cloth-ears, I said "how" not "who". How the body looked could be important. I can see that I should visit the good Father Anselm tomorrow morning.' He looked at Bradecote. 'With your leave, my lord.'

Bradecote nodded his assent. 'As long as we have no disasters to follow up, yes.'

* * *

154

It was quiet. A moonless sky gave no light in the streets, and only those with need were abroad. Father Boniface, having attended a birth that had become a deathbed, guided an old woman, who had acted as midwife, to her own door, before heading back to his little dwelling beside St Andrew's church, while in another part of the town, Father Anselm administered the Last Rites to an elderly dame with none but a neighbour at her side to see her passing. A few unsavoury souls, whose occupation relied upon the concealment of darkness, plied their 'trade', and on the morrow, three good laying hens would be found missing from a widow woman's coop, and Payn the Moneyer would be at the castle early, reporting that an unsuccessful attempt had been made to prise open the heavy-bolted and locked door to the little room that contained his dies and freshly stamped pennies.

The cloaked and hooded figure that passed along Cokenstrete shortly after two men of the night guard had passed by on their way to the riverside, was seen by no one. Approaching the house of Simeon the Jew the figure trod more carefully, and at the shuttered window stopped. After taking a pot from beneath the folds of the cloak, they smeared the shutters with the contents, and then pressed a moist cloth into the join where the shutters met, letting threads hang down below. The same process was followed upon the stout door, where a liquid was then also thrown against it. The grease pot was left at the door sill with another thin strip of cloth pressed into it. The fire-raiser stood back for a moment, surveying their handiwork, and then drew forth flint and steel and set sparks to the trailing threads. The strip burnt but when the pot was reached there was nothing but a little smoke. A second attempt was made. The third time

also to the ceiling within. Taking your warning seriously, I had every available pitcher, pail and dish filled with water and left in the hall. That gave us an advantage.' He pulled a face. 'Mind you, the whole door, window and frames have to be entirely replaced.'

'Cannot wood be used simply to repair the damage if the wood is still solid?'

'You do not understand, my lord. These are unclean. Can you not smell it?'

Bradecote stepped up to the door and sniffed. The overriding smell was that of charred wood, but above that was a smell of . . . pig. He turned to Simeon. 'Swine fat, and something faint that I cannot put a name to.'

'All things to do with swine are unclean. We cannot touch them. These must be totally replaced. I would not pass through this door and have it contaminate me and mine. I will send my family to Bristow today, my lord, and will not have them back until all this is resolved.'

'I am sorry. We have failed you.'

Simeon raised his hands, and shook his head. 'No lives have been lost tonight. That is the important thing.'

Bradecote looked about him at the idle neighbours, and was suddenly angered beyond belief.

'Why do you all stand and do nothing?'

The townsfolk looked at their feet, and said nothing. A man coughed, and it was not at the smoke.

'If this was anyone else's house you would help.' Bradecote picked up a pail and thrust it into the hand of the nearest man. 'Here. Be a neighbour. Fill it.'

The man looked to his fellows and then at Bradecote.

'I am the Undersheriff of Worcester, and I say do it. Now!' yelled Bradecote, frustrated and also ashamed of his own inability to have prevented the fire. The man blinked and went to fill the pail.

'It matters not, my lord.' Simeon was tired. 'I expected nothing else,' he said softly, wiping a begrimed hand across his eyes.

'I will see this matter sorted out, Master Simeon, as soon as is possible. You should not be parted from your family for long.' He clapped the merchant on the back consolingly, directed a couple of men-at-arms to remain until such time as the damping down was complete, and returned to the castle.

He woke late, but after confused dreams that left him feeling jaded and lacklustre. He shaved with some care, hoping his ablutions would clear his mind as well as cleaning sooty smuts from his visage, and went in search of Serjeant Catchpoll. He found no sign of him, but was confronted by Walkelin, keen to do his bidding.

'You have work for me this morning, my lord?'

Bradecote ignored the question. 'Where is Serjeant Catchpoll?'

'Not here, my lord.'

'So you have not seen him today?'

'Yes, my lord, but he went straight off to find the priest of All Saints, and told me to await your orders.'

'Did he know of the fire in Cokenstrete?' Bradecote's temper was rising.

'Oh yes. I mentioned it myself.'

The undersheriff swore, giving vent to his feelings in a string of highly descriptive expletives. Walkelin regarded him admiringly. He had been surprised to find that Bradecote spoke good English, but it was an honour to serve a lord whose mastery of the vernacular extended to inventing colourful descriptions of the absent serjeant and what he would like to do to him. The man-at-arms managed to wipe the smile from his face before Bradecote rounded on him and tersely commanded him to accompany him to Cokenstrete.

It took some time for Catchpoll to run the good Father Anselm to earth, for he was busy about his parish, visiting the sick, providing what little help he could to the indigent. His was a parish that included many of the less wealthy citizenry of Worcester, and a fair number of widows with children, for whom finding food for the infants often meant going without themselves. The serjeant eventually found him giving a cast-off cotte to a crippled youth, begging down by the quayside.

Father Anselm, priest of All Saints, was a short, rotund man of gentle mien, popular with his flock, and keen to see the best in them, while acknowledging that they all strayed from righteousness, as he did himself. His parishioners looked to their 'wealthier' friends within the parish of St Andrew's, living under the unyielding Father Boniface who gave sermons dwelling on damnation and set harsh penance, and gave prayers of thanksgiving for their own good fortune.

He greeted Serjeant Catchpoll courteously but with some concern, fearful that the serjeant might ask him to break some secret of the confessional, and he was therefore initially relieved to be asked about the death of Mistress Brewer, so recently laid to rest within his churchyard.

'Ah yes, Serjeant Catchpoll, a very sad business. I arrived quickly, and there was a deal of commotion still. The Widow Fowler, who had apparently found her, was all tears and waving her hands about, the way women can be, and Maud Brewer lay at the bottom of the stair, which is more of a ladder, it is so steep.'

'There was no doubt she was dead when you found her? I mean she held no breath when you got there?'

'Oh, no doubt at all. Her neck was clearly broken. You could see from the peculiar angle, and when I closed her eyelids her skin was cool, like someone who had been outside in a chill breeze, and her skin pale, except for the purple marks on the cheek I could see. I assumed they were bruises from the fall, but when I recall them now they were not quite like bruises.' The priest's voice had slowed and he frowned at the implication of what he was saying. 'How often does one bruise an earlobe, even doing such a thing? But why should bruises be there if—'

Catchpoll held up his hand to halt him. His mind was working quickly. 'Yes, Father, there is a problem here. Did the eyelids close easily?'

Father Anselm sat for a moment, the realisation of the implications vying with dredging the details from his memory. He clasped his hands together as if seeking assistance from Higher Authority, and when he spoke the words were measured and precise.

'It is difficult. I mean they closed without force, but . . .'

he licked his lips and paused briefly – 'I am called to many deathbeds, Serjeant. It is part of my daily life. I am often the one to close the eyes, and there is no resistance. Thinking on it, there was a little, but not requiring force, if you understand.'

Catchpoll nodded. 'Now, can you recall where the body lay and how it lay . . . arms out or whatever?'

'She was in a sort of heap at the bottom of the ladder, as if she had been a bundle dropped by mischance, and lying face down, on her front I mean, with her head on one side . . .' He paused and closed his eyes in concentration. 'And one bare foot was visible, peeping out from under her skirts, but her arms were not flung out. There were clothes, washing, scattered about from a basket, so she must have stumbled as she was bringing it down. Oh dear, this is most unwelcome.'

'Face down? Was the cheek against the ground, the one bruised?'

'No. No, that is what was odd.' His face brightened. 'Ah, but of course, I imagine her husband, or Widow Fowler, had turned her face, in the vain hope of seeing she lived.' There was something in his voice that said he was trying to convince himself, but could not succeed.

'And were her feet nearer the ladder?' Catchpoll was thinking hard, and every thought pointed to one thing.

The priest nodded dumbly, and Catchpoll continued, speaking more to himself.

'If I was coming down a ladder, and it was more like a ladder than stairs, as you say, would I come down it with a basket of washing and facing outwards?' Catchpoll shook his head. 'I'd play safe, especially in skirts, and come down facing the ladder.

161

I am sorry, Father, but I think your parishioner did not die by accident.'

'The basket could have made her spin round as she fell?' Father Anselm's tone was almost one of pleading.

'Aye, it could just about, but all things considered, I think not.'

The priest crossed himself and mumbled a prayer. Catchpoll left him shaking his head over the wickedness around him, as he set to pray for other souls than just that of the late, and lamented by a fair number of men other than her spouse, Maud Brewer.

Chapter Twelve

In the chilly light of the September morning, the frontage of Simeon the Jew's house presented a sorry spectacle. The charred remains of the woodwork already lay in the street, with dark voids where they should be set. There was no sign of Master Simeon, but a man was clearly in charge. Bradecote accosted him and learnt that the Master was down at the quay, settling his family in a craft to take them downriver. He had left instructions that all trace of the contaminated wood was to be cleared away before his return, and carpenters were measuring the window for new shutters, whilst two more were in the process of replacing the door frame, complete with its little niche.

Bradecote squatted down by the remains of the door that lay to one side, summoning Walkelin to do likewise.

'Right, Walkelin. You have to use not just your eyes and

ears in this business, but your nose also. What can you smell on this?' He tapped the charred wood.

Walkelin shut his eyes and leant forward until his nose almost touched the wood. He presented a comical figure, and a watching child giggled. The flame-topped head was bent for some minutes, and then Walkelin straightened himself.

'The main smell is clearly of burnt wood, but that would not interest you, my lord. Above that, well I would say it was most like swine crackling, but there's something else as well. I recognise it, but it isn't food. I mean I don't link it to food.' His face was serious, and his puckering brow drew together the pale freckles upon it. He sighed in concentration. Bradecote understood what he meant, but could not put his finger on the smell's origin. Suddenly Walkelin broke into a wide grin.

'Of course, my lord. That's holy oil. It's nothing to do with food. It's a faint smell, but that is what it is. Have I said something wrong, my lord?' His superior's face had contorted as if in pain.

'No, Walkelin. But I should have guessed that straight away.' He paused. 'This is Simeon the Jew's house. Can you think of why pig fat, lard, would be the thing to start a fire with?'

'Can't say that I do, my lord. Sorry.'

'No, I did not think of it either until I was told, which makes me wonder how many folk would do so. It says so often enough in Scripture, but you do not immediately think . . .' Walkelin was looking lost. 'Jews avoid anything to do with swine. I suppose I knew they did not eat them, as unclean, but it goes far further.' He paused. 'Right then, in the absence of Serjeant Catchpoll you can come with me to St Andrew's Church.'

Walkelin looked puzzled. 'We resort to prayer, my lord?'

Bradecote gave a crack of mirthless laughter. 'It may yet come to that, Walkelin. But first we find out if the priest of St Andrew's can cast any light on who may have stolen his bottle of holy oil.'

Serjeant Catchpoll returned mid morning to report his findings to Hugh Bradecote, and reached the castle only a short time after the return of the undersheriff and Walkelin. One look indicated that he was in for a rough time with his superior. Catchpoll had never actually seen Bradecote lose his temper beyond being tetchy, and he looked a man who lost it rarely but fully.

'Kind of you to join us, Serjeant.' The undersheriff's voice dripped sarcasm, and he added, without turning, 'Get out, Walkelin.'

Walkelin did as he was bid, torn between regret at missing seeing Serjeant Catchpoll berated, and relief at not being drawn into a messy argument.

Bradecote's expression was thunderous and he ground his teeth. 'When we spoke last night, I gave you leave to chase off after the possible killing of Maud Brewer on the understanding that there were no more fires started and demanding our attention. Yet I rise, having attended just such a fire during the night, to find that you have gone hunting the priest of All Saints, despite being told of the fire . . . a fire that has no feasible link to Maud Brewer, anyway. I can't decide whether you are deaf, insubordinate or just so puffed up in your own cleverness that nobody else's words mean anything to you. You may be the sheriff's man, but by heaven I'll see you shovelling the midden if you disobey me deliberately again.' His voice had risen so as to be heard by an interested gathering outside.

Catchpoll looked stolidly at the younger man, with what could as easily be insolence as an attempt to be emollient.

'No lives were lost, nor did it sound as though the delay of a couple of hours would alter what could be discovered. I made a judgement, my lord, simple as that. Finding out about the death of Maud Brewer could clear our path; take one strand from the tangle. I reckon as you don't need me to be at your side for every interview, or raking over cool ashes. You've worked alone often enough over the last days.'

'No, I don't need you to hold my hand and guide my steps like an infant, Catchpoll, but sometimes more can be gained than would be expected. You could not know what would turn up at Cokenstrete.'

'At my guess, signs, if you're lucky, that the fire was started with holy oil, probably on cloth or suchlike. We said it would make it easier to start a fire from the outside, and that is presumably what happened.'

Bradecote wanted to shake Catchpoll until his discoloured teeth rattled, and the fact that his assumption had been correct placated him not at all.

'You are a disobedient, insubordinate bastard, Catchpoll. You may have all the experience in the world, but if you work against me and not with me, then you are no more use than a holed bucket. One more trick like that and I will have the sheriff dismiss you, however much you think he values you.' He was clearly not in any way appeased.

'Understood, my lord.' By not so much as a flicker did

Catchpoll indicate how he took this reprimand, or whether he thought the sheriff would be prepared to dismiss him on the say-so of a novice undersheriff.

'Call Walkelin back in.' Bradecote turned away and took a deep breath, composing himself to think calmly.

Those listening from without made instant efforts to appear otherwise engaged as Serjeant Catchpoll opened the door, but Walkelin stood wooden-faced within a few paces. Antagonising the sheriff's serjeant was not a wise move, and he had no intention of doing so, especially having to work so closely with him. Catchpoll called him back with a jerk of the head, and he returned with a look of perfect innocence upon his face.

'Walkelin and I visited Cokenstrete. As you guessed, there were indications that holy oil had been used to start the blaze, but there was more than that. An oaken door does not catch easily, nor heavy shutters, but these were heavily damaged on the outside surface. From the smell, it seems they were smeared with lard.'

'Clever. That would not run down swiftly, like oil, even if it was perhaps a little slower to catch. You still need a good deal of heat to light it, of course, but it would work.' Catchpoll nodded to himself.

'But there is more to it even than that, Catchpoll. Swine are considered foul and unclean by Jews. Master Simeon is having the door, window and framing entirely replaced because of the contamination. He said he would not even cross that threshold until all was removed. I had no knowledge of this, but then I am from the country and never met or lived near a Jew. Walkelin says he was ignorant of it, but what about you?'

'Well, you hear odd things, of course, but what is true and what is fanciful gossip isn't always easy to decide. I know there are odd things about what they eat, but beyond not pig-meat, I couldn't say what.'

'So you would be surprised if many of Worcester's inhabitants knew?'

'Yes, my lord. Though mayhap some as have had dealings with him, borrowing, would have heard or seen more about him.'

'Fair enough. Well, after seeing the site of the fire we went to see Father Boniface. What did you think of him, Walkelin?'

The young man wrinkled his nose. 'Not a man I'd want to confess to afore my dying breath, for certain. He's a priest who believes in right and wrong, we, the ordinary folk, being the "all wrong". Makes you wonder whether priests like that ever had mothers, or perhaps were just found in cloisters, ready grown and tonsured.'

'Strange imagination you've got, lad. Best keep it shackled,' declared Catchpoll, shaking his head.

'It may be useful yet, so don't shut it down entirely,' added Bradecote. 'Anyway, we were keen to know if he had any ideas about the identity of his thief.'

'Don't suppose he helped much, other than saying they will be damned for it.' Catchpoll shrugged.

'Not directly, Serjeant, but he did say what he did the day of the theft.' Walkelin allowed an edge of excitement to enter his voice.

'Go on, then. Tell me.'

'He said he had last used it during the morning, when giving extreme unction to an elderly parishioner. He returned to the church and in the afternoon received visits from several of his parishioners, most of whom we can ignore.'

'On what grounds?' Catchpoll wanted Walkelin to be thorough.

Walkelin ticked them off on his fingers. 'Two were old dames who wanted prayers said for dead kin, one was Thorold the Wheelwright, come to arrange the churching of his wife after her delivery of twins . . . and his old mother used to live hard by where my mother and I live, so I know him and would vouch for him . . . there was blind Tosti come for alms and then,' he paused for effect, 'one Serlo, servant to Master Mercet.'

Catchpoll suddenly looked more interested. 'Did he really? Never saw him as religious. Shows how wrong you can be.' He did not look as if he felt at all wrong about Serlo. 'Came for a long confession, did he?'

'No,' answered Walkelin, unaware of the irony. 'It seems Master Mercet wishes to be a benefactor of the church and wanted to know if any particular item of silver is called for that he could commission.'

'Wonders will never cease. Item of silver, eh? Wonder if Master Mercet is intending to purchase at a fair price, or just lean on a silversmith, really hard. Was our friend Serlo left alone for any period of time?'

'Father Boniface says he cannot recall, because it was a busy afternoon. I asked about the locked box the oil would be kept in, and Father Boniface showed where it had been forced, though a repair had been made.'

Hugh Bradecote had let Walkelin make the report until this

point. 'It proves nothing because we only have understanding, not fact, but Mercet would gladly be rid of Simeon as a rival. We must reconsider Mercet as a suspect, although he clearly did not do the deed himself.'

'If he sent Serlo, who is dark and a mite taller than me, then he would disclaim any knowledge if we got Serlo to confess, and I'm none too sure he couldn't raise oath-swearers to vouch for his probity, with some strong-arm tactics.' Catchpoll was not hopeful.

'There is something else.' Bradecote did not want to focus solely on Mercet. 'Father Boniface knew all about the Jewish loathing of pigs, and said he had preached about swine possessed of spirits only a week or so ago and explained it then, so his congregation would have heard about it in the last few weeks. It increases the likelihood of it being one of his parishioners.'

'And that would exclude Edgar Brewer, unless he happened to hear it elsewhere. Pity.' Catchpoll spoke regretfully.

'So we are saying our fire-setter is not also a wife-killer then?' Walkelin looked equally disappointed.

'Not necessarily, but it seems unlikely. It would be nice and tidy, though.' Catchpoll pulled a face.

Bradecote mirrored the expression. 'Sorry we cannot arrange things to suit your idea of neatness. Anyway, the result is that we are deep into hunting the fire-setter, and I do not see that trying to follow up a murder that happened, if at all, some months back, with the corpse rotting quietly in the graveyard and the only evidence that of memory, will get us anywhere. The real evidence is long gone. So there is no point—'

Catchpoll held up a hand to halt him.

'First off, my lord, it was murder. I'm certain of it. For it to be accidental, Maud Brewer would have to have come down that ladder stair with a basket of washing in her arms and yet facing outwards.' He shook his head. 'No woman would do that, my lord. Then she has to have landed all of a heap, with her neck broke and lying on her front, not even her arms out as you would by nature, if falling. How does she do that, I ask you? Then there is the evidence of the death. I doubt not you've seen enough dead folk, my lord, but not dead some time, and I can tell you they change in several ways. Of course they stiffen after a while, and everyone knows that, though the stiffness wears off after a few days. But the thing is that the stiffness comes over them bit by bit, not everywhere all of a sudden. From what I have seen, it is often hands and feet, and a tightness of the face. Father Anselm noticed that her eyes did not close as easily as most. I would guess that was the start of stiffening, which would mean she had not been alive and well only a quarter-hour earlier. Also he spoke of marks on the upturned cheek.'

'Bruises, you mean?' The undersheriff was not finding this easy to follow, and Walkelin's mouth hung open as if he were watching a feat of magic.

'Not as such. If they were, you would have to ask how she got them in the fall if that cheek did not hit the ground. But you see, I have seen purple marks on bodies, and they are on the parts nearest the ground. A man found hanging will have 'em on his feet and lower legs, and his hands; even the nails darken; a body on its back will have them on the shoulders and in the back, except what presses hardest to the ground. I asked a physician about it once, and he said it was the blood and other humours settling back to the earth from which we are sprung, which sounds sense to me. Whatever causes it, it happens after death and in the first hours. That means Maud Brewer lay most like with that darkened cheek to the floor, not the way she was found, and was dead some hours before she "fell", or rather before her corpse was pushed down the ladder. She was described by Father Anselm as lying in a bundled heap. No living woman, or in her senses at least, would land like that off a ladder-stair. Oh yes, and he said she was barefoot. Would you not wonder why she was barefoot? The brewer is not a poor man, and even if she was going to do washing and did not want them wet, she would not take off her shoes until everything was ready.'

'And the small matter of the men all hearing her working upstairs and humming?' Bradecote wanted to be really sure if he was going to let this intrude on the hunt for the fire-raiser.

'The men heard a woman upstairs humming, not singing as she usually did, and humming, from what I have heard over the years, does not carry as well as singing. I would say the shutters of the upper chamber were open enough just so that humming would be heard, and it was. They heard a woman, but it was not Maud Brewer, who was already lying dead with her neck broken by her cuckolded husband, who had decided that a loyal wife, however plain, was better than a comely one who would lie with half the men in Worcester, and probably burnt his pottage. I have no doubt our humming dame was the Widow Fowler. She wouldn't sound the same singing, but humming is humming. When everyone is there in the brewhouse, working under Edgar Brewer's direction so he could have nothing to do with the "accident", she pushes the corpse down the ladder, because she don't like having the corpse staring at her close up, which is why it ends up feet nearer the ladder and on its front. She tosses down the basket and some clothing to make it look like dropped washing, and hangs back until it is clear nobody is going to investigate the noise of the fall. She then comes down, steps over the body and goes to the front door. She knocks, from the inside mind, calling out nice and loud, and then screams fit to bust to get everyone in to see the accident. Quite clever, and with a fair amount of planning by one or both of them.'

Walkelin stood stupefied by this feat of detection. Bradecote was convinced, and secretly also very impressed. Catchpoll had a wealth of experience and clearly used it well. 'But how do you prove that with all evidence neatly cleared away and buried?'

'My lord, we could not convict just with evidence anyways. It says so in law. I can't give you the Latin of it, but it is something like "you cannot convict anybody on serious charges from evidence only". What is needed is confession, and even two months late, that, and the witness evidence, is valid. You leave it to me, my lord, and I will see a way round this, and without halting our fire-raiser hunt. It might even be easier if they think, like you, that nothing can be proved agin them, and we are busy elsewhere. Leads to mistakes, that does. "Pride cometh before a fall" I think it says in the Bible, and this fall is like to be one into eternal darkness with a gallows rope about their neck.'

Biblical utterances were also issuing forth from the glowering visage of Father Boniface. The townsfolk were now very worried

173

by the fires in their midst, and turned, instinctively, to the Church for solace. At All Saints that is what they got from Father Anselm, but at St Andrew's the priest was berating them for their sinfulness that had brought down God's fiery wrath upon them. He had read out Holy Scripture about the chaff being cast into the flames, with relish, and was making sure every soul before him knew the peril in which they stood.

'You who are conceived in sin, born in sin, and wallow in it as swine wallow in their own filth, how can you hope to gain the mercy of the Almighty. The judgement of the Lord is upon you, and you do not repent. Such fire as you see here is but a candle's light in comparison with what you face in Damnation, yet do you change your evil ways? No, even in the presence of His will, you do not alter your sinful lives; you deceive and cheat your neighbours; you lie in disgusting lust and adultery and fornication, taking pleasure,' here his voice added incredulity to anger, 'in the foul and corrupting act; you bear false witness; you break every one of the Commandments. Worcester is become as Sodom and Gomorrah, so it is small wonder the flames of vengeance are come to raze it.' Father Boniface's voice shook, and his eyes smouldered as fierce as any furnace coal. 'Salvation is for them that fear Him, and therefore I tell you to be fearful, fearful for your very souls' sake, before God. Repent, and cast out the evil from your hearts. Prostrate yourselves before Him and plead for your souls before you are cast into the fires of eternal hell as chaff by His angels, and burn in agonies that cannot be eased, for all time to come.'

The congregation, almost in unison, lay down in penitence upon the stone floor, their faces as pale as its cold surface, and prayed for deliverance from this fate, and also, in some cases, from the terror that was Father Boniface himself. When they emerged from the church, many raised their eyes to the heavens, as if the angels of their destruction might be peering at them from behind the wisps of cloud, and the fires of God might descend upon them at any moment. Within, Father Boniface composed himself and then prostrated his own long-legged form before the altar and closed his eyes, repeating the paternoster, 'Our Father, which art in Heaven, thy will be done, in earth as it is in Heaven . . .' until the blood ceased pounding in his head, and his heart resumed its normal beat. Nobody could ever say that the priest of St Andrew's took his duties lightly.

Chapter Thirteen

The three sheriff's men spent the end of the forenoon trying to work out what possible reason could have led Robert Mercet to have organised a fire at the silversmith's workshop. None of them could come up with any answer beyond it being a decoy, and it left a worrying sense of doubt in the undersheriff's mind, however much he sought to dispel it. He still felt that Mercet's original denial of having set the first two fires rang true, however much he was 'an evil bastard' and top of Catchpoll's pet hates. It was agreed that a watch should be set on Simeon's warehouse, which seemed the next likely target if Mercet really wanted him out of business, since another attempt on the house itself would be too risky, so soon after the first one.

It was then that a question entered Walkelin's head, the answer to which, it seemed to him, might solve the problem of linking Mercet to the silversmith's fire. He made his suggestion to Serjeant Catchpoll and the undersheriff with becoming diffidence, but clearly keen to undertake the following of this strand of investigation.

'So you are going to give us the answer to our problems, Walkelin?' Catchpoll schooled his features into solemnity as he noted the eagerness in Walkelin's eyes. Once upon a time, he too must have looked that keen. He remembered the sheriff's serjeant under whom he had learnt the craft, and the key rules: to observe, not just 'see'; to listen, not just 'hear'; and, most important of all, to 'out-bastard the bastards you have to catch'. It was this last that he thought might be hardest for his apprentice. Walkelin was inherently friendly, not your natural at being mean and unpleasant. He would simply have to learn the art.

'I can't promise anything, Serjeant, but for the sake of an hour it might do just that. It only means talking to a few folk to see if the link exists.'

'And you do not wish to reveal your idea lest it prove to be the chasing of a shadow.' Bradecote nodded his assent. 'Fair enough. Off you go, and report back as soon as you have your answers.'

Dismissed, Walkelin hastened off to Reginald Ash's workshop, and there cornered Edwin the journeyman to get directions to the home of Widow Wick and her daughter. It lay close enough, down by the river, and clinging to the edge of the parish of St Andrew's.

Following Edwin's directions, Walkelin soon found himself standing in front of a row of rather dilapidated dwellings that indicated their occupants were not among the wealthy of Worcester, and could not afford to live further up the hill and away from possible flooding. He had intended to knock at neighbouring doors with a tale of being a country lad seeking a distant relative by the name of Wick, and delving into her connections from there. In truth, when he came to it, he was unsure whether this ploy might work, and he felt alarmingly self-conscious. What if some kindly soul chose to lead him to the door and stand there as the woman denounced him as no kin of hers? As it happened, he was spared the necessity of a ruse, and was more fortunate than he could possibly have anticipated.

The man who entered the cottage with the most perfunctory of knocks looked familiar, but Walkelin wanted not just his own identification. A question to a woman selling bunches of dried herbs confirmed the name, and more beside. The herb seller was taken aback with the force of his heartfelt thanks, and wondered why such mundane information should set so broad a grin upon his face. She watched him as he headed off with long strides, and shook her head. The poor young man was clearly addled. Red hair, she said to herself, was a sure sign of instability.

Walkelin almost ran back to the castle, and was disappointed to discover that his superiors were not to be found. He was left kicking his heels for an hour of increasing exasperation.

In fact, Bradecote and Catchpoll had only gone the short step as far as the priory, whence they had accompanied the newly returned Martin Woodman.

The carpenter was obviously shaken by the discovery of the disaster that had befallen his home and business during his absence in Feckenham, but he was a straightforward, practical man, as befitted his trade. When his wife's sobbed tale had been concluded, he headed to the castle to get the full account without tears. The help that he could give the sheriff's men was limited. He had rented his home and premises from Robert Mercet for the last six years, and would have chosen almost any other man in Worcester as his landlord, had he the choice.

'Needs must though, my lord, and the premises were just what I needed. The lease was set and paid for each Quarter Day, but it included my making all repairs, and his man Turgis was forever turning up and snooping around, hunting for winter storm damage, summer shrinkage or general wear and tear. Turgis the Ferret I calls him, though not to his face.'

Bradecote decided that Mistress Woodman had not told her husband about her encounter with Turgis after the fire. All in all, perhaps that was for the best. A carpenter had sharp tools, and he did not want to have to arrest the man for the perfectly reasonable act of removing Turgis's 'tool' with an adze.

'Did you not challenge the amount of repairs?'

'No, my lord,' Master Woodman smiled crookedly at the undersheriff's naïvety, 'since it was made clear to me that unspecified damage might occur to me and mine if I did not do as requested.'

Bradecote frowned, but Catchpoll was unsurprised.

'But he never threatened to burn you out?' Serjeant Catchpoll needed simple fact.

'No indeed, Serjeant Catchpoll. That he did not, for if he

had I would have gone to the other carpenters and as a body we would have come to the lord sheriff. Fire would be too great a threat to all and would not be tolerated. Even a bully like Mercet would not voice such a threat, whatever he might say about a man's flesh and bone.'

Martin Woodman's serious, honest face was greater in its appeal for justice than any pleading or hand wringing. At no point had he bemoaned the failings of the sheriff's men in finding the perpetrator of the crime. When he made to leave, he said that he was off to the cathedral priory, hinting gently that any support from 'Authority' would be welcomed. Bradecote and Catchpoll both offered to accompany him to lend official voices, should they be required in negotiations with Father Prior. This he accepted gratefully. Not that such support proved necessary, for the prior was quick to call for the details of any leases that might be available and of sufficient size for the carpenter's business. He was a man both godly in his charity and practical in his desire to see a craftsman whose work benefited his priory given premises in which to fulfil his commissions.

The undersheriff and serjeant came away, leaving churchman and artisan finalising details of a fair and amicable agreement. They had a sense that some good had been achieved, even without their good offices, and in this lightened mood they met with Walkelin, by this time barely able to control his desire to impart his news.

'You look like the mouse that's been given the run of the storeroom, lad. Best tell us before you burst from keeping silent.' Catchpoll grinned.

'I haven't solid proof, my lord,' Walkelin began in a rush,

looking from Bradecote to Catchpoll and back again, 'but I do have the connection we was looking for between Mercet and Master Ash's smithy, like I said before. Not that it gives us a reason why he would want to burn it down but—'

The words, so long held back, came out in a flow like a breached dam, and Catchpoll raised a hand to stem them. 'Whoa! If you gabble, we'll need the tale twice over. Take your time, and don't wander off into blind alleys.'

'Sorry, Serjeant.' Walkelin cleared his throat and began again. 'You see, what was getting me was that whoever set the fire in the silversmith's had to know how the premises were set out at the rear. You said Mercet had never owned the place, so he could not know by that way. I wondered if the cooking girl, dim Agnes, or leastways her mother, might have a connection. I thought perhaps their place might be rented from Mercet. Then it would be easy to get the woman to tell all, with a bit of careful questioning, that is . . . you know how women go on at the slightest chance. Well, it so happens that Mercet is indeed their landlord, but it gets even better . . .' Here Walkelin could not resist pausing for effect, although Catchpoll merely rolled his eyes in exasperation.

'Get on with it.'

'It turns out that the Widow Wick is sister to Serlo, Mercet's man. I saw him visit, and recognised the face, but wanted to be certain, so asked a neighbour who confirmed his identity and gave me all the details. He visits regular like, on account of having no nearer kin and enjoying a free meal at his sister's. No problem, then, for Mercet to know just how to set the fire, and if it was in the day, little chance of it spreading too far. If he wanted a fire he could have no obvious link with, to lead us off the scent, then this was it.'

Catchpoll rubbed the end of his nose meditatively, but was only partially successful in concealing the reptilian smile that was spreading across his face.

Walkelin looked from serjeant to undersheriff, clearly in hope of praise. Bradecote relented. It was certainly a good piece of work, and Walkelin deserved his moment of glory.

'That's certainly very useful. Well done, both for the discovery and for getting down to the nub of the problem. Now, what do you suggest we do next?'

Walkelin's blush of pleasure that set cheek at odds with flaming hair, turned to an expression of jaw-dropping horror as he realised the next move was being offered to him, a lowly man-at-arms. He blinked several times, swallowed hard so that his Adam's apple bobbed up and down, and stammered his response.

'Well, I suppose we could . . . but that wouldn't work would it, my lord? No. Then I simply suggest, humbly mind, that we visit Master Mercet and see him squirm.'

'Nice idea, boy,' grumbled Catchpoll, 'but it would take a lot more than what we have to make Robert Mercet even turn one of those fair hairs of his. If we shows him all we know he will laugh in our faces. He will simply disown Serlo and have three times the required number of oath-swearers queueing up within the hour to attest to him being as innocent as a newborn babe. Far better to take up Serlo on his own and see what we can get from him without his master on hand. He may just be persuaded to squeal like a stuck pig and implicate Mercet, but even then we are left in almost the same stew. Whatever we confront the miserable bastard with, Mercet will wriggle free. We need to have such evidence as will make any oath-swearer, however great the pressure upon him, know he is perjuring his eternal soul with a blatant lie. If we bring in Serlo and leave hints of deeper knowledge with Mercet, then perhaps, just perhaps, if we are very fortunate, he may make a stumble.'

Walkelin's cheer subsided. What had seemed a conclusive link that would bring about the arrest of the guilty party, now seemed as flimsy as a house of straw. His disappointment showed in droop of shoulder and heavy sigh.

'Don't be too disheartened, Walkelin.' Bradecote tried to sound positive. 'If Serlo was Mercet's instrument and we have solid evidence against him, he at least will face justice for the old woman and the fires, and Mercet would be rash beyond imaginings to send out another of his men to continue the work, assuming that any more fires are intended. Of course, it might well be that his aim was simply to rid Worcester of Simeon the Jew. That has failed, and his victim is going to be both on his guard and under our watchful eye.'

'Ah, now there's another problem, my lord.' This time it was Catchpoll who looked glum. 'What's been gnawing at me like a rat in a rope-house, is why the fire at the Jew's house was set as it was. True, if they had not been prepared by your warning, there might have been great damage and loss of life, but there was no attempt to block the rear exit, and that would have been the true killer's way. This was almost haphazard, almost "*Deus vult*" – as God wills. Destroying his warehouse, now that would have cut deep, or better still do both at the same time. It's the odd thing that niggles me, see. The fire-raiser seems to set a fire and not make sure of the effect. I admit I've never hunted one before, but I thought they liked to see the results of their "work", and make it as spectacular as possible, not set it and walk away, disinterested like.'

Bradecote was frowning, and rubbed his hand to and fro across his chin, as if he had a dull toothache. 'But that is changing the culprit from a hired man into one who does it for himself, Catchpoll, and we are suggesting, out of desperation, it was Mercet at the back of it. Besides, we believe that the first fire was to set us off in the wrong direction and draw suspicion from Mercet, and that the second was another, since the first was still accounted a possible accident, but with the added bonus of Woodman's place to rebuild and lease anew. Neither required a death, even though the second caused one. It is thus only this last fire that falls into the category of one not followed through. And perhaps the fire-setter was disturbed in some way, or even got oil and grease on themselves and was too scared to attend to the back or the warehouse.'

Catchpoll nodded reluctantly. 'You've a fair point, my lord, but there's something in this somewhere that just doesn't sit right, and I for one will not be content till I find out what.'

'Serjeant's instinct, eh?'

'Easy to mock, my lord, but it's an instinct that's served me well over the years.'

Bradecote sighed. 'Until that instinct has a revelation then, let us do something practical. We'll take the first opportunity that arises to take up Serlo, as long as he is out of Mercet's tender care. We want him alone and feeling vulnerable.'

'Then best try an alehouse, my lord, and since young Walkelin here is proving so clever, we will send him.' If the lord Bradecote entered an alehouse everyone present would be staring open-mouthed at him all evening, and Catchpoll would have every man wondering why he was there. Also, he had no wish to return after a possibly fruitless evening, smelling of ale, and to a sharp-tongued spouse. Walkelin was not known as other than one of the castle guard amongst the townsfolk, so he would blend in, even with his red hair. What Walkelin's mother might say about his evening's work did not worry the serjeant in the least.

'Sit there all evening, Serjeant?' Walkelin wondered how slowly he could drink.

'If needs be.' He gave a wry smile. 'Not all galloping around being heroic, our job. As much time is spent waiting and watching, and getting sore feet and chilled to the bone. Best you get used to it early on, young Walkelin. Now, off home and eat, since an empty stomach leads to a thick head.'

Walkelin returned to his mother with his brain awhirl with hopes, ideas and a sense of amazement that he, Walkelin, son of Hubert, had become one of the select number of sheriff's men looking to the law in the shire. He hoped his mother would be impressed by her son's elevation, but found that telling her he had orders to spend the evening in an alehouse brought down choice words upon his head, and those of his superiors, that were not approbation. However, he asserted his male authority, which was difficult in the face of his mother, and as the afternoon became evening, headed for the nearest tavern to Robert Mercet's house. He bought himself a beaker of ale, and then sat doing a fair impression of a young man with things upon his mind, and not there for a laugh and lewd tales.

His eyes and ears were on the alert for Serlo, but his brain was racing with thoughts. He was on approval, and doing quite well, but if he could bring the murderer of Maud Brewer to trial, he would bask in the approbation of the undersheriff and, somehow more importantly, Serjeant Catchpoll. That murder, he felt, was 'his'. After all, it had been his work which had made the discoveries that set Serjeant Catchpoll to confirm it as murder, and the lord Bradecote and Serjeant Catchpoll were primarily involved in the hunt for the fire-raiser. He permitted himself to daydream of being lauded for his craftiness, boldness and outstanding abilities, and was only brought back to reality by the tavern keeper asking sourly if he was going to drink his ale or watch it dry up over several days. It was another beaker later that Serlo ambled in, greeting several of the drinkers in a friendly way. It occurred to Walkelin that getting Serlo out of the tavern might be opposed by his 'friends', so he was forced to wait, stifling the occasional yawn, until his quarry lurched gently out of the door, rather late. Walkelin took the man by the arm, but turned a friendly gesture into one of control.

It was very late when he got to his bed, but was more fortunate than his superiors.

Chapter Fourteen

The bakehouse to the rear of Widow Bakere's small dwelling along Frog Lane was nearly always still warm and sweet-smelling at night. A tomcat, who had won the right through many skirmishes, would often doze upon the roof in between hunting the mice that scuttled about the yard. At dawn, the widow, or now, on occasions, Drogo the Cook, would make up a fresh fire in the oven, so that when it reached the appropriate temperature as judged by the flames, the fire and ash could be raked out and the morning's loaves inserted and blocked up inside to bake in the residual heat, while Widow Bakere turned the more quickly cooking oatcakes and honeycakes on a heated hearthstone. Those who baked their own bread did so in the communal ovens owned by de Beauchamp, but there were those, like Reginald Ash, in womanless households, and those also who came into Worcester and purchased sustenance rather than brought it with them.

Nesta Bakere baked for such, oatcakes and honeycakes more than loaves, and if it was not a messuage of size, it did at least bring in good profit.

Tonight, however, the fire had been relit well before midnight, and not to bake bread. The only smell was acrid and throat-catching. Kindling had been scattered over the bakehouse floor, in the small yard, and piled against the back door of the little house. The striker of flint and steel had set spark to the kindling and then clambered over the side wall of the property and into the alley. This alleyway divided the bakery, as much for safety's sake as for a thoroughfare, from its neighbours. For a few minutes the flames grew in near silence, surreptitiously licking up the walls and timber framing, savouring their prey like silent assassins. The bakehouse was tiled, but the dwelling was thatched, and this eventually caught from the underside, charring at first and then growing red as the fingers of flame tugged and took hold of it.

It was a castle guard who caught the smell of burning drifting towards him on the night breeze. He had been half asleep even as he made his tour of the bailey walkway, but sprang to wakefulness at the sight of the red glow spreading near the eastern side of the castle.

Serjeant Catchpoll was woken from heavy slumber by the insistent hammering at his door. A hammering in the night always boded ill news. The man on his doorstep did not say anything, for the scene behind him told all that was needed. The castle guard had turned out to a man. Those not armed with hooks and rakes were formed in bucket lines and casting water at the building, from which smoke billowed at the front, while flames from the rear framed it in silhouette, black against infernal red. He scrambled into clothes.

Catchpoll saw Hugh Bradecote already directing the soldiery, and had almost got within speaking distance when a figure darted forward from the throng. Drogo the Cook, one shoe on and half dressed, was shouting incoherently at the top of his voice. Suddenly, before anyone could stop him, he charged the front door with his shoulder. The first time it merely shuddered, but on the second blow the latch inside gave way, and he almost fell into the open doorway. As he entered, a gush of smoke eddied past him. Before anyone could do more than cry out, he had disappeared within. Catchpoll half moved towards the door, but was restrained by the hand of the undersheriff gripping his shoulder.

'If the smoke takes him,' yelled Bradecote, 'it'll take any that follow. No use, Catchpoll, I'm sorry.'

That Drogo would not return was a reasonable assumption, but within a few moments a cry went up as a soldier saw movement and dashed forward. A dim shape was visible low in the doorway, and the soldier hauled at it. The cook's bulk almost rolled out into the street, and within the clasp of his right arm was the limp form of the baker's widow. Serjeant and undersheriff pushed their way to where the soldier, coughing and spluttering, was bending over the two figures.

Catchpoll clapped the man-at-arms on the shoulder in commendation as much as assistance, but his eyes were on the bodies. He rolled Drogo onto his back, fully expecting his friend to be dead, but in the unnatural orange light some slight movement of his chest showed that Drogo was harder to kill than expected. Catchpoll snatched a pail from one of the fire fighters and dashed it over the singed and blackened cook.

'Here, give me a hand to sit him up,' cried Catchpoll, heaving him under one armpit. The soldier did so, and Catchpoll commenced thumping his friend so hard upon the back that his fist ached. After some moments, Drogo caught a deep, jagged breath, coughed and retched. His eyes remained shut, but he was clearly conscious.

'Come on, Drogo, you old bastard, keep breathing. Not dead yet.' Catchpoll's tattoo upon his friend's back did not abate until the man's eyes opened, reddened with the smoke.

'Nesta?'

Catchpoll said nothing, but looked to where Bradecote knelt beside the slight form of Widow Bakere. Even in the dim firelight she presented a horrible sight. Her face was blackened, her clothes smouldered, and the right arm that Bradecote was laying across her body was clearly badly burnt, the skin sloughing away, leaving a patchwork of black and red. Bradecote, perhaps sensing he was being watched, looked up.

'My lord, is she . . . ?'

Bradecote's face was solemn. 'Not quite. She breathes, but badly, and the burns, well, I'm no physician but . . .' He shook his head doubtfully.

Catchpoll squeezed Drogo's shoulder. 'She's with us still, friend, at least at present. Now let's get you to a cot and fetch a physician.'

'You'd be best calling the infirmarer from the priory,' suggested a voice close at hand. 'They say Brother Hubert did wonders for them that was burnt in the Great Burning.'

Bradecote sent a man to the priory with the urgent request. He had another man fetch a cart in which to carry the victims into the castle. Drogo was placed in his own bed, and room found for the widow in the serving maids' chamber. Once the injured were removed, the fire was kept in check to prevent its spread, but beyond saving the front wall of the cottage, there was little to salvage, and the fire largely burnt itself out.

As the first pale streaks of morning smeared greasily along the eastern horizon, the sheriff's men were alone among the smoking ruins, prodding and poking in the pathetic remnants of the bakery.

'Could have been an accident, of course,' mumbled Catchpoll without any conviction. 'The ovens never really get cold, or mayhap a thread of breeze caught some glowing embers from the last rake-out.'

Bradecote yawned, and inadvertently trailed a charcoal smudge across his brow with a grimy finger. 'I wish I could believe that, but I don't, and nor do you. If it was an accident, how did a woman who has been in the trade so long make so dangerous a mistake, and even if she did, why is there a very definite heap of ash in the yard. That could not have got there by accident, even if you say the bakehouse caught and then spread the flames to the house, and the breeze is light.'

'I'm not saying anything, just trying to find some way this is not tied up with the others. Jesu, this is a right tangle, and my head's got to the spinning stage.'

'Best we turn in for an hour or so, then meet up. Did Walkelin bring in Serlo?'

'He had not when I left. If he did so just after, then Serlo cannot be our man.'

'Indeed, Catchpoll. I'll see you when we've taken some rest, and maybe we'll know then if we've also got more murders to solve. I wouldn't give much for the woman's chances.' Bradecote shook his head, and turned back to the castle. He stopped after a few paces and turned. 'By the by, it does at least prove that your friend the cook can have nothing to do with the fires, doesn't it.'

'Aye, but small consolation that is now, to me, or to him,' sighed Catchpoll.

Three hours later, still jaded and hung about with the smell of stale smoke, Bradecote and Catchpoll stood at the end of a narrow cot. It had been hastily vacated by a sleepy kitchen maid, and was now the resting place of Widow Bakere. The elderly Benedictine brother, who had been attending her since summoned from the Priory of St Mary long before the bell for Prime, had a face of compassion blended with grim determination. Life, he would instantly aver, was in the hands of God, but his clear duty was to keep those who could be kept alive living, and to give physical comfort and some spiritual ease to the end of those who were called to death. At this moment, he was uncertain which he was attending.

The woman lay as still as if laid out for shrouding, but for the hesitant breathing and the single arm laid across her breast where two would be crossed after death. Her face was pale, with a faint tinge of blue to the lips that brought a tightness to Hugh Bradecote's chest. Ela had looked like that, but more so. Perhaps this woman would not die, would not slip almost imperceptibly from the grip of life, but it would be in the balance for some time yet.

'I take it she has not woken, Brother?'

'No, my lord, and best it is so in some ways. I have been able to dress the burns, but I am not sure she would be strong enough to take a draught for the pain as yet, were she awake. Sleep is a gift from God that can bring us quietly to the gates of the hereafter, and let us take the step within without pain, but as easily draw us back without knowledge and fear. We must wait to find out which in this case.'

'And her chances, Brother?' Catchpoll spoke in a hushed whisper, as if normal speech alone might rouse her to pain.

'My friend, I do not wager, but I can say she will be fortunate to recover, and think herself most unfortunate in the process. The burns are very bad to the arm, and to a degree on one side of her neck. I have dressed them with my own paste of sweet briar and cleavers, which I would replace with honey at a later stage, to keep suppuration at bay, but such wounds turn bad very easily and take long to heal. If she lives, the disfigurement will distress her, being a woman and prone to the vanities of Eve, but it will be the contraction and loss of movement that will be most disabling. The arm will not be easy to turn and twist, and turning her head will forever be difficult. Moreover, there are internal problems from breathing the foul smoke and not God's good fresh air. I cannot get more air into her to flush out the smoke, and it chokes the lungs as soot coats the eaves. Also the heat sears the throat and makes it swell, which is another reason her breath is laboured. For this I have no cure but time. In three or four days, if she has not succumbed, I would then say she would be more like to live than die, but until then we can only pray.'

'And the other patient?' Catchpoll had avoided seeing Drogo until he knew how Nesta Bakere did.

Brother Hubert gave a wry smile. 'Ah, he is strong in body, loud of voice and sinful of tongue. He has burns, but they are not so deep, and if they stay clean he will recover well enough. The sole of one foot is burnt so that he will hobble for a week or so. He will complain, as men do, more than women when ailing, but afterwards it will be forgotten, just as women do not forget. You may see him, but do not tire him overmuch. Peace aids recovery.'

They found Drogo in his own chamber. He was propped up in bed, coughing and cursing, and looking much the worse for wear but very much alive. If peace aided recovery, murmured Catchpoll to his superior, then Drogo's would take longer than the monk envisaged. At their approach he grew silent, watching them very carefully, as if he could tell by their demeanour whether they were the bringers of bad tidings.

'Rest easy, Drogo, my friend. The Widow Bakere may be small but she is clearly strong, for she breathes still.' Catchpoll permitted himself a small smile.

Bradecote noted the relief crossing the injured man's face.

'She's not out of danger, mind. The good Brother Hubert says it will be three or four days yet before we know, but so far the news is fair. So you can say your prayers and turn your mind to getting your smoke-addled brain to come up with something helpful for us.' Catchpoll did not appear sympathetic, but Drogo knew him well enough to see behind the facade.

'Ever the truth-hound, you single-minded old reprobate,' he wheezed. 'Well, if you find out who did this, then you'd better find out before I am back on my feet, because I swear to God, Catchpoll, if I get him he'll die a slow and painful death.'

'Unshriven but well seasoned?' Catchpoll tried to be frivolous, but Drogo did not smile.

'Yes.' The single word had a depth of meaning.

Bradecote felt vaguely sick. Violence was one thing, but this sounded ghoulish. He had no wish to dwell on Drogo's murderous plans.

'Do you know if Widow Bakere's place is leased from Robert Mercet?'

'Aye, that it is, but I know she paid the last quarter on time and the next is not due till Michaelmas in a fortnight. She's always been a good tenant, as was her husband before her, God rest him.'

The sheriff's pair were relieved to hear the Mercet connection had survived, even if it was seemingly growing tenuous.

'Who collects the rent?'

'Nobody. It has always been her way to take it to Mercet herself. Shows she's not afraid of him, she says. Makes no difference, as I see it, but it's her lease.'

'And is there anyone who might hold a grudge, against her, or indeed against you?'

'Against her, why none of course, my lord. Never caused harm to anyone, my Nesta. As for me, I doubt many knew of our connection. We've been careful not to set tongues wagging, even over a goodly time, and I am not with her every night. If only I had been . . .' He sighed and coughed. 'If Catchpoll here has barely discovered us, we have done well till now.'

'But you've not wed her yet. No idea of making "an honest woman" of her?' Bradecote could see that this hit home. Drogo bridled.

'She's "honest" enough, wed or no. It did not seem needful, her being past childbearing, and both of us with sad memories of marriage. She lost a husband young, and two sons, and another babe that was stillborn and cost her the chance of others when she was married to Bakere. I've buried three wives and never seen a child I sired come to birth. We felt wedlock unlucky, but if she lives . . .'

Drogo closed his eyes and said a silent prayer.

'Don't you fret before you have to, friend. When she's fit enough to leave the maids' chamber, she can be brought to my place. She'll be cared for well enough till she can start her trade again.' Catchpoll refrained from saying how little Mistress Catchpoll had taken to the idea.

'What trade? The bakehouse is gone and we know what Mercet is like. If he rebuilds it will be with a greatly increased rent. No, when . . . If . . . she gets well, I'll take her to wife proper and she can live here with me. A good baker is never wasted in a castle this size.'

Bradecote and Catchpoll departed in grim mood. Walkelin met them in the bailey, and announced that he had had Serlo in the cells since late the previous evening.

'He gave trouble all the way, last night. First he cried he

was being attacked by a thief, and I would have had trouble if one of my mother's kin hadn't come to her door to see what the noise was, and announced me as one of the lord sheriff's men. Saved by an aunt! Huh! Then he tried to make a run for it as we came up along Bocherewe and I felt a right fool haring after him.'

'He can languish in the cells a few hours more, though he could not have set the fire in the night if you had been watching him.' Catchpoll sound regretful.

'So why keep him, Serjeant?' asked Walkelin.

'Because offal like him need to learn we are more to be feared than Mercet.'

'Ah.'

The three men walked out to the scene of the night's conflagration. In the clear light of the September morning the remnants of Widow Bakere's existence looked forlorn and irreclaimable. The breeze picked up flakes of wood ash and tossed them playfully before discarding them like grey snowflakes. As before, the sooty puddles, charred beams and baked daub depressed the spirits. The odd survival stood out amongst the wreckage; an iron griddle pan, a small copper scoop and a girdle clasp that Catchpoll felt dig into the sole of his boot and picked up. It was blackened and a bit twisted, but recognisable and, after a bit of spit and rubbing, revealed a small cabochon garnet set in the middle. Catchpoll grunted.

'I'll keep this and any other scraps that's worth holding on to, in the hope Widow Bakere will be able to claim them. It's not much, after what must be at least a score years living here. All she can call her own.' He shook his head, despondently.

Bradecote nodded, but he was not fully attending. He was trying to see the events as they must have unfurled in the darkness.

'The fire was at the back, and not caused by something tossed over the wall on the chance it might catch. Therefore our fire-raiser must have climbed in, made his preparations and left once the flames took. We did not check the side alley first thing, so we'd best do so now. I'll take the inside of the yard and you two take the outside.'

The wall itself was something under five feet in height; enough to keep out stray curs and small children, but easy enough for a grown man. In the yard Bradecote peered carefully at the surface of the wall and the ground, though both were disguised by soot. He found a footprint, only to find that it matched his own exactly, and snorted his disgust.

'Anything that was here is either burnt to ash or mixed up with our own presence this morning,' he called. 'Any luck your side?'

Catchpoll's head, which had been hidden as he bent to inspect the wall and ground, popped up. 'There's footprints sure enough, but not with any detail. Whoever was here was either fairly tall, or a small fellow with unusually big feet. Come over and we'll compare 'em with yours, my lord.'

Bradecote climbed over the wall with an ease, Catchpoll reflected, that he himself no longer possessed. The footprints were nearly as large as the undersheriff's, but unusually narrow and with a poorly defined heel mark.

'I'd stick with a tall man, probably not of stocky build, Catchpoll. Heavy-set men rarely have narrow feet.'

'And it's something you've noticed is it, my lord?' Catchpoll raised his brows in mock enquiry.

Bradecote grinned. 'Not that I've made a study of it, no. But if I think of big men I've come across, they all had clumsy great feet. As a squire you can quite literally be underfoot, or on the receiving end of a lordly boot.'

'I never thought it so tough to be a lordling. Poor little souls.' Catchpoll shook his head and tut-tutted ostentatiously.

Bradecote's eyes narrowed in amusement. 'Indeed, and I thank you for your sympathy.' He grew serious once more. 'Yet this does no more than confirm we are looking for the man who set the fire at the Jew's house, for we know he was tall and leggy.'

'And wore a long, dark cloak, my lord.' Walkelin, who had played deaf to the mild jest between his superiors, put thumb and forefinger together and delicately extracted a coarse black woollen thread from a jagged crevice in the wall. He held it up for inspection, and grimaced. 'You know, my lord, I don't see Serlo striding around in a long, black cloak, ever, do you?'

'True, and unless it smouldered for hours he could not have set this fire. But then, what is the point of a disguise if it is not to make you seem different from normal?'

'Or like someone else who is different,' added Catchpoll, which made both his companions stare at him. 'I mean, if different men were sent to light fires but each wore the cloak to make it seem one.'

'You are clutching at straws, Catchpoll,' Bradecote sighed.

'I am that, but if I go and find the girl who saw our man on the night of the storm, and see if she recognises Serlo, it makes it certain it was not him at all, and it is a tidy reason to keep him nice and worried a few hours more.'

'True enough, Catchpoll, but it almost takes Mercet off our list of suspects, and, Jesu save us, what if we have been following the wrong scents?'

'What else could we be missing? When it began we had two fires; now we have four. It ought to be easier, if we only look at what we have in the right way.'

'Let us see Serlo, and then you try and find the girl.' Bradecote made his decision.

Chapter Fifteen

They heard Serlo in the castle cells long before they saw him. The sound of his flat-toned voice, alternately pleading and threatening, floated to them. They entered the cells to find Serlo, his wrists bound, in a crumpled heap at the end of a length of chain.

'Stand up,' commanded Walkelin, but Serlo just rolled his eyes and cried innocence of all misdeeds.

'Isn't the dog obedient, Walkelin?' His serjeant grinned, but then glared at Serlo. 'Stand up before the lord Bradecote.' He yanked the chain, and Serlo scrambled to his feet.

'I feel dizzy. I need bread,' Serlo whined. 'I need water. I need . . .'

'. . . to shut up moaning,' growled Walkelin, and kicked the back of his knees so he collapsed. 'Now you can faint and not hurt yourself as you fall.' He looked to Bradecote. 'He won't hurt himself if he faints from down there, will he, my lord?' His voice was all mock solicitude.

'No, Walkelin, he will not. A wise decision.' Bradecote spoke sombrely, but his eyes danced.

Catchpoll was impressed; this was young Walkelin thinking like a serjeant, keeping the prisoner off balance in more ways than one. He looked down on Serlo with a contemptuous sneer, and then kicked him with almost casual violence. 'Nice of you to come and see us.'

Serlo yelped, and whimpered, 'I'm an innocent man, Serjeant Catchpoll.'

'Innocent!' Catchpoll nearly choked on the laugh. 'You was born guilty, Serlo. Our only difficulty is proving whether you're guilty of this one particular crime. Now, let's have your shoe off.'

Serlo's eyes widened, imagining some evil torture. He rolled his eyes, and cast Bradecote a look of entreaty.

'Whatever it is I didn't do it, my lord. Don't let him maim me, I beg you.'

Bradecote feigned boredom, and turned away. 'Nothing too messy, Serjeant, that's all I ask.'

'Right you are, my lord.' Catchpoll sounded as if about to enjoy a rare treat, as he bent for the shoe.

Walkelin was unsure what exactly was going on. Serjeant Catchpoll was known to have a mean and miserable streak, as those given extra duties and demeaning tasks would verify, but Walkelin had not expected torture of suspects, even guilty ones. And the undersheriff had seemed very upright and not at all vindictive. He frowned.

Removing the shoe from the trembling Serlo, and casting it aside, Catchpoll caught the man-at-arms' expression and his thin lips twitched.

'You keep an eye on this maw-worm, Walkelin, and I'll be back before you could heat a hot iron nice and red.'

Walkelin's jaw dropped, and Catchpoll gave a slow wink, then mouthed, over the prisoner's head, 'If he tells us anything useful, let me know.'

He and Bradecote left, to the sound of Serlo gibbering.

Once outside, he nodded to his superior and smiled. 'Thank you for that, my lord. Did me a power of good, that did. Even though we can't get him on this, it will have been useful to make him more afraid of us than of his master. And a nice touch, the lack of interest.'

'Thank you, Catchpoll. In this case I think your reading of the man quite accurate. But for reference, I do not approve of confession by force. There is too much scope for error.'

'Quite, my lord, and a confession under duress does not count under the old King's laws, so I only use it in really exceptional circumstances.'

'No, Catchpoll. On any investigation where I am involved it will not happen at all, however "exceptional" the circumstance. Be clear on this.' There was no levity in the undersheriff's voice.

'As you command, my lord.' Catchpoll's smile died. He disliked having parameters put upon his actions, and made a mental note to be careful that Bradecote did not see his less genteel methods in action.

Catchpoll headed into the busy streets of Worcester and Bradecote went to ask Drogo if he had seen anyone loitering near the bakery and wearing a long, black cloak. As he expected, the answer was negative, and he returned to the cells.

'Has his fear loosened his tongue to give anything of merit?' Bradecote enquired quietly, when Walkelin came to him.

'Not sure, my lord. He rambled on about how influential his master was, and hinted that Mercet had the ear of Earl Waleran, though I think that mere fancy. He did say as how Mercet was hoping to clear the hovels down by the river, and put up more warehousing, though I will be bound Serlo would find another place for his sister. Not that he, Mercet, was thinking of burning 'em out, just leaning on those too weak and poor to resist bully-boy tactics. I never knew this went on in Worcester, my lord. Such meanness by a man who has so much. I tell you, if the lads in the guardroom heard it, well I wouldn't give much for Mercet's own property staying upright.'

'Best not let it be known then, Walkelin, because lawlessness cannot be allowed from those within the castle. If the sheriff's men misbehave, what can we expect from the common folk?'

Walkelin looked disappointed.

'Mind you,' the undersheriff suddenly brightened, 'what you say may yet have a good use. It is we who could "lean" on Mercet over this. If we let him know we know what he is about, and suggest what would happen if the soldiery found out, that could well put paid to this particular scheme. Yes, I think this will make Serjeant Catchpoll a much happier man. Well done, Walkelin.'

The young man looked cheered, and a faint blush tinged his cheek at the praise.

* * *

Serjeant Catchpoll was in need of cheering. He was looking hard enough for Huw's sister, but his mind was not fully on the task. The thought that Mercet might not be behind the fires after all filled him with gloom, and worried him at the same time, as it did the undersheriff. Mercet was a connection, and they had found no other. Had his loathing of the merchant blinded him to some other thread that pulled all together? A small voice in his head said that he was missing something. He had kept trying to ignore it, but it would not go away, and its words now seemed to hold true.

In part this touched his pride. He was Serjeant Catchpoll, who knew Worcester inside out. This was his place; these were his people, criminals and innocent alike. He knew those who committed crimes and could even select those most likely to be victims of crime; he knew most of the feuds and grudges between families, and tradesmen, and even parishes. Yet here were events he could not link. He turned the thought over and over until he felt almost dizzy. What was there that had given rise to these events happening now? And why had he no inkling of it? Two words, a germ of an idea, stirred in his brain, but gave rise to questions he could not begin to answer. In desperation, he tried to concentrate purely on the matter to hand.

He espied Huw, apparently making friends with a mangy, flea-riddled cur of indeterminate colour and decidedly malodorous, matted coat. The child did not notice Catchpoll's approach until his new canine friend, with uncanny intuition, adopted a belligerent pose and began to growl, its hackles raised. Huw turned, and jumped guiltily. It was one of Serjeant

Catchpoll's unnerving attributes that he could make the most saintly feel they had erred.

'I wasn't stealing him, my lord,' piped Huw, plaintively.

'I know that, boy. I was looking for your sister. Is she hereabouts?'

Huw thought for a moment. 'She said she was busy this morning, but she would bring me some bread about noontide, and said I should not stray from here. She cannot be far away.'

'You stay as she said, then, but if she is a little late do not fret. She may have to come to the castle to help us for a short time, but she will be back.' He smiled at the boy, at which the dog growled more menacingly.

The girl was found sat upon an upturned and damaged barrel to the rear of one of the brewers' premises. She was wiping her eyes on her grubby, tattered skirts, and sported a split lip and reddened cheek. Catchpoll's expression grew very hard. He was rarely perturbed by the failings of his fellow man, even when they resulted in murder, but he was revolted by the thought of what supposedly God-fearing and honest men assumed they could do to a slip of a girl.

'So who did this?'

She shrugged. 'They don't generally tell me their names, for they aren't here for talking. It matters not, anyway. He paid, so we'll eat when what you gave is gone.' The voice was dulled, and matter-of-fact.

'You'll eat for the rest of the week if you can come and help the lord undersheriff at the castle. We've a man we want you to see. You can tell us if it is the man you saw before the house in Cokenstrete.'

'And you'll pay even if he is not?' The girl sounded doubtful.

'Yes. It is important we know if it is the right man. We are paying for the truth, not a particular answer.'

'Will he see me? The man in Cokenstrete scared me.'

'He need not see you, girl. Now, come along with me.'

She followed, almost beside him but carefully not 'with' him, and was ignored by those against whom she brushed or passed; excepting one man who gave a small, tight smile and jingled coin in his scrip; and the priest of St Andrew's, who emerged from a house and saw the retreating figure of Serjeant Catchpoll, and noted the girl. He stared for a moment, frowning, and then turned away, muttering about 'daughters of Eve' and the sinfulness of the young. Oblivious to the censure, the pair made their way along the main thoroughfare and shortly thereafter arrived at the castle gates, where the girl hesitated.

'I've never been within,' she said in a small voice.

'I should hope not,' replied Catchpoll, the voice of virtue, 'but this is helping the law and a good thing.'

She entered the gate as if the bailey were the haunt of monsters and ravening wolves, chewing nervously upon her damaged lip and with her eyes darting to left and right.

Catchpoll led her to the door of one of the storerooms on the bailey's perimeter, adjacent to the kitchens. He bade her wait just within, and with the door open enough for her to view the bailey. Then he sought out the undersheriff and had Walkelin fetch Serlo from the cells, while he and Bradecote returned to the storeroom. The girl was pale-faced, and her eyes watchful. Bradecote nodded his acknowledgement of her presence but let Catchpoll explain that all she had to do was say whether the bound man brought across the yard was the one she had seen on Cokenstrete.

Serlo was reluctant to leave the perceived security of the cell, and Walkelin did nothing to disabuse him of the idea that something unpleasant awaited him. He was pushed, wrists bound, across the outer bailey, blinking in the daylight, and was only persuaded to move by Walkelin shoving him, none too gently, in the small of the back. He crossed the bailey to the guardhouse and disappeared within. Catchpoll's eyes had not watched his progress, but had remained fixed on the girl's face, seeking to read any sign of recognition that she might, in fear, attempt to conceal. He noted the flicker of her eyes, but when she turned to them there was no fear, merely contempt.

'I know him alright. Tight-fisted and heavy-handed he is, but not, I swear before God, the man in Cokenstrete. If it had been him, I would have led you to him straight, for he is another of Master Mercet's men. He's but a *nithing*, not worth a second glance. He can't even manage what he pays for, sometimes.' She thought for a moment. 'The man I saw was important, at least to himself, my lords. This man is no better than a whipped cur, who likes to think he is a man because he can attempt a man's "pleasure" upon a girl, but the hooded man feared nobody. He walked as if he had a God-given right to go as he pleased, and yet he was no lord I've seen in Worcester these last months.' She looked from Catchpoll to Bradecote and read the disappointment on their faces. 'I tell you true, but it's sorry I am if it is not the answer you wanted.' Her voice was uncertain.

'No. You did right by us and we'll do right by you.' Catchpoll looked meaningfully at Bradecote, and surreptitiously held up two fingers. Far better the largesse came from the wealthiest present. Bradecote raised an eyebrow by a fraction, but dug dutifully in his scrip and drew forth two silver pennies, which he handed to the girl. Her eyes widened in delight and she bobbed a curtsey to him, but looked to Catchpoll for dismissal.

'You get back to your brother, and remember there's more if you bring us news of the hooded man.' Catchpoll nodded at her, and she disappeared with a mumbled promise to bring any information she had gathered.

'Any other monetary commitments you have in mind for me, Catchpoll?'

The serjeant's eyes narrowed. 'My lord?'

'Anyone else you'd have me pay to give you information?'

'Ah, be fair, my lord. The information was for the both of us, and I am but a poor serjeant.' He spread his hands placatingly, but the death's head grin ruined the effect. 'Besides, my lord, you saw her face. Two more silver pennies will keep her from such as the "friend" who gave her those marks, at least for a few more days.'

'Only a few days, Catchpoll.'

'In her world, that is as far as you look, my lord – to the next meal, or lack of it, to the next time she has to lift her skirts to earn coin for food.' Catchpoll shrugged.

Hugh Bradecote felt sullied, not by the girl's having been at his side, but for being male. If he thought about the women who sold themselves at all, he thought vaguely of those who seemed to throw out their lures from choice. He disliked them. It was better than the truth: that there were young girls, and widows too, no doubt, who had nothing else to sell. They were condemned by 'decent folk' for whoring, more than the men who paid them, and it was wrong.

Catchpoll watched Bradecote's face. Some realities of life passed the high and mighty by, but the sheriff's men saw all. The undersheriff would have to get used to the dirtier bits, physically and morally, because it came with the job, and the quicker the better.

They crossed to the guardhouse, where Walkelin had Serlo concealed. Catchpoll was reluctant to end his enjoyment, and so stood stony-faced and arms folded, the picture of icy retribution.

'You are sure of this, my lord?' He addressed the undersheriff but kept his eyes on Serlo.

'Yes. Best make an end to it straight away. He is of no further use to us.' Bradecote's voice had a callous chill to it. He could play this game as well as Catchpoll, and he was recalling what the girl said about him.

Walkelin, privy now to the ploy, wondered how they kept such straight faces. He was having to bite his lip to avoid laughing. Unconsciously, this made him look nervous, which in no way alleviated Serlo's rising panic.

'I beg of you, my lord, have mercy.' Serlo's eyes rolled, and his lower lip trembled.

Bradecote stared, unmoved.

Catchpoll reached out and grabbed Serlo by the throat. With great deliberation, he drew a very serviceable knife. Serlo whimpered. Catchpoll could smell the fear on him, augmented by a hint of urine. With no trace of emotion, he cut the rope bonds that tied Serlo's wrists.

'Get out,' he snarled.

Serlo stood rooted to the spot, uncomprehending.

'Get out. Now. And remember the only reason you leave here is the merciful, and to my mind, over merciful, attitude of my lord undersheriff. So when he comes, all civil like, and next asks you a question, be sure and give him an honest answer. For my part, I am going to be trying to persuade him not to be so soft with vermin like you.' Catchpoll spun Serlo round and sent him staggering out with a well-aimed kick to the backside. Serlo needed no third command. He scurried off, too relieved to wonder why he had been held in the first place, and with an inflated idea of Bradecote's power over life and death, just as Catchpoll intended he should.

Chapter Sixteen

'Now that's over, what do we do next?' Walkelin wondered, when Catchpoll's guffaws of delight subsided.

Brought back to earth, Catchpoll sighed, and sucked his teeth.

'Well, on the sad assumption that Mercet is not the instigator, we go back to the beginning and look at everything we have, trying not to make the same connections as before. It grieves me, that does. Even if Mercet is not our man, it feels as if he has slipped through my fingers again.' He shook his grizzled head despondently. 'And it looked so promising.'

He was mildly revived by the thought of thwarting the merchant's clearing of riverside properties, as explained by Bradecote, but it was a small consolation.

'Do we still take it that all four fires are linked, for a start?' asked Walkelin, who had taken the serjeant literally and was mulling over the case from first principles.

'We have to, as I see it.' Bradecote attempted to focus his thoughts. 'I am sure that none were accidental, and it is surely stretching the imagination too far to have two fire-raisers in Worcester this Michaelmastide.'

'We have no motive, no link between all the victims, and no probable suspects to follow.' Catchpoll pulled a face indicative of frustration and misery.

'But those things must exist, mustn't they?' Walkelin was nothing if not dogged. 'Men don't plan fires without a reason, and these must have some planning to them. Is there another man apart from Mercet who would want to rid Worcester of Simeon the Jew? Other than priests, of course. They must see them as pagans, or heretics or something.'

'Even if there was a papal edict put out, I cannot imagine the clergy running round setting fire to other things as practice.' Catchpoll dismissed the idea, but had considered it seriously.

Bradecote held up a hand. 'Wait.' He shut his eyes in concentration. 'There's something in this.'

'What, my lord?' Walkelin could not hide his incredulity.

'Oh, not monks wandering the streets with burning the town in mind, but a reason based on something religious. Remember the holy oil stolen from St Andrew's? Why could it not have been stolen, not just as oil, but actually because it was holy oil?'

'And the swine fat used to make a point, not just as an insult.' Catchpoll nodded. 'It might be a link, but then, what could be the religious connection with the others?'

'Drogo and Widow Bakere are having a sinful union,' noted Walkelin, with a degree of relish. 'The bakery fire could be a warning against furni . . . forni . . . lustfulness.'

'He's a widower, she's a widow, and it isn't as bad as adultery, which goes on in almost every street most nights if you was to listen hard, and I do not suggest you do, being young and innocent.' Catchpoll did not sound taken with the idea.

'Does it?' Walkelin was surprised, and not uninterested. He had never thought of adultery 'going on' on such a scale.

'Don't corrupt the young, Catchpoll,' remarked Bradecote, drily.

'You understand though, my lord. In the scale of sinning, why pick on them?'

Bradecote shrugged. 'It was a case known to the fire-raiser, not just gossip?'

'That would narrow the hunt. I did not know of it until a few days back.' Catchpoll sounded vaguely aggrieved, as though the sin was him not knowing of the affair long since.

'And if the ever-vigilant Serjeant Catchpoll doesn't know about something it must be a well-kept secret?' Bradecote queried.

'Something like, my lord.' Catchpoll almost blushed.

Walkelin was too lowly for badinage, and, in consequence, was single-mindedly persistent.

'So that would cover the last two fires, but what about the first two? If the old healing woman was the intended victim, it could be because she helped women lose unwanted babes, but that still leaves Master Ash, the silversmith. Of course, that will be it.'

'What will be it, Walkelin?' Catchpoll was beginning to find the man-at-arms' enthusiasm jarring.

'The fire-raiser objected to Master Ash because of his trade.

Judas was paid thirty pieces of silver and to our man that is enough to mark a silversmith as victim.'

'One of the moneyers would be more fitting, but it would work at a stretch.' Having begun this theory, the undersheriff was finding it ever less likely. 'This means we are hunting some form of religious maniac. Seen any about the town?'

'We have a few odd folk . . . Mad Meurig comes to mind . . . but I'd swear they are harmless.'

'Mad Meurig?' Walkelin and Bradecote chorused.

'Oh yes. He's Welsh, of course, and they can have some dismal ideas. Probably because they live in a land of rain and mist so much of the time.'

'I went to Wales once, I think, and it was bright and sunny every day I was that side of the border,' Walkelin chipped in, and received a withering look from his serjeant.

'Well, you were in the wrong bit, then. Mad Meurig has thought the world was about to end "any day now" for the last twenty years. He tells everyone who comes to his smithy, and even accosts people in the street, but he never causes harm.'

'Odd behaviour, but mad?' Bradecote pulled a face.

'Yes, when he also tells you that he knows this because he is visited by angels; angels with long tails that scamper about his floor and squeak.'

'Ah. Fair enough. He's mad. But does a person like that turn killer?'

Walkelin pursed his lips, assuming that it was part of the profession to pull faces.

'He might not have seen it as killing, just purging by fire, perhaps,' he suggested cautiously.

'It doesn't get us past the question "Why now?" though, and the only answer seems to be because our fire-setter is new to Worcester.'

'Which,' noted Catchpoll, 'would account for them not being amongst our "known" madmen. Trouble is, if they are only recently come here, how have they found all these different targets so quickly, and how do they know their way about?'

Bradecote made a decision. 'Right. We therefore find out who has come to Worcester in, say, the last six months or so. They must be male, living alone, and not apprenticed. We then narrow that down by who is tall and not fair-haired.'

'That'll take some doing, my lord.'

'I know, Catchpoll, so you and Walkelin set about it first thing. Walkelin had a late night, and we got barely any sleep at all, so we'll make an early night tonight.'

The trio dispersed; Walkelin and Catchpoll ultimately to their hearths. Catchpoll wanted to see his friend Drogo before returning to his wife, but Walkelin delayed him.

'How do you get folk to confess without force, Serjeant? And for that matter, what is "due-ress"? I can't see how the laws work.'

Catchpoll scratched his ear and considered his red-haired apprentice, judging whether he was fit to hear a proper explanation. Apparently he did, for he patted him on the back in an avuncular fashion and steered him to the brewhouse to lubricate said explanation. Leaning comfortably against a sun-warmed wall, Catchpoll tried to pass on some of the workings of his craft.

'Duress is, as I see it, heavy-duty threatening along the lines

216

of "Say or do this, or I'll drown your children, break your neck, throw your mother down the well". That sort of thing. It's not nice, and while it may get the answer you want it might not be the right answer . . . if you see what I mean.'

Walkelin was concentrating hard. 'You mean a man will say something that's not true to avoid the threat becoming fact.'

'Exactly so. Now the tricky bit, and it is what comes with years of doing the job, is putting the pressure on without it being duress.'

'So frightening Serlo until he pissed himself wasn't duress?'

'Oh no. Firstly, that was for pleasure.' Catchpoll grinned. 'Perks of the job, you might say.' Then his face became serious. 'Now, he was not told what to admit. Also, no specific threats were made. I mean, did you ever hear me tell him I was going to do him a permanent injury?'

'No-o, but that's what he thought.'

'Not my fault if the man's stupid though, lad. Hinting at extreme violence isn't the same as direct threat. Mind you, you have to get yourself a nice healthy reputation for being unpleasant for it to work a treat.'

'I'm not sure I could threaten a woman, Serjeant.' Walkelin sounded apologetic.

'Wouldn't ask you to. You see the craft is in judging how to get your criminal to admit the crime. Brute force and ignorance has its place, but if that were the only thing a good serjeant needed, Hammon would have been given the job long ago. But Hammon hasn't got the wits, or the innate distrust of his fellow man, nor the memory neither. Now I picked you because you have a good eye for detail, which is a healthy start.

Distrust you'll have to pick up, just as you learn the finer points of serjeanting. Vermin like Serlo understand violence because that's the world they work in. He therefore sees the opportunity for others to inflict pain upon him because that's what he would try and do with others. He's also stupid, so we could have tried tricking information from him, but I'll admit frightening him felt so much better, and this job needs a few moments like that. Bakers get extra bread, butchers offcuts of meat, and serjeants get to scare the criminal brotherhood.'

Catchpoll was warming to his theme, and took a long draught of ale. He then drew the back of his hand across his mouth before continuing.

'With women it is getting them into letting their tongues run away with them, and, Holy Virgin, don't they do that; riling them so they admit it in a temper; or frightening them by making them think you know everything, or even that your idea is worse than the reality. Of course they'd all of 'em do better to say nothing at all from start to finish, but it is mighty rare for a criminal to be that clever.'

Catchpoll stretched and gazed at the bottom of his empty beaker. The lesson was over, and he went to check upon Drogo the Cook. Walkelin disappeared off home with his mind working overtime, going over everything he had heard. His mother found him distant and absent-minded, even finding him sitting with spoon suspended halfway to mouth during dinner. She was beginning to worry that all the new thinking might overheat his flame-topped brain, and recommended he retire with a cool cloth upon his brow.

* * *

Drogo was fretful, in enough discomfort to make him ill-tempered but not enough to keep him quiet. He was railing against being kept from Nesta Bakere's side, and was prey to the growing fear that an awful truth was being kept from him. Catchpoll tried to reassure him that the widow still breathed, but it took several avowals and some strong language before this was accepted.

'You think me foolish, I doubt not, but we have our happiness, not like the heat of youth, but strong nonetheless. The thought of having it snatched away now is an awful thing to bear. She's a good woman, a comfortable woman, my Nesta; not as fair as my Emma, but that was more than a score years ago when we were both young, nor as witty as poor Judith, but a woman to grow old with peaceably, see.'

'No need to persuade me, Drogo. I wish you well of her, God's truth. You just keep from fretting while there's nothing you can do. The quicker you are up and able, the quicker you can fend for her. Think on that, and don't swear at poor Brother Hubert when he comes, for it's God's grace and his skills as keep your woman alive.'

The undersheriff sought solitude up on the battlements, gazing out over as much of Worcester that was not obstructed by the mighty bulk of the cathedral, in hope of inspiration. He had no proprietorial feeling, although he could now identify the churches rising above the general roof line, and had an idea of the main thoroughfares. Some of the roofs were tiled but a majority were thatched, and the variation in colour told the story of a firing of the town by Earl Robert of Gloucester's men only four years past. Bradecote wondered idly what Catchpoll felt, looking over Worcester, and surmised that it was much as he felt atop the little scarp that overlooked Bradecote; a sense of protective belonging. He shook his head, for instead of being inspired he had merely become maudlin.

His hopes of being left in peace were of short duration. A servant sought him out with a message from the castellan, summoning him without delay, and, groaning inwardly, Bradecote descended to hear the castellan's litany of complaints, starting no doubt, with the incapacity of his cook. Much to Bradecote's surprise, this was almost treated as an irrelevance. The castellan, in more than usually poor temper after the drawing of a tooth, did of course bemoan the continuation of fires, noting that the last had occurred within view of 'his' castle. This was clearly seen as a personal affront, which the undersheriff had failed to prevent, but the main cause for his peevish anger concerned a man whom Bradecote had never met.

'Why, in the name of heaven's saints, have you dragged the good name of my poor son-in-law into the mire of your incompetent hunt?'

Bradecote's face registered bafflement, for he could not imagine any of the suspects being related to the castellan. 'Your son-in-law?'

'Yes. Jocelyn FitzGuimar, the husband of my eldest daughter. I have heard that you have been sniffing like hounds round Worcester, asking impertinent details about him, suggesting he consorts with whores and . . .' The castellan halted at Bradecote's upraised hand.

'Neither I nor my men have once mentioned this man. I

have never heard of him until this moment. So you are in error, my lord.'

Simon Furnaux was not in any way mollified. 'You say this to me, but it is a lie. You have been hunting a man already burdened by disaster and misfortune; one whose honour and courage deserve better than having his name dragged into a criminal case.'

Hugh Bradecote was at the point of losing his temper, but he was assailed by a sudden thought that kept it just in check.

'What is this misfortune?'

'Why, that he is maimed after the fire at his manor last All Souls. A brave man, Jocelyn, who risked all to save his wife and children. He reached home after the blaze had started, and found his servants, witless cowards to a man, making no effort to reach the solar where the family was trapped, because the hall roof was ablaze. They even tried to hold him back, but he threw them off. Part of the roof collapsed as he passed through, and he actually cast flaming timbers aside to reach the chamber. How he did so defies understanding, though it is said a man can do great things in time of emergency. He found my daughter and the children collapsed because of the smoke; forced open the shutters and dropped the smaller children to those below, and then, with burnt hands mind, battered the embrasure with the brazier to make it large enough to get Isabelle out. He himself grew faint, and was pulled from the building by the steward, using a ladder, but his hands will never hold sword again, and his face bears unsightly marks, not that Isabelle cares. And rightly so.' He paused for breath in his righteous indignation, and Bradecote took the opportunity to interject.

'My lord Castellan, I said true. The name means nothing to me, but we did follow up a visitor to the healing woman who died in the Corviserstrete fire, because he was unknown and a mystery. We never found his name because we went no further, once we found out that he was a burnt man, and not so recent as to have been harmed while setting the first fire. If your son-in-law's good name is offended, I will willingly make him my apologies and have it known he is beyond doubt unconnected with these crimes.' Bradecote wondered how Simon Furnaux had heard of their quest for the gauntlet-wearing man and worked out who it must be, and then made no mention of it to him. 'We would have done so immediately had we known his identity. What pity it is that you did not mention him, that we could have eliminated him from our investigation before any rumour spread.' He did not mention that they would only have done so after checking his story for themselves.

The castellan sniffed, ignoring the implied criticism. 'He comes rarely to Worcester now, disliking unknown company and staring eyes, but you apologise to his lady, for she is come to me but yesterday, and I told her of the insult.'

I bet you did, thought Hugh Bradecote, and felt pretty certain that the impugning of the man's honour had gone no further than his father-in-law and now wife.

'You may certainly make your apologies to her. I shall call for her.'

Lady FitzGuimar was probably only in her very early twenties, but care and worry had added to her years and she looked older. She was thin and birdlike, with anxious, periwinkle-blue eyes, but she held herself proudly when she came to the hall to receive the apology on her lord's behalf. Bradecote would have far preferred to make any apology without the castellan's presence. He had no objection to apologising to the lady herself, but he had little regard for her sire.

She listened, attentive and grave, and bowed her acceptance. Her voice, when she spoke, was at variance with her looks, for her speech was firm, low and measured.

'I will convey your words to my lord.' She then confirmed Bradecote's suspicion. 'There is no need to make a public pronouncement unless it should be known that scandal is being attached to him. I am sure the matter can be considered at an end.'

'Thank you, my lady.' Bradecote paused, and then the seed of an idea made him add, 'Would you object to telling me how the fire started; some accident with cooking fires, perhaps, or a branch of candles?'

'Oh no, my lord Bradecote. It was no accident. I do not know whether it makes it the worse for being intentional. Someone loosed flaming arrows into the roof thatch. Afterwards, one of the men found his bow and a quiver of arrows missing. The men-at-arms had been at the butts that very afternoon, while my lord had been hawking. It was not one of the men, for each could be vouched for by others, and there is no cause of discontent among them. My husband is a fair man.'

'So was nobody found to have committed this deed?'

'No. Suspicion did fall upon the monk who stopped to have his blisters attended to, but he was never found. He said he was from Winchcombe and on his way to Evesham, but no Brother

Laurentius was known in Winchcombe. The lord Sheriff of Gloucester himself went to discover him.'

'What manner of man was he? Did you see him yourself?'

Lady FitzGuimar glanced enquiringly at her father, puzzled. 'My lord, how is this of importance? It was last year, and Dumbleton lies in another shire.'

The castellan shook his head.

'Nevertheless, my lady, it might be relevant,' Bradecote persisted. 'Please, tell me all.'

She shrugged. 'Well, the steward saw he had food and drink while my tirewoman dealt with his poor feet. She said the blisters were real enough, so how he could have walked fast enough to be beyond finding is a mystery. He was just a cowled Benedictine, not old. She never saw his face. Indeed her only description was of his feet; long, blistered and bony. I must say the connection was made only because he could not be accounted for. There was no cause for the man, and a man of God too, to commit such a crime. He was unknown to all within our walls.'

'Thank you, my lady.'

'Surely that is enough for you, Bradecote,' announced the castellan, peevishly. 'As my daughter says, the fire was not even in your jurisdiction. What interest it can be to you, when you have more than you can cope with dealing with fires here, I cannot imagine.'

'No, I don't suppose you can, my lord.' Bradecote bowed to lady FitzGuimar, and turned to leave.

The castellan was not quite sure whether or not he had just been insulted, but on balance, thought that he had.

224

'I will be sure to report this to the sheriff, and to my friend Guimar of Shapwyck also,' he threw after Bradecote's back, trying to get the last word, and was taken aback when the undersheriff spun round.

'What?' Bradecote almost bellowed at him.

'Guimar of Shapwyck,' reiterated the castellan more hesitantly. 'He has the right, as Jocelyn's brother and head of his house.'

Hugh Bradecote's expression was grim, but there was excitement in his voice. 'My lady, you may tell your lord that whoever caused his injuries and loss may yet come to justice, and in the shrievalty of Worcester.'

With which, and to the consternation of both father and daughter, Bradecote strode out.

Chapter Seventeen

Catchpoll was awaiting his dinner with no small degree of anticipation. The smell of the fish and the herb dumplings in the pottage made his mouth water, and, after a day that had, despite some entertainment, proved depressing, he was glad to empty his mind of all but thoughts of food for a while. The arrival of the undersheriff was therefore less than welcome. He invited him in reluctantly, but Bradecote's desire to discuss his news prevented him noticing the forced hospitality.

'Don't you see, Catchpoll?' asked Bradecote, as he drew to the close of the incident at Dumbleton. 'The elusive "Brother Laurentius" could easily be our fire-setter. He was not seen bare-headed, and I'd vouch that in reality his head had never seen tonsure. This was a good disguise to get him into the manor. Who would not give ease and assistance to a holy brother? Those who went after him found no trace because they were looking for a Benedictine on foot, not a man on horseback, and a horse he surely had to aid his escape. He fits the description as tall and with long, bony feet, just as would fit our footprint in the alley.'

'All very good, my lord, and I wouldn't deny the likelihood of anything you've said thus far, but what does it add to our knowledge beyond the fact that our man has spread his net wider than expected.'

'But listen further, Catchpoll. The man whose home he tried to burn down and whose family nearly burnt to death, is the brother of Guimar the Younger of Shapwyck, and where has that name turned up before?'

'The lordling with an eye to Emma the silversmith's widow! But we have discarded Drogo as a suspect after last night, and I can tell you his feet are wide and stubby. Aye, and smell to high heaven in the heat of his kitchen, not that it is a help.'

Bradecote shook his head. 'No, that is not at issue. Drogo, besides being a man with smelly, stubby feet, would be noticed if he went absent for several days. Also if he had held a grudge against the man it would have been way back when the youth was smitten with the woman, not nigh on two decades later, when the man has manor and family. The point is that there is suddenly a link between the burning of a manor last autumn, the fire at the silversmith's, and with Drogo, and this grudge or whatever it is, goes back a full score years. That would account for you not knowing of it.'

'But you cannot bring in the fire at Simeon the Jew's house, or Martin Woodman's yard.'

'I can fit in the latter, because the wood yard was merely

the method of starting the fire. The target was Old Edgyth, the healing woman.'

'Who treated Drogo's wife and couldn't save her?' Catchpoll's face contorted in thought, and Mistress Catchpoll took the opportunity to bob a curtsey and ask if the lord undersheriff would be staying to eat with them. Bradecote was suddenly aware of the delicious smell from the pot over the hearth, and his empty stomach, and assented willingly. The lady of the house set a bowl and spoon before him and began to ladle out her culinary delight.

Catchpoll was only dimly conscious of his meal being shared out with his superior. His brain was sorting information at speed, and extracting the most important facts.

'We do not have a link with the Jew, but that does not mean there isn't one somewhere. What we do have is an old, old cause for very current events. Our man has to be old enough to have been part of those events; who left and has at long last returned; a spurned rival for the lady's affection, perhaps, who adored her from afar and blamed these people for her death. Drogo, according to gossip that lingers to this day, killed her because the child she carried was fathered by the young Jocelyn FitzGuimar, and Old Edgyth either tried to rid her of the child, or failed in her healing potions. It is an empty tale, but was juicy enough to linger in memories. Trouble is, Drogo has said that he did not think his wife would have known Reginald Ash, because he would have only been a journeyman then, and he could not be the jealous suitor because he didn't set fire to his own property. Of course, much of the rumour need not have been true, just believed by our culprit.'

Mistress Catchpoll, having set a steaming bowl before her husband and brought bread to the table, sat down primly.

'Seems to me, Catchpoll, as you needs speak to Aldith Merrow,' she commented.

'Who?' Bradecote queried.

'An old spider, my lord, who has, or rather had, for she is crabbed and aged now, the gossip of Worcester set out like threads of a web, and with her in the middle, awake to every tremor. She would indeed know every scandal that has raised its head in Worcester these last thirty years, though her mind sometimes drifts nowadays.' Catchpoll turned to his wife. 'A fair idea, but you keep all of what you've heard this night within these walls, mark you.'

Mistress Catchpoll sniffed. 'What do you take me for, husband?'

'A woman like any other, who cannot bear the thought of not letting her friends know that she knows more than they do. But keep this very quiet, love, for lives do depend upon it.' He turned back to Bradecote. 'I'd best also find out the name of his wife's first husband from Drogo as well. I'll speak to him in the morning, since we can do nothing tonight.'

'My lord,' Mistress Catchpoll cast her spouse a swift glance before hesitantly offering Bradecote another thought, 'could not the span of years be come about because the man went on crusade, or at least followed the soldiering trade. Some Worcester men go off and never return or come home so as you'd not know them.' She turned back to Catchpoll. 'You remember Edgar Oakes who went away for must be twenty year, and when he came back his father at first refused to believe it was him, having grieved for him dead all those years without word. He only proved himself by recounting tales of his childhood that none but he could have known.'

'A good thought, wife, but don't have too many more or the lord undersheriff will be drafting you as serjeant and I will be left to keep house.'

She giggled almost girlishly, and as she got up and gathered the empty bowls, Catchpoll tapped her playfully upon the rump. Bradecote, suddenly ill at ease with a domestic Catchpoll, made his excuses and retired, well fed and confident that at last they were not hunting shadows.

Walkelin lay in his bed, very awake. He tossed the clammy, damp cloth aside. His mother had pressed it to his brow, despite his protestations, complaining that he was in danger of succumbing to a fever of the brain, but he felt foolish, lying there in the dark like a sickly child. Tonight it did not worry him that sleep would not come, for he again let fantastic thoughts of stunning his superiors with his wily cunning, heroic bravery and clear-sighted intelligence, turn over and over in his head. His first effort had won approval, even if it had not proved ultimately successful, and his suggestions today had won praise. The future seemed full of promise and plaudits. One day he would be not just Walkelin, son of Hubert, but Serjeant FitzHubert, which sounded grand as a name, and be as respected, feared and, in certain quarters, loathed, as Serjeant Catchpoll.

The stable was not locked, merely latched, and slipping silently within was easy. There was the strong smell of sweet hay and warm horse, and the sound of contented and vacuous munching came from the stalls. A rat scuttled across the floor, making one of the horses stamp in irritation, but nothing else disturbed the preparations. It took a while to become accustomed to the intensity of the darkness, where the moon's silvery beams did not penetrate, but it was merely the work of minutes to create a small bonfire of straw and kindling beneath the hayloft, and with every other flammable item laid close to hand. The hands that lit the fire did not tremble in the slightest, and the fire-raiser, smiling in contentment, let themself out and latched the door to conceal the mayhem that was beginning from such an innocent little flame worming its way between the kindling within, and spreading like a red contagion.

Hugh Bradecote was definitely sleeping better, and his dreams, while frequently convoluted, were not haunted by a white face and scarlet sheets. It must have been the middle of the night, for he was deep in slumber when his shoulder was shaken and an urgent voice called his name.

'Not again, please,' prayed Bradecote out loud, as he surfaced to full consciousness, but his prayer was not answered. As he pulled on his boots, the undersheriff wondered what fresh incendiary disaster awaited him. The servant who had woken him could give neither direction nor detail, excepting that one of the watch had raced back to the castle with the cry of 'Fire' upon his lips. Bradecote went to where the man waited, and set off, leaving instructions for Serjeant Catchpoll to be similarly disturbed. He would be damned if he should spend yet another wakeful night and yet have Catchpoll snore through it in peace.

* * *

231

The wooden stable building burnt easily and swiftly, and had caught well and truly before neighbouring townsfolk turned out to prevent its spread, or, in the case of the very old and very young, to be excited by the spectacle.

It was Huw's coughing more than the agitation of the horses that woke his sister, and when she opened her eyes she was confused by the thick darkness. As she took a yawning breath, thinking she had been dreaming, the smoke reached her, and she sprang to full wakefulness. Her first thoughts were panic-ridden and jumbled. She sat up, pushing her brother, nestled against her, from her body, and choked. She crawled towards the ladder of the hayloft to look down, but never reached the edge, for the heat, and sound of crackling burning, told her that any escape by their normal route would be impossible. She tried to think, though the thought that hammered in her brain was that they were trapped. It was fast becoming difficult to breathe, and she shook her brother's shoulder, calling his name. He woke befuddled, rubbing his eyes and grumbling, and she had to shove him to move him towards the front wall of the building, where small gaps between the wooden planks gave access to snatches of clearer air. She heard the sound of a horse lashing out at the panel of a stall in its panic, of people shouting outside, of splintering wood as men hacked through the wooden planks to reach the tethered beasts, but doubted any would guess their presence, or would hear them if they managed to call out.

'Stay by the cracks, Huw, and keep your face to them for air. I will be back soon.'

She took a deep breath and crawled back along the eave edge of the loft, praying that her memory did not deceive her, and giving silent thanks when her hand touched the tine of a pitchfork. Dragging it back, at what seemed a snail's pace, she began to prise and kick at the planking. She knew her strength would not last, but she prayed fervently to heaven that it would be enough. In answer, the first plank splintered, and she used the pitchfork to try and lever another to make a hole large enough to lean out and attract attention.

It was a woman's scream that alerted the firefighters to the presence of the child. All attention had been on the seat of the fire behind the main doors, and attempting to save the horses. A couple had been rescued by men taking axes and breaking in the side of the building where the stalls were located, but the others had been too panic-stricken to control, and the whinnying had now become laced with the ghastly sound of equine screams. The woman's scream, at a different pitch, and accompanied by a pointing, waving arm, drew eyes to the left, where Huw's tousled head had been thrust through the hole by his sister, and he called out piteously in a choking treble.

Catchpoll and Bradecote were only just upon the scene, and Catchpoll's heart missed a beat. Of course, this was where the children holed up at night. He surged forward, calling for a ladder, but was beaten to it by a tall figure that showed itself as Father Boniface. Grim-faced and muttering Latin in a monotone, the priest tucked the hem of his habit into his rope girdle, baring the hairy legs and knobbly, pale knees that Catchpoll had seen in Corviserstrete, along with an axe thrust into his hand by a helpful bystander, and began his ascent of the rickety ladder. All eyes followed him, even as men threw water on the blaze, and shouts of encouragement from the crowd added to the noise.

At the top of the ladder Father Boniface steadied himself, and leant back to get a good forceful blow at the planking. Huw shut his eyes as the axe bit close and splinters scratched at his face. The priest was not a bulky man but showed strength in his arm, and after a couple of minutes dropped the axe, with a shouted warning to the men holding the foot of the ladder, and reached forward to haul the boy by the shoulders through the enlarged hole.

A ragged cheer went up, and people clapped. Catchpoll took the child from Father Boniface's arms as he reached the ground, coughing and with sweat dripping from his tonsure, but the serjeant's face was taut, not congratulatory.

'What of the girl?'

'What girl?' the priest replied.

The flames had risen to the loft edge by now and the heat seared the throat and was uncomfortable to skin. The relief at seeing her brother disappear through the enlarged opening drained the girl of much of her remaining strength. She had fulfilled the task her mother had set upon her, and taken care of Huw. She was breathless in the smoke, and part of her wanted nothing more than to take the easy way, give in and let the grey swirls take her, but the flames were reaching out to her also, with hot claws, and she did not wish to perish by fire. The horses' screams sounded to her like the damned in hell and she did not want hell. It was barely a couple of feet to crawl forward to the hole, but it seemed to take her an eternity. She was praying, not for salvation in this life, for she was resigning herself to its end, but that God would forgive the sins of the flesh she had been forced to commit to keep her sibling from starvation. Holy Mary would intercede for her, since it had been for a child. She repeated the line in her head as even whispering it made her choke the more. '*Sancta Maria, Mater Dei, ora pro nobis peccatoribus, nunc et in hora mortis nostrae.*'

As she reached the opening, the light diminished. Someone was there for her. '. . . *nunc et in hora mortis nostrae.*' Now and in the hour of our death. Perhaps this might yet not be that hour. She held out her hands to the figure who darkened the opening, and looked up into the face of her rescuer in the firelight. She saw the reflection of the fire tinting the censorious eyes in the grim face.

There was a crash as the floor gave way behind her.

'Oh no, Holy Mary, please no . . .' The cry of horror was cut short by the scream, echoed by that of women in the crowd below, and the priest leant back as a tongue of yellow flame licked forth from the embrasure.

He descended the ladder swiftly, helping hands steadying him as he reached the bottom. His brows were singed, but also clearly furrowed. He looked straight into Catchpoll's eyes, his own as hard as granite.

'It is the will of God, Serjeant.' The voice was emotionless.

Catchpoll had no words with which to respond.

Other hands clapped the priest upon the shoulder, praising his efforts. 'You tried your best, Father, and it was a brave deed . . . At least the boy was saved . . . There was nothing else could be done . . .'

Catchpoll turned to look at the child, hunched, and with sacking draped round his thin shoulders. His eyes were wide, like a mouse in the gaze of a snake, but there was comprehension as well as horror.

'Catchpoll.' Bradecote repeated his name before he responded.

'My lord?'

'I asked what should be done with the boy.'

'I'll take him home with me for tonight. We can think of something later. Do you need me here still? If not, I'll get him away from all this.' Catchpoll jerked his head at the red and yellow inferno that had been the stables.

Bradecote nodded his agreement, and turned to direct the preservation of nearby buildings, as Catchpoll lifted his small burden and walked away into the dark, the crowd parting silently to let him through.

Walkelin reported before his time to the castle, so keen was he to get to work. The night had brought not counsel, but a plan, one which would use the newly gained advice of Serjeant Catchpoll to good effect, and have his superiors marvelling at his 'serjeanting' skill. Not finding Serjeant Catchpoll or the undersheriff yet about, he left a message with one of his fellow men-at-arms to let them know what he was up to, and to come along to Edgar Brewer's as soon as they could. He had been expecting to have to share his glory, if not find much of it purloined by seniority; but he now judged that their absence

236

should give him enough time to have reached the climax of his efforts and prevent the more senior and experienced sheriff's men stealing all his thunder. He left whistling and in confident expectation, but also in blissful ignorance of the dramatic and tragic turn of events that had occurred during the night.

Chapter Eighteen

Catchpoll did not sleep late, but before meeting the undersheriff, he went, heavy-hearted and grim, to speak with Drogo, whom he found more cheerful than before, having had good news from old Brother Hubert about the condition of Nesta Bakere. He was surprised by Catchpoll's query, but supplied the name Catchpoll sought without hesitation.

Hugh Bradecote did not feel like breaking his fast, though his throat, still lined with the bitterness of smoke, would welcome cool liquid. He was sick at the thought of another life wasted, and in such a horrific manner. The girl's cry and scream had haunted his disturbed slumber and at that moment he doubted whether he would be able to bring the fire-setter to trial for the simple reason that he thought he might kill the man himself. He told himself that the taking of a life was the same crime, no matter the age or gender, whether the willingly sinful Maud Brewer or the unwillingly sinful . . . he did not even know her name, poor girl, and yet it did matter. It touched him emotionally. Catchpoll, he decided, would condemn such feelings and be impervious. In this instance he was wrong.

The sight of the castellan, sat at the high table and tearing bread with evident pleasure, gave him further reason to go without breaking his fast this particular morning. He would have no patience with the man's wittering, this day of all days.

The meeting of undersheriff and serjeant was taciturn, being merely the exchange of a nod and a grunt. They walked in silence and by some unspoken mutual consent to the guardhouse at the gate, where they ascended to the battlements, and there leant with Worcester spread before them.

'How's the boy?'

'In body, fair enough. He coughs a bit, but then that's all he does; no words; no movement. He's in shock, but how long it will last, heaven alone knows.'

'And for the future?'

'We'll keep him until this is all concluded, and be sure we end this soon now, my lord, but thereafter I wouldn't like to say. Neither the wife or me really want a child of that age about the place. Went through all of that in our time and are past the age for it. I wondered if the cathedral priory might take him, even without a gift, out of charity.'

'Father Boniface might put in a good word.' Bradecote did not sound as if he thought it likely.

'I doubt a good word is ever forthcoming from him,' Catchpoll snorted. 'You can't say he's without guts, but there's not a jot of humanity in the man. He's some hollowed-out religious stick. There was no sign of horror last night, no compassion, no regret, just "*Deus vult*".'

There was an unnatural silence as both men realised what had just been said, and made connections.

Bradecote shook his head, disbelieving. 'No, we must be wrong to think it. He's a man of God, however unfeeling. If we follow this through we'll see it cannot work. For a start, he is probably younger than I am, so he could not have been in love with Emma. Jesu, he would only have been a—'

'Child, my lord?' Catchpoll grimaced. 'We considered a man, true enough, but not a loving son. Think of it. He's seven or eight, much the age of young Huw. His father dies in shaming circumstances and his loving and adored mother sends him to the Benedictines to keep him from that shame. So he grows and is devout, remembering his mother almost as the Lady Mary, and chooses the ministry of the priesthood over the cloister. Then chance sends him back here, where the vague memories are rekindled and idle gossip burns his ears, and he becomes her avenging angel. It fits, right down to the holy oil.'

'And he gave us Serlo, so now we know that it was not he who stole the oil, who else is there who could have done it? Nobody, because the priest himself used it. Of course. And the fires take their course as God's judgement like you said.' The undersheriff paused. 'Tell me there's a flaw to this, Catchpoll,' groaned Bradecote. '*Mea culpa*, what else have I missed?'

'*Mea culpa*,' echoed Catchpoll, growing pale. 'That's what he was muttering last night when he went up the ladder for the boy. I was so taken with someone rescuing the lad I took no heed, but if the fire were the priest's fault, and he had no knowledge of the boy's presence . . .' Serjeant Catchpoll closed his eyes and fell silent for some moments. When he spoke again his voice was very quiet.

'The girl. She must have recognised his face at the very last minute. Remember what she cried, "Oh no, Holy Mary, no," except the last word was cut short. It was not "no" at all but "not"; it would have been, "Holy Mary, not you." Think about what happened exactly, my lord. When the crash came, did the priest reach out to try and grab that poor girl's arms?'

Bradecote tried to cast his mind back. 'I was not best placed to see, but no, I think not.'

'But the normal reaction would have been to lunge forward in an effort to grab her. He made none, I'll swear, and when he came down he was so cold and calm it was unnatural. "God's will" he said it was.' Catchpoll ground his teeth. 'I'll give him "God's will". I care not for your commands about how I gets a confession on this one, I am going to make that bastard long for the rope before I finish with him. To let her die . . .'

Bradecote understood Catchpoll's anger but was striving to stay calm and analytical. 'But wait a moment. How would Boniface know of what happened once he went to the monks? He might remember the names of who ruined his father but . . . This fits and yet does not. Could we be making it fit as we tried to make Mercet's plot against Simeon the Jew fit? Simeon.' Bradecote repeated the name, and groaned. 'Catchpoll, he might have given us the key long ago if we had but known it. He said he once lent money to a "godly woman" whose husband had killed himself when brought to ruin by some scheme. The woman had shown kindness to Simeon's wife and he charged her no interest. She used it to send her son to the brothers in a religious house. He made a joke about a Jew funding a Benedictine. He said the woman paid it all back, despite having only a menial job, and then she married and he knew no more of her. There's our connection with Simeon. No doubt Boniface found out about the loan and assumed the obvious. She may even have taken him with her to see him. He saw his mother as a serving maid to pay off the interest, and taking the work in the castle, where she met Drogo and Jocelyn of Shapwyck, to do so. Now, how could he have heard of Shapwyck?'

'Gossip dies a slow death, my lord. Agnes Whitwood told that very tale to my wife, and I doubt not it is a favoured one.' He closed his eyes as if in pain, and groaned, 'and she prays at St Andrew's.'

'And since the priest wanders at night to "think", he might have seen Drogo at the Widow Bakere's? Everyone who has a connection with his mother has to pay the penalty, because it was their fault she came to a sad end.'

'We haven't found the link to Mercet or the silversmith, but Mercet might be a false trail. It could be that the priest knew of the girl's hideaway and wanted to be rid of her. He need not have known of the brother, and would have striven to save him.'

Bradecote ran a hand through his hair, trying to ensure all avenues were covered. 'There can be no doubt when we do this and bring him in, Catchpoll. Think of the reaction of the Church if we are wrong.'

'But think of what further damage he could do if there are others he blames that we know nothing about.'

Bradecote crossed himself devoutly. 'Holy saints preserve us from that.' He drew a deep breath, having reached a decision. 'Right then. You go swiftly to the "spider" woman, the aged Aldith Merrow, and check what you can of the old tale. I will go to the priory and see Father Prior. Meet me at the remains of Mercet's stable as soon as you can. First one there can ferret around, not that we need to know much. The girl's body was removed, I know, but afterwards?'

'I spoke to Father Anselm of All Saints. He offered to hold the body and have it buried in the churchyard there. Many of his parish are too poor for fancy funerals and he is a good man. Why do you go to Father Prior though, my lord?'

'Churchmen know about who is where, especially if they have the say in who is sent to a particular parish, and we need to find out about Father Boniface. Between us I think we should be able to draw enough together to bring in the priest of St Andrew's. We can always send Walkelin to keep watch on him.'

'Walkelin . . . now, I've not seen him today, which is peculiar. He didn't look like he was sickening last evening. I wonder where he's got to?'

The man-at-arms to whom Walkelin had spoken had been sent to the smithy with a horse that needed shoeing, and so Catchpoll did not see him. Walkelin's whereabouts remained unknown, and brought down curses upon his absent flame-haired head.

The young man himself, in blissful ignorance of being in bad odour with Serjeant Catchpoll, had arrived at Edgar Brewer's, and then been struck by a problem that he had not foreseen. Having previously broken bread with the brewer's workers, he had no desire to be recognised as the nosey toy seller. He pondered his problem, and as he did so it was solved by the same two men emerging from the rear of the brewhouse rolling barrels, which they loaded onto a cart pulled by a morose and underfed horse. They led it away at its own pace, which was funereal. Here was his opportunity. He approached the front door, wiped his damp palms down the front of his cotte, cleared his throat, and knocked.

Widow Fowler opened the door by no more than a crack, and peered at the young stranger.

'Yes?'

Father Prior was not a man who rushed things. He greeted the undersheriff with calm courtesy, which in normal circumstances Bradecote would have appreciated, but today he had little time for offers of refreshment and animadversions on the effect of the recent weather upon the apple crop in the priory orchards. He needed to cut the pleasantries short without seeming churlish, and if the prior thought his smile more of a fixed manic grin and his responses overbrief, he gave no outward sign. At long last the sheriff's officer was able to pose his important questions.

'Father, I have need of information that I think only you, in Worcester, can provide. Lives may depend upon a swift resolution.'

'This certainly sounds very serious, my lord. Tell me how I may assist you.'

'I need to know as much as possible about Father Boniface and St Andrew's.'

'Ah. You know it is strange how becoming a priest, rather than a monk, affects some men. We had no cause to think . . . And if he is rather "rigorous" . . . After the death of Father Ambrose last year – and he was a fine man, very much loved and respected by his flock – we sent the parish this new, young priest. I believe he is most devout and a strict shepherd, although from report his manner is a little too . . . er, forbidding. The enthusiasm of the young, no doubt. I am sure he will mellow.'

'So he is of this house? Tell me about him, since he entered the priory.'

'I . . . he came to us as an oblate. In his case . . . It was many years past, and . . . there was some great need in the family. I did not deal with novices much. I was the sacrist before I was elected prior, and in those days not even an obedientiary. He was a Worcester boy, though our brothers come from all over the shire and beyond. It is one of the reasons he was given St Andrew's. A young man desirous of bringing God's word to his own people, you know.'

'One other question, Father. Do priests use their own names?'

'I'm sorry?'

'When men take the cowl do they keep their baptismal names?'

'Sometimes, but others choose to take a new name to signify their new life, or are given them if they are oblates. Not that committing boys to the conventual life is encouraged now. It is better if they come when they are of an age to decide for themselves. God must call you to the cowl; you must not be forced into it.'

'Thank you. Father, you may hear distressing news about the

incumbent of St Andrew's, but be assured we would not act if we were not sure.'

'That sounds very official, and unpleasant.'

'I am sorry, Father Prior, but it is. Very.' He rose, made a polite obeisance, and left.

Aldith Merrow had lived in Worcester all her long life, which numbered over three score years and ten, and she now lived with her son and his wife, with whom she maintained a state of verbal war. For the better part of five decades she had been the repository of Worcester gossip, trading her knowledge for further snippets, which she filed in her memory as either wild talk, truth wrapped in tales, or simply weapons, barbs to be cast at those she disliked. These days her only barbs were for her daughter-in-law, and her memory, while vivid for the distant past, could not tell you what she ate for yesterday's dinner, other than she must have disliked it because 'the idle good-for-nothing' had cooked it. She greeted the announcement that the sheriff's serjeant wanted words with her with a grunt, and a grumbling complaint about letting the aged sit quiet, but she was secretly delighted, and responded to his enquiry about the silversmith who had killed himself nigh on a quarter century past, and whose widow had gone to work at the castle.

'Remember? Of course I remember. That was the talk of Worcester for half a summer.' The old woman grinned toothlessly at Catchpoll, and her watery eyes sparkled at the memory. 'Such a tale, it was. Waltheof was a fool, of course, but that was not gossip, just good plain fact. He was a good craftsman with his hands, it must be said, and you'll see his work proudly shown by those who own it, but in all else a fool. William Long and his cousin, "young" Mercet as he was then, embroiled him in some foolish scheme that left Waltheof with all the risk and them with any chance of profit. So naturally, when it went wrong it was Waltheof who was ruined, and the other silversmiths, thinking of the probity of their craft, would not help him. Long managed to come clean from it somehow, and Mercet cared as little then as he does now what folk think of him. In fact he was probably quite pleased.' The old woman then described Robert Mercet in pithy and unsavoury terms that matched Catchpoll's own views, though he was vaguely shocked at hearing them on the lips of a frail-looking dame of advanced years. 'Waltheof could not face either the shame or telling his wife, and took the coward's way. The poor widow, and the boy, were left with nothing but debt, which took both business and home. Emma was a good, kind soul, far too good for the likes of Waltheof, and sent the lad to the monks. It was a sensible decision, giving the boy a secure future, for the scandal would have tainted his life outside the cloister. Boys are not known for their kindness, and rubbing in the fact that his father was not even entitled to holy ground to rot in would have been a cruel thing for a child his age. I never heard how she found the wherewithal to find the gift for his admission, so it must have been a very tight secret, but sending him from her forever, well, it broke her heart for sure. And then she took work in the castle, where she turned heads of course. A pretty woman, Waltheof's widow; pretty and pious. She married the undercook, though she could have had a lord for the snapping of her fingers, and

of elderberry and whatever it is the potion-pedlar puts in it.'

The audience was at an end, and Catchpoll was conscious of a desire to bow himself out. He smiled when he emerged into the street again, but it was fleeting. Matters were beyond any jest now. He set off, at pace, to the remnants of Mercet's stable.

Chapter Nineteen

He stood by the ashes of the stable for a short while, awaiting the undersheriff, but despite Bradecote's suggestion, made no attempt to root among the remains. The smell of burnt flesh lingered, and although sense told him it was most likely the dead horses, he had no stomach for it. Bradecote had only seen the girl twice, but Catchpoll was pricked by the uncomfortable feeling that he bore some responsibility for her, even though chances were that she had not been in a position to be saved until that last moment. The fact that she had had little likelihood of a long or happy existence did not help. Catchpoll vowed to set a candle for her when all was done, and it was a contemplative serjeant that Bradecote found upon his arrival.

They exchanged information without preamble, and had, without thinking, begun to head for St Andrew's before they had finished.

The church was empty when they entered by the parish door. As with all church doors, it creaked as it opened; the sound was amplified by the acoustics of the building, and their footfalls sounded in their own ears like an advancing army. They heard sounds in the vestry and approached as stealthily as they could, wincing at every echoing step and finally flinging open the door so hard that they almost fell through it. There was a clatter, and a woman screamed.

In front of them a short, rotund dame stood with her hands over her mouth and her eyes wide with surprise. A broom lay dropped at her feet.

'I'm sorry to frighten you,' apologised Bradecote, attempting to hide the fact that he had come very close to launching himself at the unfortunate woman. 'We seek Father Boniface.'

The woman blinked several times and opened her mouth, but let it hang open.

'Father Boniface, woman.' Catchpoll had no time for politeness in this situation, and cast the undersheriff a fleeting look of scorn.

'He'll be out sick visiting, as I should guess, my lord. I saw him only for a moment this morning.'

She bobbed a nervous curtsey, incorporating the retrieval of the broom in the action.

The sheriff's men turned to leave, and saw the black-garbed figure in the nave.

'Oh, there he is, come back,' remarked the woman, needlessly.

Father Boniface eyed the two men calmly, and folded his hands before him. He was completely calm, and said nothing.

'Good morning, Father. We were wanting to have words with you.' Bradecote spoke slowly and distinctly.

'We've come for confession,' growled Catchpoll.

The priest looked squarely at him. 'I imagine you have plenty to confess, and telling a falsehood is just another added to the list.'

'It isn't our confession that needs to be heard.' Anything less amicable than Catchpoll's tone would be difficult to imagine.

Father Boniface looked past them and addressed the cleaning woman. 'Go now.'

'But I've not—'

'Go.'

The little figure bobbed a hurried obeisance to Bradecote, then to priest and altar, and scurried out.

The three men stood in silence until the parish door shut with an amplified click of the heavy latch.

'You know why we are here,' Catchpoll growled. 'The trail of ashes, the trail of dead, leads to you, and ends now.'

Father Boniface did not flinch.

'Tell us why.' Bradecote could feel Catchpoll stiffening as his wrath reached boiling point. The priest's lack of concern rankled.

'Really, I have no time for this. I must be about my Father's business. I am His servant and His work must be done without let or hindrance.' The priest did not sound alarmed, rather mildly irritated, as though they had come to him at an importune moment to arrange a christening. Then, quite suddenly, he turned, and with a speed that neither Bradecote nor Catchpoll had anticipated, covered the few paces to the door; to their surprise, he did not open it but rather vanished through a smaller door in the shadows.

'The tower,' cried Catchpoll, already running. 'We have him trapped.'

The two men ran up the spiral stair, breathing heavily, lungs complaining as they approached the top. They paused for a moment and took a deep breath before flinging themselves at the door, expecting resistance, and instead found themselves stumbling onto their knees into the sunlight. The top of the tower was empty.

'The bastard's jumped,' gasped Catchpoll, and they both rushed to the parapet to look down, expecting to see a broken black figure at the base of the tower. There was nothing. It was then that the tower door shut with a snap. They looked at each other and scrambled for the door, which would not open.

'He's wedged the latch with something, but how did he get behind us?' complained Bradecote, heaving at the door in vain.

Catchpoll groaned like a soul in torment. 'This'll get out faster than we'll get down from here. The shame of it.' He ground his teeth. 'When we catch this murdering bastard of a priest, I warn you, my lord, you'll have to let less than a whole man be handed to the bishop, 'cos I'm going to pull his legs off, slow as I can. And don't try that, my lord, for you'll just damage a good weapon.'

Bradecote was preparing to try and lever the door off its hinges with the tip of his sword.

'Quicker, if more embarrassing, to call down and get someone up from below.' Catchpoll leant over the parapet. Perversely, there was nobody visible in the street. He swore with great vehemence, which was not appropriate in an ecclesiastical building, but he was technically outside, and the situation desperate. After a couple of minutes a woman, holding a small child by the hand, came into view. Catchpoll shouted and waved.

The child heard first and tugged its mother's hand, pointing upward. She looked up, then gathered the child up into her arms, and helped it wave happily at the irate serjeant, who cupped his hands, shouted, and then began a peculiar mime show. The child laughed and clapped at the entertainment. Eventually she seemed to grasp what he meant because she put the child to the ground and disappeared from view beneath them. A few minutes after that they heard the sounds of laboured breathing and the clump of heavy pattens.

''Tis jammed shut,' announced the voice, 'with a big metal key thing. I can't budge it. You wait till I fetch a man. Don't go away,' she added unnecessarily, and the clomping grew more faint.

By the time a strapping youth with a mallet had knocked the obstruction free, both Catchpoll and Bradecote were nearly jumping up and down in frustration. The door opened, and Catchpoll almost dragged the lad through the doorway to give room for their descent.

'Sheriff's business. Important. Thank you,' cried Bradecote as he too dashed past their bemused rescuer.

'That's how he did it,' shouted Catchpoll, as he passed a small door that they had ignored three-quarters of the way the way up. 'Door to roof.'

At the bottom, they rushed out into the street as if chased by fiends. Catchpoll bent forward, gasping for breath and making a peculiar whistling sound as the air was dragged through the irregular gaps between his teeth.

'Where first? The gates?'

Bradecote nodded, breathing almost as heavily through his long nose.

'Well, we'd best turn out men from the castle, then.'

'You do that, Catchpoll, but I'm straight for the Foregate and Bridge Gate. They're close enough for him. Meet you at the Foregate as soon as you're able, and bring a spare horse.'

Catchpoll set off, too breathless to curse, wishing that his legs felt twenty years younger, and that his lungs did not feel like bursting. The thought also crossed his mind that this was a job Walkelin should have done.

At the Foregate, on the north side of Worcester, Bradecote began to ask everyone whether they had seen the priest leave, and realised after the first few shaken heads that he must appear demented. He pulled himself together, and seconded a pedlar to stand by the gate and keep his eyes open until such time as relieved by a man-at-arms. He then passed on to the Bridge Gate, with little hope of receiving any positive answer, though a man mending a fishing net swore no priest had been that way all morning. Bradecote doubled back to the Foregate to await Catchpoll, who arrived with a clatter of hooves and several mounted men. He dismounted before his horse had even halted.

'I've set men to the gates and a second to report back here as to whether any sign has been seen of the priest. What has hit me as I came along is that it is always possible he has not tried to leave at all. Had you thought, my lord, about how he was in the

255

church . . . very righteous and calm before he duped us. If he sees himself as the agent of God's vengeance, well, if his task was complete he'd be as likely to ignore what we might do as not.'

'You mean that he escaped because he hasn't finished?' Bradecote groaned.

'Exactly. And although most of the fires have been at night, he knows we are after him so the next one will be as soon as he can set it.'

'The old woman.'

'What, my lord?'

'Your "spider". The only lead we will get is if she recalls anyone else connected with his mother. Otherwise we are looking for a needle in a hayrick, and a hayrick that is about to catch aflame.'

Catchpoll and Bradecote arrived outside the home of Aldith Merrow's son in an impressive haste, and hammered firmly upon the door. Her daughter-in-law answered it, ready to berate whoever it was, and swiftly altered her demeanour. She ushered the undersheriff and serjeant in, but told them 'Mother Merrow' was asleep.

'Then we'll wake her,' said Catchpoll. His face brooked no argument. The woman announced them loudly and slowly, as if to an idiot, and shook the old woman none too gently by the shoulder. Second time round Aldith Merrow opened her eyes.

'I'm not deaf,' she lied in a loud, strident voice, shaking off the hand and focusing on Catchpoll and then Bradecote. 'Didn't expect you back so soon, Serjeant, and in smart company too.' She looked Bradecote up and down. 'This'll be the new undersheriff. Does he understand God's good English?' She was addressing Catchpoll, but Bradecote answered.

'Yes, Mother, and speaks it also. We need your help, and quickly if we are to avoid more deaths and more charred buildings.'

Her eyes narrowed, and sparkled a little. 'Better than the last one,' she muttered, appreciatively.

'That's because he called you an interfering old witch,' commented the daughter-in-law, with relish, 'and in Foreign too. You had to ask Father Jerome what it meant.' The woman smirked. 'And—'

She would have continued but for Catchpoll's raised hand.

'We have to know everything about what happened when Waltheof the silversmith died. So far, fires have been started at the smithy that passed from Master Long to his journeyman, Old Edgyth the healing woman, Simeon the Jew, the bakery of Drogo's bride-to-be, and Mercet's stable.'

He saw the old woman smile at the new information that this gave her.

'Well, that's interesting. Now, that's more folk than I'd have supposed, but have you missed any? Let me think.' Thinking involved her shutting her eyes for several minutes. Bradecote wondered if she had fallen asleep, and leant forward just as her eyes sprang open.

'Not asleep,' she announced vehemently, 'but if I thought I'd get a fine young man's hand upon me again it would have been worth dozing off.' She cackled, and her rheumy eyes twinkled in a remarkably lascivious manner for one so old. Bradecote actually coloured. 'When Waltheof died, the business was sold to pay the debts. The purchaser was no smith, but a brewer. He died within the year, and the business was taken over by his brother Edgar.'

'Edgar Brewer, husband of the late lamented Maud?' Catchpoll was incredulous.

'Lamented by more men than just her husband,' grinned the old woman, 'and not for the quality of her beer.'

'And anyone else?'

'She had no women friends. Her sort rarely do.'

'No, I meant other people connected to Emma, Waltheof's widow.'

She pursed her lips. 'Ah. Mmm, now let me see. It was so long ago, I could not swear an oath on it, but I do not believe so.'

'Thank you, Mother. We owe you a debt.' Bradecote made her a small bow.

'Send me one of that Drogo's coney patties and I'll be content. Make up for the midden-fare I get from her.' She pointed a bony digit at her daughter-in-law.

'Be sure we will.'

They turned to go and were in the doorway when Aldith threw a last question at them.

'So is it an old admirer or the boy?'

Catchpoll turned his head so quickly it cricked his neck.

'The son, but how did you . . .'

'Call it woman's wisdom, Serjeant. Now be off.'

They did not need a second command.

It had all been going so well. Walkelin felt perfectly in control of the situation. He had rehearsed the manner he would adopt according to gender and likely involvement, as recommended by Serjeant Catchpoll. Having gained entry by means of the truthful statement that he was the sheriff's man, he proceeded to weave an almost labyrinthine tale of larceny, swapping of barrels and, bizarrely, a lost dog. He wondered if that was going too far, but his last embellishment left his auditor as confused as he had anticipated. Reeling from the tangle of information, the widow did not appear at all on her guard.

After a minute or so she mustered her wits enough to enquire what exactly the sheriff's man thought she could do to help.

'Well, Mistress Brewer,' began Walkelin, the picture of innocent ignorance, 'I—'

The woman coloured and interrupted him. 'I'm not Mistress Brewer, not yet.'

'Truly? That's not what we expected.'

'What do you mean, "we"?' She peered at him, suddenly suspicious.

Here was a decision. Did he go for the flattery approach, or try to frighten her? Unsure, he tried an amalgam of both.

'Such a woman as yourself, Mistress, would have much to offer a lonely widower, unused to caring for himself, and with an unhappy background.'

'What do you mean?' she repeated. There was no doubting that she was now on the alert.

'Oh, just having lost his wife in such very unfortunate circumstances. Fell down the stairs, didn't she? Must have lain right there at the bottom, all spread out like washing on a bush. So unusual an accident, too.'

'People fall down ladders often enough.'

'But not while facing outwards and carrying a pile of washing. That would be begging for mischance.'

Widow Fowler's eyes narrowed. 'Perhaps she threw herself down, then. She was certainly stone dead when I saw her.'

'Of course, and she used the washing as a cunning device so that nobody could accuse her dear husband of having done away with her. So thoughtful. Don't suppose she was thinking of him when she entertained the other men, do you? Or was she the tidy sort? Did she think he'd forget to bring it down in the mayhem afterwards? I would I could find so excellent a wife.'

'I could wish just that for you,' sneered the widow, maliciously, but Walkelin noticed that she was gripping her skirts with her left hand so tightly that the knuckles showed white. He felt confident he could get an admission from her, but suffered a setback with the arrival of Edgar Brewer from his brewhouse yard. Brewer cast a swift interrogative glance at Widow Fowler before asking Walkelin's business. The man-at-arms swore inwardly. Going over his tale once more would give the woman time to regain her poise and concoct a good story, and he was not sure that his reason for his presence would sound as convincing on the second outing. Certainly the brewer was watching him very closely, and was suspicious of every word. Like the woman, he listened to the tale and then announced that he wanted to know what he was meant to do about it all, but it was clear that he was only paying lip service and believed none of it.

'Since I do not think we can be of use to the lord sheriff, I suggest that you try elsewhere. I'm a busy man, and Widow Fowler here was come to collect my washing for me and will be wanting to get down to the river on a fine day like today.'

A seed of doubt in his own abilities was germinating in Walkelin's brain, but he was not one to shirk a task and continued doggedly.

'But Widow Fowler here was telling me all about your poor wife's fall, Master Brewer. It made such interesting hearing.' That, he judged, would cast a rift between the pair, and he had the pleasure of seeing Edgar Brewer glare suspiciously at the woman.

'I did no such thing. You know I would say nothing.' Her voice was outraged, but her eyes were on the brewer, and pleaded understanding.

Walkelin opened his eyes wide in mock surprise, and his lightly freckled brow furrowed. 'Strange then, that you said she was "stone dead" when you found her, and "stone dead" implies cold, yet you were heard to scream only minutes after the heavy thump of something weighty falling from a height had been heard in the brewhouse.'

'Shut up!' Edgar Brewer spat, and though he might have been addressing Walkelin, it was clear the injunction was aimed at the widow, whose breathing was quickened and whose face blended panic and fury. The brewer, without turning his head, yelled for his workmen in the brewhouse.

Young Walkelin was now hoping that his superiors were about to make a timely appearance. He was a handy sort of chap in a fight, but numbers were likely to be against him. Edgar Brewer's shout for aid was answered, but not as he expected. Cries of alarm carried into the dwelling. Walkelin gave silent thanks. Serjeant Catchpoll had obviously decided it was easier to approach via the brewhouse, and judging by the noise, he had brought reinforcements in case of need. Brewer half turned, unwilling to leave Walkelin in his chamber, but worried by the cries.

'Sweet Jesu,' he exclaimed, seeing the smoke billowing forth from the brewhouse, and ran towards his burning workplace.

Father Boniface had no need of concealment or guile. This was the culmination of his mission from God. Apprehension mattered not, for he was an instrument of the Almighty, and would be saved by divine intervention. The upended handcart he had appropriated from outside the stable a few doors away was just the vehicle he needed, and providence had supplied him with all he required for a fire. Next to the stable was the shop of a coracle maker. The man himself had disappeared within on some task, but withies and a pot of hot pitch remained by the coracle under construction. With a few armfuls of straw, set alight with flint and steel, and a bundle of withies splashed with pitch, a fire was started in seconds. He had but to open the rear door of the brewhouse, whence Walkelin had so recently seen the barrels rolled out, and half the job was done. Any attempt to thrust the burning cart back out was prevented by the simple act of jamming the latch with a stout stick. Even if they broke out, the fire would have taken good hold and drawn anyone from the front lodging. The priest nipped back to the front door of the premises, the part empty pot of pitch half concealed by his habit, waited for a minute after hearing the commotion from the rear, and opened the door in the misplaced confidence that it would be empty within. He drew up short at the sight of Widow Fowler, arms upraised and in the process of lobbing the cook-pot at Walkelin, who was caught in the act of ducking, The cook-pot clattered into the corner. Both looked at him in consternation, Walkelin because he had expected the undersheriff, and Widow Fowler because she had expected nobody at all. Walkelin was confused. The woman had been throwing household utensils at him from the moment Edgar Brewer ran out to his brewhouse. Several items had narrowly missed the man-at-arms' head, and he was unsure how best to respond. Fighting women did not come easily to a young man for whom the opposite sex were either inexplicable but fascinating, or mothers whom it was unwise as well as disrespectful to disobey. And now, in place of the undersheriff, here was the hangdog-faced priest of St Andrew's.

For her part, Widow Fowler, bosom heaving with exertion and anger, bobbed a curtsey while reaching towards the poker.

The trio stared at each other in silence for several moments before Father Boniface recovered himself enough to speak.

'I am sorry, but I was passing, and I saw . . . I mean . . . Mistress, there is smoke and flame coming from your brewhouse. I thought I should alert you.' He sounded every inch the perplexed cleric, surprised by the altercation going on in the chamber.

'Thank you, Father.' The woman saw her chance, abandoned thoughts of the poker and made to exit, thinking Walkelin would not hamper her in the presence of the priest, but he blocked the doorway.

'No, you don't. I am taking you before the undersheriff for murder.'

He was dimly aware that both the people looking at him

flinched, but he put the priest's reaction down to shocked horror.

'Fool,' spat the widow, coming at him with clenched fists and flailing at his head and chest. 'I never killed her, before God I swear it. She was already dead and cold when I—' She caught herself on a gasp and clamped her mouth shut.

'When you pushed the body down the stairs and dropped the washing after it.' Walkelin finished the sentence for her. He did not pose it as a question but rather as a statement of known fact, and grabbed her wrists. He noted the spasm of fear that crossed the woman's features, and did not see the look upon the face of the priest, who muttered something under his breath that Walkelin assumed to be indicative of moral condemnation.

In reality, Father Boniface was overwhelmed by the knowledge that this final task laid upon him encompassed the punishment of another mortal sin. A glow of righteousness as fierce as any flame surged through him. He threw the pitch pot against the door, where it smashed, and pointed an accusing finger.

'Jezebel!' He flung the insult at Widow Fowler, who turned her head in surprise at his vehemence.

Walkelin too was taken aback. The priest seemed possessed. His eyes flashed, and his arms flailed wildly. Then Walkelin noticed the pitch dripping down the door and the flint and steel in the priest's hands. Father Boniface shouted at them.

'"*Mihi vindicta: ego retribuam, dicit Dominus.*" And I am the instrument of that vengeance; God's own instrument. You cannot harm me.'

Walkelin was a good lad who had always paid attention in church, and he knew the text. Just the sort that a priest like Boniface would use, he thought bitterly, letting go of one of the widow's wrists and drawing his sword. He edged towards the priest.

'Wrong, Father. Vengeance is God's alone. Now you just come away from the door and put out the flame.' His calm voice belied the confusion in his brain.

Seizing her chance, Widow Fowler pulled herself from Walkelin's grasp upon her wrist and lunged for the rear doorway, only to find that the now thick and billowing smoke in the small yard threw her back, choking her. Walkelin, dealing with problems on two fronts, took his eye from the priest for a moment as the woman escaped him. It was all the time that Father Boniface needed. The scrape of flint and steel was followed by his cry of triumph as the flame took to the tarred door. Then the cry became a scream as his habit, which itself had been smeared with the contents of the pitch pot, caught alight.

Walkelin was fighting his own rising panic. The rear exit was not viable, the front door was burning and in front of it the priest was twirling around, arms waving like a swan trying to get airborne, trying to put out the flames engulfing his person and achieving the opposite effect. The screaming was an unnatural pitch and core-chilling. Widow Fowler was choking and appeared almost unhinged by fear, flinging herself on the floor. Walkelin, coughing, and with his eyes watering, made a snap decision, and ran at the priest, dragging him down onto the floor and trying to roll him in the rushes, but some of those too were now smouldering, and all that diminished was the screaming.

The smoke was thickening, catching in Walkelin's throat and eyes. His chest felt constricted. He realised he had but one chance remaining. Abandoning the priest, he lifted the now inanimate woman in his arms, and made his move.

Chapter Twenty

Hugh Bradecote, Serjeant Catchpoll, and their clattering entourage arrived at Edgar Brewer's already aware of a fire from the smoke rising into the pale blue of the September sky. Neighbours were in the process of forming parties to fight the flames, which came from both brewhouse and domicile. Men with axes were hacking at the brewhouse door to aid the men who were shouting and coughing within, and fearing to be burnt to death, or asphyxiate in the smoke-filled yard, which was little more than a few yards between the two.

Bradecote dismounted before his horse had even been pulled up, and thrust the reins into the hand of an old man too frail to be of use in fighting the flames.

'Is there anyone within the house?' he yelled, as he ran towards the sound of the trapped men in the brewhouse.

Before any answer was returned, the shutters of the lower

chamber of the house burst open, and Walkelin, with an inanimate Widow Fowler in his arms, half rolled and half threw himself out into the street, coughing and retching.

Bradecote turned back, and Catchpoll ran forward and relieved the gasping Walkelin of his load, whom he dumped unceremoniously in the street, then thumped the spluttering 'serjeant's apprentice' hard upon the back. After which he cuffed him smartly round the ear. Bradecote returned his attention to the rescue.

'Ow, what's that for, Serjeant?' Walkelin complained.

'Breaking rule number two.'

'Which is?' queried Walkelin, eyes streaming. He rubbed his ear and grimaced.

'Disappearing without me knowing what you're up to. Telling someone to let me know, if they happen to bump into me, isn't good enough. You were a fair way to getting yourself killed in there, and while it'd be no more than a halfwit deserved, I picked you out and don't like to be shown up foolish, which I would if you ended up a corpse on your first task.' Catchpoll sounded as if he was only concerned that his reputation might be dented by Walkelin's demise.

'Sorry, Serjeant. And the first rule?'

'Never do anything to upset Serjeant Catchpoll. In fact, since that covers number two, just remember that at all times and you might just stay alive.'

'Right, Serjeant.'

'And did you get a confession from the sack of bones you've just carted out?' Catchpoll jerked a thumb at the inanimate form of Widow Fowler, around whom several women were fussing, attempting to bring her round from her swoon.

'Sort of. She certainly made it clear that Maud Brewer was very dead before she arrived on the scene, and since she is meant to have discovered the body just after the sound of the fall, well, the fall must have been of a corpse. This clearly shows—'

'That she died in her upper chamber, and that her husband has no proof he was not there. Who else could have been up there and not caused her to scream?' The serjeant mumbled the last part almost to himself.

'Well, judging by what has been said, it could have been half of the men in Worcester.'

Catchpoll shook his head. 'No, that doesn't work. Firstly, the husband would not have dismissed the thump of the fall. He would have gone to investigate, not made an excuse. Also, from years of dealing with this sort of thing, she wouldn't have entertained other men in the marital bed when the husband was close by and liable to discover her.'

'So we have him.'

'Aye, and the widow too, since she clearly would not have pushed Maud's body down the stair if she had found it unexpectedly. She would have screamed, a proper scream, not a pretence. You made a good taking, Walkelin, but you put success before safety. Don't be a fool again.' Catchpoll turned to send a man-at-arms to keep a hand on Edgar Brewer, who had emerged, singed and breathless, with his workers from the brewhouse, but Bradecote was before him.

Walkelin was vaguely pleased, but as commendation went it seemed muted. He was also confused. The smoke, he thought dimly, must have got to his brain. He felt suddenly very tired and sank down on to his haunches.

'Where is Father Boniface?' The undersheriff, now that the emergency was over, feared the priest had escaped once again, and there was urgency in his voice.

Walkelin shook his head, and immediately regretted doing so as his senses swam. 'He's still within. He'll be dead, was flaming when I grabbed . . . I had no choice. Sorry, my lord.' He looked to Catchpoll. 'I don't understand. What was he doing?' He rubbed his brow.

'Setting fire to the place, you mean?' Bradecote looked down at his man. 'Well, that might be because he did that a lot. Walkelin, the priest of St Andrew's was our fire-raiser. I'll explain why later. Let's get you and the surviving culprits back to the castle.' He turned to address another man-at-arms. 'If you find the priest's corpse, get something to cover it, fast, in case it is recognisable as a cleric. Much as I would like to crow our success from the rooftops, the Church will find this embarrassing, and an embarrassed Church is a "complaining to the sheriff" Church.'

Catchpoll smiled. 'He's beginning to sound like me,' he murmured, half to himself.

'I don't like it, Catchpoll. It's unnatural the way he sits there like some drooping gargoyle off the cathedral roof, with never a word, nor a sign he hears what I say, though it's simple and his mother tongue. You'd think I was talking Foreign.' Mistress Catchpoll was watching the boy, Huw, who sat in a corner. 'He's like some sick animal, waiting for the end. It's unnerving me, good and proper. How long is he going to be with us?'

'Mother tongue,' repeated Catchpoll slowly, ignoring the last part of his wife's complaint. 'Of course. You know, I might have the answer to that. I'm off back to see Brother Hubert and find out how Widow Bakere goes on.'

'But, Catchpoll . . .' Mistress Catchpoll found herself addressing the open doorway and shook her head as she shook out her broom.

Brother Hubert again reported improvement in the widow's condition. 'But it is important for her to want to recover, really want to. The spirit can be worse wounded even than the body, and if the spirit fails . . .' He shook his head, but then brightened. 'The cook visited her for the first time this morning, and he was, I will say this for him, both soft of word and kind in manner, though she wept after his departure.'

'Could she be moved yet, Brother?'

The monk considered the matter gravely. 'It is not what I would recommend, though I know the girl whose bed this is would be glad to have it back.'

'What if I could give you a good reason? Listen.' Catchpoll expounded his idea, and the old Infirmarer, after a few moments, nodded and smiled.

Having returned home and cast his house in uproar by announcing that Widow Bakere would be arriving in a litter within the hour, Catchpoll escaped his wife's voluble condemnation by disappearing to find Drogo.

'I've arranged for your Nesta to be taken back to my home this morning.'

'She's not fit, surely?' Drogo looked concerned.

'Perhaps not, but I have my reasons, and I'm hoping you'll not be put out by them.' He sat down and set about putting Drogo in the picture. It had occurred to Catchpoll, only on the way to visit him, that the plan might not be entirely to Drogo's taste, but he took it very well, and a little later was seen limping beside the litter when the small entourage arrived outside Catchpoll's cottage.

Mistress Catchpoll made a show of hospitable welcome, though she cast her spouse a look that spoke volumes. He merely smiled back at her. The invalid was set down tenderly and lifted, not without tears and groans, into a cot borrowed from the cooper's next door. Revived by a drop of Mistress Catchpoll's fermented elderberry, which only appeared on special occasions, she began to look less pinched and faint. All the while, Huw the orphan sat curled in a corner, his hands clasped round his knees and his face a blank mask. Catchpoll drew up a stool and spoke very softly to Nesta Bakere.

'I know you must be thinking of your hurts and losses now, but we need your help. The lad in the corner, well he's the victim of the fire-setter too, and though he looks unhurt, he suffers mortal bad. His parents died some while back, and there was just his sister to care for him, and her not of an age to take the task. They were reduced to sleeping in a stable, and that was burnt to the ground. The girl did her best, and Huw here was saved, but she was lost to the fire. He has said nothing since, nor shown sign of interest in the world. We haven't even discovered the sister's name, and we need to get what there is of her buried decent.'

Nesta Bakere did not turn her head, but swivelled her eyes in the boy's direction.

'How can I help?' she queried, faintly.

Catchpoll smiled slightly; it was just a quivering of lip and extension of the line of his mouth. 'His mother was Welsh, and I thought if you spoke to him, in the language his mother used, then he might respond.'

The injured woman's eyes filled with sudden tears. 'There's tragic. Poor little soul.' She grasped Drogo's hand with her sound one, and he patted it consoling.

'*Huw bach, dere eistedd gyda fi,*' she called gently, patting the stool vacated hastily by Drogo.

The little boy looked up, his face still impassive, but the eyes registering understanding. She repeated her plea for him to come and sit by her, more request than command, and after a few moments he uncurled himself and trod nervously towards the cot, his eyes not leaving the woman's face. The sympathy he saw and the trembling of her lips as she whispered soft endearments, broke the shell of his grief; he slumped on the stool and all of a sudden he leant forward against her bosom and began to sob in great gasps. Catchpoll said nothing but indicated the pair should be left alone by a jerk of his head, and everyone drew back in respectful silence; Mistress Catchpoll to sweep her yard and Drogo and Catchpoll to take a draught of ale.

The cook looked back at the weeping pair, frowning. 'Will it do her any good, do you think?'

'Give her something to mother that's in a worse state than she is and instinct will do the rest. Mind you, she may want to keep the lad by. I may have lumbered you with an adopted son, Drogo.'

He pulled a face, but it was half smile. 'If it gives her something to get well quicker for, how should I complain? And besides, he's of an age when a father could be the moulding of him. Mayhap he'll turn into a fine cook, or a baker like Nesta. No, you've not lumbered me, just given a new turn to life perhaps.' He sighed. 'I never thought to have a son to raise at my time of life. We'll see soon enough.'

Later in the morning, Catchpoll was able to go to Father Anselm, who had offered to have the girl's remains interred in his churchyard, and give him her name. In the afternoon, Nerys Ford was laid to rest, with her brother standing between Catchpoll and Drogo, to whose cotte he surreptitiously clung, and in the presence of the undersheriff and a turnout of parishioners who either never knew of her occupation, or were inclined to disregard it, especially in view of the manner of her death. Catchpoll had hidden nothing from Father Anselm, knowing he was a good man and a realist.

"Tis only fair you know, Father, since you have offered her "room" in your consecrated earth. I can tell you it was not a life she followed from choice or with any pleasure. It was all she possessed and all she could sell, and she kept what she had to do from her little brother, kept him from seeing and learning things he ought not, and from what little the lad has said, she did everything she could to save his life when the fire took hold, not caring for her own. There could be no more selfless act than that.'

'God sees all, God judges all, and I am but a humble parish priest. It is not for me to judge, and her end was brought about by one whose calling . . . Oh dear. I will pray for her soul, assuredly, and see no reason why she cannot lie among my parishioners.'

Father Anselm shook his head in sorrow that a child should be reduced to such a sinful life, and at the wickedness of lustful men. At the graveside he made much of God's grace and forgiveness, and said not a word about how she had been forced to live. Hugh Bradecote stood very pale and silent, reliving the last burial he had attended, and conscious both of guilt at how long ago it seemed and relief that it had passed swiftly into aching memory rather than lingering as a current pain. The pitiful remains were shrouded only, so at least he was spared the heavy sound of earth upon planks. At the end Drogo hoisted Huw, a little stiffly and with a grunt of discomfort, onto his broad shoulders to take him back to Catchpoll's house. He gave a promise to arrange matters so the boy could live in the castle even before Nesta Bakere could take her place as his wife. Catchpoll greeted this with relief, for his wife was far from unsympathetic but none too comfortable with her home becoming 'a refuge for orphans and the sick'.

He hung back and waited for the undersheriff to come up beside him. Bradecote's face was contemplative and serious, and Catchpoll thought a shadow crossed it, but then it broke quite suddenly into a wry smile.

'You know, I am beginning to think you a fraud, Catchpoll.'

'And why might that be, my lord?' Catchpoll's voice was full of suspicion and his eyes narrowed warily.

'Because you make a great effort to show yourself to the world as a miserable, cynical, suspicious and cold-hearted bastard, and I believed it as much as the next man. Yet here, in Worcester, in your own place, there's been a human side to Serjeant Catchpoll I had not imagined.'

Catchpoll looked aggrieved, almost insulted.

'I don't see as how you should think that, my lord, and I'd appreciate it if you didn't spread such a rumour. This isn't a job where being "human", as you call it, is a good thing. You have to be able to stand back, and stand firm, and the lawbreakers have to know that however hard and mean they may be, you are harder and meaner. If I have seemed otherwise, well, it's a bad thing. I admit I have tried to help Drogo, but even a serjeant can have a friend, "off duty" so to say, and as for the girl,' he sighed, 'perhaps there I am growing soft. It was a bad end to a hard life, and she had tried her best. I admired her for that, I admit. I hope you'll not have cause to notice any other weakness, and I'll be on my guard against it. Thank you for the warning.'

Bradecote was surprised by the reaction. He had expected Catchpoll to treat the matter as a mild joke, and was taken aback by his serious, and clearly genuine, response.

'It was not intended as such, but no matter. I would have thought understanding people would have been an advantage, but—'

'Oh, understanding 'em is fair enough, but you can't get involved. It is too messy and makes you prone to mistakes. It ain't an easy thing to master, and it will be one of the things I have to teach young Walkelin. The last undersheriff, my lord de Crespignac, he kept from it by being involved with the whole process as little as possible until the last moment. It worked well enough. You, my lord, are clearly not of the same mind, and that's your right. You think straight, which is good, but, begging your pardon, you've not learnt to think nasty, nor to stand back far enough. It leads to sleepless nights and fatal mistakes, but no doubt you'll get better time by time.' Catchpoll conveniently forgot the disturbed rest this case had given him.

The undersheriff put his head a little to one side and the twisted smile returned.

'And I thank you for your warning, Serjeant. A fair exchange, I think.' He nodded and turned the conversation to practical matters.

They came upon Simeon the Jew by chance in the main thoroughfare, and the merchant bowed and gave Bradecote a broad smile.

'I have sent word to Bristow, my lord. As you foretold, I have not had to be parted from my family for long. I thank you for your diligence.' His glance encompassed both sheriff's men. 'It is perverse, is it not, that I have suffered in this from an act of charity.'

'One misconstrued, mind you, and in the mind of a madman.'

'Very true. Yet God has been merciful to me. I give thanks for it.'

Bradecote smiled back. 'And I am glad you have received it and can recall your loved ones to you. May your business prosper, Master Simeon.' He nodded his acknowledgement of the merchant's obeisance, and Simeon turned away down a side street.

William de Beauchamp arrived back in Worcester two days later, still limping and in less than joyous temper. The castellan ensured that he was brought up to date with events before ever he called for his undersheriff and serjeant. He might do little, but Furnaux loved to talk. It was a beetle-browed and tight-lipped lord sheriff before whom they came, and with a nervous Walkelin hanging back at a suitable distance to the rear.

The sheriff sniffed and glared at his representatives.

'Well, there's still some of Worcester standing, so I suppose I should be pleased,' he grumbled. He paused for effect. 'On the other hand,' and he lifted his left hand and began to tick off fingers with his right. 'There have been seven fires . . .'

'One of which was the result of a bolt of lightning, my lord,' interjected Catchpoll.

'All right, six fires; the destruction of several premises; damage to others and the deaths of an old woman and a girl. On top of which, you have caused grievous insult to the castellan's son-in-law. The only good thing is that the culprit did not come to trial. According to the lord Bishop of Hereford, in whose company I have spent far too long, the Archbishop of Canterbury is increasingly determined that no cleric shall come before the King's justice, even for killing. It will cause problems, with no blood sentence.'

Catchpoll was outraged. 'But my lord, it was always understood. The ecclesiastical courts tried those under their jurisdiction but cast out those guilty of capital offences so we could deal with 'em after.'

'Well, I am not sure we can trust to that much longer. Might be best, if you are sure of your case, that clerics get real justice, and don't come to court at all.'

Bradecote could not but remonstrate. 'Without trial, my

278

lord? How can that be justice if it is our decision? And besides, last time we brought you a corpse and you berated us for it.'

The Pershore case had ended in what might be termed trial by combat, and a body to present. De Beauchamp would not normally have objected, except that the Empress Maud had directed that the same man be taken into custody for breaking his oath to her.

'Well, I'm not berating you for doing it this time.' The sheriff had little time for niceties, believing rather in pragmatic law-keeping. 'Saved everyone embarrassment. I have had the prior here, and he is hoping to make as little as possible of the whole thing. He has already sent a message to the lord Bishop of Worcester, suggesting the name of an older, more experienced and worldly wise incumbent for St Andrew's. That should settle the parish at least, and the townsfolk will calm down soon enough. Thankfully, the dead were not of any note.'

Catchpoll kept his mouth clamped shut, but Bradecote saw his jaw working, and tried to diffuse the situation by changing the subject.

'My lord, we did also secure the murderers of Maud Brewer, whom you can at least arraign without any trouble.'

'A woman whose death was not even murder before you started digging.'

'Oh it was murder from the moment her neck snapped, my lord. It was just that we were all away when it happened and nobody thought to make anything of it at the time.' Catchpoll had a point to make.

William de Beauchamp made a growling noise that might be considered grudging acceptance.

Catchpoll continued, calling Walkelin forward with a gesture of his hand. 'And in the solving of that murder I would like to bring to your lordship's attention your man-at-arms, Walkelin, son of Hubert, whom I selected, in your lordship's absence, as worthy of training in the craft of serjeanting.'

'"Craft",' the sheriff snorted, 'more like some black art.' He studied Walkelin, rather in the manner of a man deciding upon the purchase of a horse. Walkelin was struck by the sudden idea he might be asked to trot up and down and bare his teeth for inspection. Whatever he saw, the sheriff clearly did not have any objections to Catchpoll's choice.

'So Serjeant Catchpoll thinks he can train you up to follow his footsteps, does he?'

'Yes, my lord,' enunciated Walkelin with great precision and loud volume. The sheriff had never addressed him personally before, and he was so keen not to appear pusillanimous and overawed that his response was completely the opposite.

'Well, see you attend to him. I doubt there's a better serjeant to be found for sniffing out law-breakers.'

Serjeant Catchpoll looked at his feet and shuffled in embarrassment.

Emboldened, Walkelin responded. 'Indeed, my lord, and I have learnt the first rule.'

The sheriff looked quizzically at him.

'Don't do anything Serjeant Catchpoll wouldn't like,' announced Walkelin.

William de Beauchamp glanced at Catchpoll, whose face bore an agonised expression, and schooled his own features into severity.

'You are wrong. That is the second rule.'

'My lord?'

'The first is never to do anything that I would not like. Eh, Serjeant?'

'Correct, my lord,' mumbled Catchpoll, casting Walkelin a glance that he correctly interpreted as 'you just keep your mouth shut, or else'.

Hugh Bradecote suddenly felt as if he were watching a performance; a dance that was both a bonding and a re-establishment of rank. There was something almost formulaic in the ritual, and he was not part of it. He supposed that sprang from the long association of sheriff and serjeant rather than any intention to hold him at a distance, but he was aware of it rankling.

'My lord, if the case is now closed, and I am not needed to give evidence in the Brewer trial, am I at liberty to return home? I would like to be there for the Michaelmas feast.'

The three men stared at Bradecote, conscious of having forgotten him.

'I do not see why not. You are not due for service with me until All Souls. No, go home to your w . . .' De Beauchamp paused for a fraction of a second before covering his lapse, 'wailing brat and your celebrating tenants. I intend to remain in Worcester, or at least hereabouts, for some time.' He coughed, and said stiltedly, avoiding Bradecote's eye. 'I am sorry for your lady. Happens, of course, but a bad business. Furnaux told me.'

Furnaux would.

That was the only reference the sheriff intended to make to Bradecote's bereavement, and having made it, he was keen to change the subject. He commented upon the general state of the year's harvest, hoped that Bradecote would also be able to join him for boar hunting before Christmastide, and nodded dismissal.

Hugh Bradecote felt slightly empty. He had performed the task allotted to him and was stood down; and for all that he longed for the clean air, open horizons and simple comforts of his manor, he realised that part of him was now part of the world of de Beauchamp and Catchpoll, and he half envied Walkelin his permanence among the law-enforcing fraternity.

Catchpoll had been reading his expression, and part of his superior's thoughts were clear to him. He understood, but it was not his problem.

For all his request to be released from duty, Hugh Bradecote did not leave Worcester immediately. He went to the priory and sought out the prior, who shook his head over the turn of events.

'You were right, my lord Bradecote. This has been a terrible business, and the involvement of a priest . . .' He sighed. 'He was clearly warped of mind, to do such things.'

'Indeed so, Father. But it is not upon that matter that I have come back to you.'

Bradecote told the Benedictine of the death in childbed, and took a scrip of coin and placed it before the cleric.

'It is all I have remaining, here in Worcester, Father. I will bring more when next I come upon my duty, but it should be sufficient for several Masses for her soul.'

Father Prior did not actually lay hands upon the money. It

would have looked mercenary in the face of bereavement. He nodded.

'It shall be done, my son, and I will have your lady's name mentioned in our prayers for the remainder of the month. God has taken, but God has given also, and I shall pray additionally for the good health of your son.'

'Thank you, Father. It is appreciated.' Bradecote sighed.

The undersheriff departed before noon, parting from Catchpoll with as little ceremony as he had shown on arrival. His big grey horse lipped gently at his sleeve as he made his farewell, as if eager to be on its way.

'If there are any more fires in Worcester, Catchpoll, please make sure the lord sheriff is on hand himself.'

'Aye, my lord, it was a messy business start to finish.' He paused. 'And I am sorry . . . You'll be glad to see your . . .' Catchpoll suddenly realised he did not even know the gender of Hugh Bradecote's baby, 'child.'

'I have a son, Catchpoll. His name is Gilbert Bradecote, at his mother's dying wish, and yes, I will be glad to get home to see him.'

Catchpoll nodded. There was nothing he could say, nothing he really needed to say. Sympathy would sound hollow, and achieved nothing. Grief and loss were something that hit everyone, and had to be coped with as best they could, each in their own way. Privately, he thought coming away here, and concentrating upon something totally different, had helped the man. Despite the disturbed nights, he looked a lot better than when he had arrived, and perhaps it had broken the cycle of helplessness. He could not have prevented what happened to his wife, but what they had achieved might well have prevented more deaths in Worcester, excepting the loss of little Nerys Ford, and he had been brought back to the reality of everyday life, after staring into the dark abyss. There was a moment of silence, when each looked at the other, and then Hugh Bradecote nodded at Catchpoll, and swung himself up into the saddle.

As the undersheriff wheeled his horse round and trotted out of the castle gate, Serjeant Catchpoll climbed to the top of the gatehouse, where Walkelin had, in the absence of other instructions, returned to guard duty. Catchpoll came and stood silently beside him as they both watched the figure on the grey horse trot out through the Sutheberi gate and set off up the hill at a gentle canter.

'Seems a fair man, does my lord,' commented Walkelin meditatively. 'Not one of the high-and-mighty sort who look down on us ordinary folk as if we was midden. I reckon we're lucky to have him.'

Catchpoll was still watching the horseman in the distance. 'Could do worse. Not that any undersheriff has ever looked down on me though, at least not more than once. What you've got to remember is that he's lucky to have us to ferret for him. On their own no fancy lord would have a hope of maintaining the law, him included.'

'Do you like him, Serjeant?'

At this Catchpoll turned, his face a picture of stunned disbelief.

'Like him? What in the name of all the saints has that to do with anything? He's him and we are us. Being "liked" means nothing. If he respects me and knows his position, and I gets to respect him and knows my position, all stays sweet as honey and we work as a team. And as you are now to be part of that team, you'll do the same. With luck, he'll see some improvement in you when he comes next.' Catchpoll was not going to admit that he was warming to the undersheriff more than he had expected, and was indeed beginning to respect him.

Walkelin was pondering a deep thought. 'I know my position easy enough, but is it you or the undersheriff who is really in charge?'

Catchpoll's mouth lengthened into his skull-like smile, and his eyes twinkled. 'What do you reckon?'

'Right, Serjeant.'

'Now, since we have no murders to detain us, I thought I would take you around this fair town and point out the criminal element so that you know which stones to look under when crimes are committed, and there's a report in of the theft of a ham from a smokehouse. Come on.'

The grey horse disappeared from view.

Historical Note

Fire was Worcester's great enemy, but the fires in this book are of course fictitious. The basic street layout of the city has not altered in the area that lay within the walls, but many of the street names have changed. If you look at the map at the front of the book and one of modern Worcester you could follow in Bradecote and Catchpoll's footsteps but you have to imagine buildings nearly all single storey, made primarily of wattle and daub walls and with thatched roofs. The churches are in the same place, though much altered, and in the case of St Andrew's, only the later tower and spire (known as The Glover's Needle) remain.

William de Beauchamp was the lord Sheriff of Worcestershire, and we have some details of his life in the histories, but his physical look and character are my invention. The greatest fiction is, of course, that there were men dedicated to the taking of criminals. The sheriff was primarily the King's tax gatherer and militia organiser, and the sheriff's serjeant would have collected those taken up by hue and cry to bring before the justices, but would not have spent his days 'policing'.